# WATCHING AMANDA

## PRELUDE TO A KISS

Amanda stood and paced the room, then sat back down on the chair, then stood, then sat back down. Lord, what was wrong with her? She knew it'd been a long time since she'd been with a man, but c'mon.

It had been a long time. Pre-pregnancy long. Paul Swinwood long.

Suddenly she imagined Ethan coming out of the bathroom, wrapped in a tiny towel, his body slick, his hair damp. The towel would fall, and he'd be naked, and they'd both reach for it at the same time, and then they'd play tug of war with the towel, but he'd win because he was so much stronger, so much bigger, and he'd tug and tug until she was pressed tight against him, her breasts crushed against his chest, her pelvis pressed against his erection. He'd undo her pants and slide them down, remove her panties with one finger, and then he'd—

"Amanda?"

She started and blinked and looked up, and there he was, damp and half naked under the tiny white hotel towel. "I-I was just thinking about something . . ."

**ALSO BY JANELLE TAYLOR**

Dying to Marry

Don't Go Home

Can't Stop Loving You

Defiant Hearts

Destiny Mine

First Love, Wild Love

Forbidden Ecstasy

In Too Deep

Lakota Dawn

Lakota Winds

Night Moves

Not Without You

Passions Wild and Free

Savage Ecstasy

Someday Soon

Sweet Savage Heart

Tender Ecstasy

Wild Winds

# WATCHING AMANDA

JANELLE TAYLOR

ZEBRA BOOKS
KENSINGTON PUBLISHING CORP.

ZEBRA BOOKS are published by

Kensington Publishing Corp.
850 Third Avenue
New York, NY 10022



ISBN 0-7394-5989-9

Printed in the United States of America

# CHAPTER 1

A beautiful dark-haired woman wearing an ankle-length fur coat and matching ear muffs was throwing a temper tantrum—complete with foot stomps—in the lobby of the Metropolitan Hotel. While her two children played tug of war with a silk flower plucked from a previously lovely display, the woman wagged a manicured finger in Amanda Sedgwick's face.

Amanda, one of the Metropolitan's many front desk clerks, sat on her uncomfortable little stool behind the mile-long, granite reception counter and resisted the impulse to jump up and grab the woman's finger. She forced herself to smile "the Metropolitan way" and checked her computer monitor again. "I'm sorry, Ms. Willington, but your reservation is for only one room and we're completely booked. I can have a porter send up two cots for your—"

The woman narrowed her cold blue eyes. "Did

you say *cots*? I don't think so. You are to find me two suitable rooms—my usual suite and an adjoining double with two full-sized beds for my children. *Immediately*. And it's *Mrs.* Willington. Not *Ms.*"

Amanda mentally referred to the Metropolitan Hotel Handbook she'd received when she began working at the hotel eight months ago: *Metropolitan Hotel front desk clerks are Guest Specialists. Metropolitan Hotel policy is that the guest is always right—even when he or she appears to be in the wrong or is exceedingly difficult.* To Amanda it seemed that "exceedingly difficult" was a euphemism for obnoxious.

Hmmm, so since there was no suite with an adjoining double room available anywhere in this entire huge, thirty-two-story hotel, how exactly was Amanda to produce one?

"I wish there was—" Amanda began.

Mrs. Willington stepped closer, removed her ear muffs, and slid the band around her wrist. "Clerk, I don't care what you wish. I want two suitable rooms, adjoining, *now.*"

*How dare you, you pompous prima donna!* Amanda yelled back—silently of course. *I want this, I want that! Well, I want my baby boy to wake up healthy tomorrow. I want to be home with him right now instead of arguing with you. I want so many things . . .*

Amanda said none of this. It wasn't the Metropolitan way. The Metropolitan was one of the most expensive hotels in Manhattan. And as a "guest specialist," Amanda's job was to make Mrs. Willington happy.

The problem was that there weren't two adjoining rooms available. Mrs. Willington could have a double for herself and a double across the hall with two twin beds for her children, or she could have the one suite she reserved for all of them. The Metropolitan was hosting three different conventions this weekend, and the annual Christmas tree lighting at Rockefeller Center—just blocks away and a major attraction in a city full of attractions—was scheduled for this Tuesday. The hotel was booked.

Period.

Amanda forced another smile and explained to Mrs. Willington that she had two options: the one suite or the two non-adjoining doubles.

Was that steam coming out of Mrs. Willington's ears? *Yes, I do believe it is,* Amanda thought. The full force of the woman's anger was about to be let loose on Amanda, but luckily, Mrs. Willington's children had chosen that moment to chase each other around their mother, grabbing her fur coat to stop themselves from falling.

Mrs. Willington let out a shriek. "Stop that right now!" she yelled to her children, who stuck out their tongues at each other but listened. The woman smoothed the ruffled fur and turned back to Amanda. Or, rather, she turned back to Amanda's counter and began pounding on the call bell next to Amanda's computer monitor.

Amanda could feel her cheeks burning. The lunatic woman banged on the bell with unnecessary force. People in line and milling about the marble and glass lobby stopped and stared. Even Mrs. Willington's own children stopped throwing jelly beans at each other to stare at their mother—and they had to be used to her by now.

Amanda counted to three (one of the Metropolitan employee handbook's suggestions for dealing with "exceedingly difficult" guests). "Mrs. Willington, if you'll—"

*Ding! Ding! Ding! Ding! Ding!*

She pounded on the bell with all her strength.

"Mrs. Willington! How lovely to see you again!"

Uh oh, that was the voice of Anne Pilsby, the front desk manager. Amanda's boss.

Amanda glanced behind Mrs. Willington to find Anne rushing up to the woman. Anne's mouth was drawn into a tight coral line as she shot Amanda a withering look.

"Mrs. Willington," Anne gushed, smoothing her fitted tweed jacket. "I do hope everything is to your satisfaction this afternoon."

"It most certainly is not," enunciated Mrs. Willington, who launched into a tirade about Amanda's lack of skills, initative, hospitality, and diplomacy, especially when dealing with the wife of F.W. Willington.

Amanda had no idea who F.W. Willington was. And it was a shame that his wife seemed to think she had no other identity.

"Step aside, Ms. Sedgwick," Anne snapped, practically pushing Amanda out of the way to ease behind her computer. A few minutes and clicks of the keyboard later, Anne smiled. "Ah, I have found the perfect set of adjoining rooms for you, Mrs. Willington. Miss Sedgwick should have known there is always a set of rooms on reserve for our treasured guests. A suite for yourself, as always, with an adjoining double room with two full-size beds for your beautiful children. How big they're getting!" Anne added, smiling at the kids, who were now taking turns flying the silk flower through air as though it were an airplane.

"Ow!" yelped a woman, whirling to see what had poked her sharply in the back. The flower dropped to the floor at her feet. She glared at the children, now giggling and hiding behind their mother's legs. The woman waited for the mother's apology.

There was none.

"Brats," the woman muttered and stalked away. Anne ignored the incident, so clearly the injured party was not a wealthy repeat guest of the Metropolitan Hotel.

"I expect to be compensated for having to ring this bell so hard," Mrs. Willington said. "My hand is hurting now."

*Oh, brother!* Amanda thought, rolling her eyes. Was she kidding?

"Of course," Anne replied with a consoling smile. "A complimentary hand massage in our spa should do the trick."

No, she wasn't kidding. Neither was Anne, who lied about "on reserve" rooms. Yet she'd done some fast and clever guest reassignment.

Satisfied, Mrs. Willington grabbed her children by the hands and headed for the elevator. Anne snapped her fingers high in the air, and a porter rushed to help Mrs. Willington with her luggage.

Anne turned to Amanda, the bright white smile now replaced by a frown. "Amanda, I'm very disappointed in the way you handled one of our best—"

The phone rang at Amanda's station. As any of the front desk clerks could answer the ringing line from their stations, Amanda decided this wasn't the time to interrupt her boss's *That Wasn't the Metropolitan Way* speech.

"Well, answer it!" Anne barked, shaking her head.

I *hate this job. I hate this job. I hate this job,* Amanda silently chanted, picking up the phone.

"Metropolitan Hotel, front desk," Amanda said in the Metropolitan way—which meant with forced good cheer.

"Amanda, thank God I got you," came Lettie Monroe's panicked voice. "Tommy is burning up with fever. It's over a hundred and four! And he's so listless. I'm worried, Amanda."

Oh no. Lettie, Amanda's neighbor and her eleven-month-old son's babysitter, wasn't prone to exaggeration. Amanda squeezed shut her eyes for a second and tried to will the panic away. "Lettie, take Tommy to the emergency room in a cab right now. I'll meet you there."

"I'm on my way," Lettie responded. "See you soon."

Amanda hung up the phone. "Anne," she said to her boss, "I'll need to lea—"

Anne put her hands on her hips and surveyed Amanda. "You've needed to leave early two other times this month. Babies get sick, Amanda. It's what they do. I've raised two of my—"

*Babies get sick. It's what they do. . . .*

"Tommy was a month premature, Anne," Amanda interrupted through gritted teeth as she gathered her purse and checked her wallet for cab fare. "He's prone to—"

Anne dismissed her with a wave of her own manicured hand. "Maybe if you'd breastfed, you wouldn't have such a sickly child."

Amanda recoiled as if slapped in the face. How dare she! "For your information, not that it's any of your business, I did breast—"

"I'm not interested in your personal life, Amanda," Anne said, raising her chin in a show of dismissal. "If you abandon your post, I'll have no choice but to permanently relieve you of your employment at the Metropolitan Hotel. Your frequent absences leave us short-staffed without proper notice, per the Metropolitan Employee Handbook."

No. Amanda couldn't lose her job. No job meant no health insurance. And Tommy's frequent ear infections and high fevers meant constant trips to the pediatrician.

There was no way Amanda could afford COBRA on what meager savings she had.

"Anne, please." Amanda abandoned her indignation and flat-out pleaded. "Tommy is very sick. He has a fever of a hundred and four, and he's—"

"And it seems your babysitter is fully capable of taking him to the hospital," Anne interrupted. "If I ran home every time my child got a cold I would not have achieved the position I hold now."

Amanda refrained from taking the glass of cold water on her desk and throwing it in her boss's face.

"Tommy doesn't have a cold," Amanda said. "He could be seriously ill and—"

Anne held up her palm in Amanda's face. "I've now wasted ten minutes of my own day and this hotel's time in dealing with you, Amanda. Enough is enough. This was the third time I've had to warn you about your attendance record. Pack up your locker, return your name pin and uniform, and see payroll about picking up your final paycheck. I'll alert them that you're coming. You're fired."

*Who are you, you monster?* Amanda thought numbly.

This wasn't happening. This couldn't be happening.

"The only place I'm going is to the hospital," Amanda told Anne. She took off her name pin and thrust it into the woman's hand.

"Ow!" Anne yelped. "You pricked me."

The phone rang at Amanda's desk. Amanda grabbed it, praying it wasn't Lettie with more bad news about Tommy.

It wasn't. It was a guest wanting information.

"It's for you," Amanda told Anne and shoved the phone at her before running across the lobby, praying she could get a cab.

Only when she was outside in the chilly December air did she realize she forgot to get her coat and hat.

Amanda frantically raised her arm to hail a taxi in front of the hotel. *Please, please, please,* she prayed to the fates of the universe.

*As if this is my lucky day*, she thought, letting out a frustrated breath as occupied taxi after occupied taxi sped past. Finding a cab in midtown Manhattan was never easy, let alone at the start of rush hour and during the holiday season. The streets were crowded with New Yorkers and tourists coming and going in every direction

Amanda shivered in her thin uniform. If a taxi didn't come soon, Amanda would have to waste more time running back inside for her coat, which was on the basement level in the "hourly employee" locker rooms.

*Please, please, please,* she prayed again, extending her arm as far as it could go, her eyes darting to check for available cabs.

Yes! A taxi was pulling to a stop right in front of the hotel and right in front of Amanda. *Thank you,* she whispered to the darkening sky. She rushed over to the cab and claimed it by holding onto the door handle, prepared to pull it open the moment the slowpokes inside appeared ready to emerge.

*Hurry up, please!* she silently shouted at the occupants of the back seat, who were taking their sweet time. The man had his hand in his wallet, and the woman, who was facing the other way, had a silver cell phone pressed to her ear.

As she watched the male occupant pay the driver and await his change, she decided she would try to talk to Anne tomorrow, when she went back for her coat. Maybe Ms. Scrooge would be in a better mood. Or find an ounce of holiday season compassion in her heart.

*Come on,* Amanda urged the couple silently. Finally, the man turned to open the door, and Amanda pulled it open for him. *Out, out, out!* she coaxed mentally. He was yakking into his own cell phone while extending a hand into the taxi to help the woman, also still gabbing on her phone.

Finally, the woman emerged. And Amanda froze.

It was her sister.

Her half sister, acutally. Olivia Sedgwick.

Without looking in Amanda's direction once, despite the fact that Amanda was standing a foot in front of her sister, Olivia dashed onto the curb, saying something into the phone about a "layout." As Amanda stood there open-mouthed, her hand barely still touching the cab's door, the man pressed something into Amanda's hand, then joined Olivia on the curb and escorted her into the hotel.

Amanda opened her fist to find a five dollar bill.

*Well, isn't that humiliating,* Amanda thought, darting into the taxi and giving the driver her destination. Olivia's companion clearly took Amanda, dressed in uniform, for a front-door valet, whose job it was to greet arriving guests.

As the driver flipped the meter and pulled away from the curb, Amanda glanced out the window just in time to see Olivia and the man greet some well-dressed people who were seated at a grouping of plush sofas in the lobby. She watched Olivia smile and laugh and shake hands, and then as the taxi swerved into a lane that was actually moving, she lost sight of her sister and turned back around.

Whoa. Olivia Sedgwick in the flesh. She felt a stab of envy and longing that startled her. She thought she had accepted the very different lives her sisters led and put them in their proper perspective years ago.

*When was the last time I saw her?* Amanda wondered. *When was the last time I saw my other half sister, Ivy? Or the only person we all have in common: our father, winner of the I-Can't-Be-Bothered-To-Be-A-Father award, William Sedgwick.*

It had been years since she'd spoken to her father, but Amanda could pinpoint the exact day she had last spoken to her sisters: eleven months ago, on the day her son, Tommy, was born on a snowy January morning.

Because he'd been premature, she barely had a look at him before he was whisked away to the neonatal intensive care unit. And while they were separated for that short while before she could go see him, she was so overcome with longing for her family—and overcome with longing to provide her newborn son with family—that she picked up the phone in the room and called Olivia and immediately got her answering machine. Amanda had left a message, informing Olivia that she was a brand new aunt and that mother and child were doing well at Lenox Hill Hospital.

Amanda had left the same message for their other half sister, Ivy. And then she called her father's office, which was the only number she had for William Sedgwick. Though it was only eight o'clock in the morning when she'd phoned, William's secretary had answered. William had been in, but in a closed-door meeting and had asked not to be disturbed for any reason. Amanda didn't want to reduce the birth of his grandson to a message on a While You Were Out pad, but she wasn't sure William would call back if she didn't leave a message of magnitude. The secretary, a very pleasant-sounding woman, congratulated Amanda heartily, and assured her she'd let William know the great news the moment the conference room door opened.

It must have been some long meeting.

# CHAPTER 2

From the beginning of her pregnancy Amanda knew that Tommy's extended family would have to come from her side; there was no other side. Tommy's father wanted nothing to do with her or their child.

*Don't think about him,* Amanda cautioned herself. But of course she did. Too often. Paul Swinwood's good-looking face, his warm brown eyes, that one dimple in his left cheek, appeared before her mind's eye. And as always, she had to blink back the sting of tears that accompanied any thought of him.

She'd loved him.

She'd known him only a few months, but she'd been crazy in love with him.

"I can't, Amanda," he'd said when she told him she was pregnant with his child. "I'm sorry, but this isn't what I want. I am so sorry."

That was it. She'd told him she was pregnant, and five minutes later he'd left her apartment. She never saw him again. She'd tried to call him during her pregnancy, and when Tommy was born. His phone had been disconnected. And her letters had come back marked "Return To Sender."

Amanda had always considered herself a smart woman, a good judge of character. She'd truly believed that Paul had loved her too.

*Yeah, so why did he abandon you the minute you told him you were pregnant? Why did he change his phone number and flee his apartment? Yet she had refused to phone or visit him at his company.*

"Maybe he was just too scared," her best friend, Jenny, had said. "Jerk! Coward! I don't care if the two of you were only dating for a few months. So what? A decent human being doesn't run away from something like that! Jerk!"

Jenny sounded off on the issue of Paul Swinwood for days, weeks, months. Finally, right before she had given birth, Amanda told Jenny to let it go. Paul was gone, and that was the only issue on the table. Amanda's future and her baby's future were what Amanda had to focus on. Not the merits or lack thereof of a man she didn't know as well as she thought she did.

And so, with no father handing out cigars the moment Thomas Sedgwick came into the world, with no grandmother knitting baby booties—Amanda's beloved mother had passed away several years ago—with no family in the world other than her long-estranged father and her long-estranged half sisters, Amanda wanted desperately for her son to have the family that Amanda had never had.

And so she'd called her half sisters. And she called her father.

And she'd received the same response from all three.

A "Congratulations On Your New Baby" card, inside which was a check. One thousand dollars from William Sedgwick, and one hundred dollars each from Olivia and Ivy. In addition to the checks, her father and sisters had also each sent flowers and a stuffed animal. A plush teddy bear from William and one from Olivia and an adorable giraffe from Ivy.

Tommy loved all three.

Neither sister visited Amanda in the hospital or asked to see Tommy, their nephew. They had both called back the day Tommy was born, each congratulating her, and each with a reasonable excuse as to why she couldn't come to the hospital. Olivia, a features editor of a national women's magazine, was going on location somewhere for an important photo shoot with a supermodel. And Ivy, a police officer in New Jersey, was working around the clock on a stake-out.

And Amanda's father, the venerable William Sedgwick, simply sent another check, this time for two thousand dollars, when Amanda left a second message telling him she would love to see him, would love for him to meet his grandson.

Amanda had sent back the first check, hard as it was to turn down a thousand dollars. Perhaps he'd thought its return meant Amanda was saying a thousand bucks wasn't enough. Perhaps the second check, which she also returned, was simply "please leave me alone" money.

Amanda didn't know. Couldn't know.

Because she didn't know her father at all.

The wealthy William Sedgwick, a man her mother never married and a father Amanda barely saw her entire life, had never been interested in Amanda or any of his daughters as far as Amanda could tell. If he were a true father to her, as she always dreamed, she might have kept the first check and opened a college fund for Tommy. But to accept what seemed like guilt money, not that William Sedgwick appeared to feel guilty for anything, was just wrong to Amanda.

She'd hoped the birth of an innocent child would sway her sisters into forging a new relationship. But neither Olivia nor Ivy seemed interested.

Born to different mothers, only one of whom was married to William, the three Sedgwick sisters led very different lives. Amanda's mother, a former secretary of William's until her pregnancy and lovestruck gazes got her transferred to another office, also refused his "keep quiet" money and raised Amanda single-handedly in Queens. Olivia's mother, a wanna-be socialite, furious when William wouldn't marry her when she became pregnant, famously sued him for millions in child support and won a comfortable living. Ivy's mother, who often bragged that her daughter was the only legitimate one, divorced him when his frequent affairs humiliated her to the point that being his wife was more embarrassing than prestigious. She too made out handsomely financially, and was able to raise Ivy in style.

William never married again. A brilliant businessman with no interest in family life, William rarely saw his three daughters except for a two-week summer vacation at his cottage on the southern coast of Maine. The mothers were not permitted on the property, and as each woman had her own motive for wanting her daughter invited back every year, the mothers complied.

Despite her negative feelings about William, Amanda's mother felt it was important that Amanda get to know her sisters. Olivia's mother wanted to make sure her daughter was exposed to her father's rich-and-famous lifestyle. And Ivy's mother wanted to make sure the other Sedgwick daughters, *illegitimates* as she called them, received no more, preferably *less,* than Ivy.

Over the summers, Amanda got glimpses of goodness in both her sisters, but generally, the three girls treated each other as rivals.

And grew up as strangers.

*What different lives we lead,* Amanda thought as the taxi sped through the Midtown Tunnel toward the New York City borough of Queens, where Amanda lived. Olivia was as glamorous as her job—beautiful, stylish, and very well-off in her own right. Ivy, much to her snooty mother's dismay, was a policewoman in a small New Jersey town and was also beautiful, but in a different way than Olivia. Ivy was earthy and natural, preferring jeans and sweaters to Olivia's cashmere and gold.

And then there was Amanda, who could hardly make ends meet, but whose son Tommy was worth the heartache his father had caused. If Amanda let herself think about it, the parallels between her own situation and her mother's love affair with William Sedgwick so many years ago would be particularly painful.

The family's lack of interest in getting to know

Amanda and her baby was also painful, but Amanda was so fulfilled by motherhood that she stopped feeling so alone in the world.

*I have my son. I have good friends. I have a roof over my head,* Amanda told herself.

*Well, I have a roof over my head if I can convince Anne not to fire me,* she amended as the taxi bumped and swerved its way along.

Tommy was going to be all right. He'd been admitted to the hospital and had been kept overnight for observation and treatment, but it was just a bad virus.

As Amanda watched him sleep in his crib, which was against the wall in her bedroom, Tommy stirred and pressed his tiny fist against his cheek. Her heart squeezed in her chest.

*I love you, my sweet boy,* she whispered. *I love you so much.*

Leaning against the crib, on the baby blue round rug on the floor, was the big giraffe Ivy had sent and sitting next to it, the bear from Olivia. The sight of the stuffed animals sitting side by side made Amanda happy, made her feel as though her sisters were almost in the room, in spirit, if not physically. When she looked at the giraffe and bear she believed her sisters did care about Tommy, did want to know him, did want to be his aunts.

There was simply too wide a gulf between them for her sisters to put aside years of estrangement simply because a child had been born. But if not a child, an innocent baby, a new Sedgwick, then what?

Amanda bent over Tommy's crib and kissed his forehead, which was cooler now. He was still wheezing a bit, but at least his cough didn't sound so dire, Amanda thought as she watched his little chest rise and fall under his blue-and-white pajamas.

Amanda glanced at her watch. It was almost eight-thirty. Anne worked until nine on Fridays. Perhaps if she called her boss now, begged—yes, begged—for her job back, Anne could be swayed. This was busy season at the hotel, and perhaps Anne needed Amanda at work tomorrow more than she needed to train a new hire.

Amanda picked up the phone and dialed. A receptionist transferred her to Anne's direct line.

"Metropolitan Hotel, front desk manager Anne Pilsby speaking."

Amanda took a deep breath. "Anne, it's Amanda Sedgwick. I wanted to tell you how sorry I am for what happened yesterday. I understand how important it is for your staff to be reliable, and I want you know I'm taking new steps to ensure that I won't have to leave work again."

That was true. Even if those steps were baby steps. Lettie, her neighbor and Tommy's sitter, felt terrible that Amanda had gotten herself fired.

"I feel so guilty!" Lettie had said. "I should have just taken Tommy to the hospital and left you alone. The result was the same, whether you had been there or not."

But it wasn't. At the sight of his mother, Tommy had stopped crying and had sagged into her arms. If Tommy had had a bad cold or a mild fever, Amanda would have stayed at work. But a fever of one hundred four was dangerous, as was dehydration. And besides, Lettie had children in school; it wasn't fair of Amanda to ask Lettie to bring home Tommy's illnesses to her own kids.

Amanda had assured Lettie that she'd work on her boss or try to find a job that would pay the rent and allow her more flexibility. She'd yet to find one of those, though.

*Please be understanding,* Amanda prayed into the phone. *I need the benefits. I need the week's vacation I have coming to me.*

"I'm sorry, Amanda," Anne responded without a shred of feeling in her voice. "But I have already replaced you. Please empty the contents of your locker within a week or they will be removed and discarded. You may pick up your final paycheck, which will include your vacation pay, docked from the extra personal days you've taken this year. Human Resources can tell you how to extend your health insurance. Good-bye."

Amanda listened to the click and the buzzing dial tone for a few moments and then finally replaced the phone. She stared up at the ceiling, mentally subtracting the four extra personal days she'd taken.

Well, one day's vacation pay would still cover the electric bill and a few small Christmas gifts.

*I'll get through this,* she told herself. *I'm a resourceful person. If I nursed my mother through the final stages of cancer, I can do anything.*

That was hard. And at least her mother had still been alive, her warm hand still able to hold Amanda's. Her mother had been sick for over two years, and Amanda had dropped out of City College after only three semesters in order to care for her mom and also work full time. She'd never built up any kind of longevity in one industry because she needed flexibility to deal with the fluctuations of her mother's treatment. Once, she'd wanted to be a nurse, but the requirements were more than Amanda could sign on for at the time. And then her mother lost the battle and Amanda got pregnant. On her own in every sense of the word, she couldn't very well afford to go back to school for any kind of career training.

The phone rang, and Amanda jumped to answer it. Perhaps it was Anne, calling back to say she didn't want to be such a Scrooge, after all.

"Amanda Sedgwick?" asked a male voice she didn't recognize.

"Yes, this is she."

"My name is George Harris. I'm an attorney at Harris, Pinker and Swift."

Was Anne suing her? For being a bad employee?

"We represent your father, William Sedgwick," the man continued. "I'm so sorry for bothering you at this sensitive time, Ms. Sedgwick, but I do need to inform you that the reading of the will is scheduled for—"

Amanda blinked. "Excuse me?" she interrupted. "The reading of the will?"

*Sensitive time?*

"Your father's will," Mr. Harris explained.

"My father's will? I don't understand," Amanda said.

Silence.

"Ms. Sedgwick," the man continued, "I am very sorry. I was under the impression that you knew that William—that your father—had passed away."

*What?*

Amanda gripped the phone. "My father is dead?"

"Yes, unfortunately," Mr. Harris said. "He died last night. Late-stage cancer was discovered some months ago—he didn't want anyone to know. I'm so sorry."

As the air in Amanda's lungs whooshed out of her, she dropped the phone. She sat numbly, blankly staring at her lap, where the receiver lay.

"Ms. Sedgwick?"

Amanda picked up the phone and put it to her ear, but all she heard was the rushing beat of her own heart.

*My father is dead.*

*My father is gone.*

*The father I never really knew is now gone forever. I'll never have the chance to know him. Tommy will never have the chance to know his grandfather.*

Tears welled in Amanda's eyes. "I'm here," she told the lawyer.

"Ms. Sedgwick, do you have a piece of paper and a pen? You'll need to jot down our address and the date and time of the reading of the will."

Amanda picked up the notepad and pen on the side table and numbly wrote down the information the lawyer gave her. He offered his condolences again, and for the second time in fifteen minutes, the phone buzzed in her ear.

She glanced down at the address in midtown Manhattan, on the East Side. She shouldn't have bothered writing it down.

There was no way she was going to the reading of her father's will.

# CHAPTER 3

As Ethan Black settled another piece of wood in the old coal stove and the flames flickered back to life, he could have sworn he heard a knock at the front door of his cabin.

Not likely.

The howling winter wind must have knocked down another tree branch, sending it crashing against the door or the window. This was his third winter in Maine, and he was almost used to the bitter cold, the frigid wind. Where he used to live, on the thirty-second floor of a Manhattan skyscraper with an entire wall of windows, he could actually feel the building shake on windy days, but the wind never sounded so fierce as it did in Maine.

He liked the sound.

He listened to the branches rapping against his door again, and then got back to work, fixing the Marrows' toaster, which probably cost ten bucks ten years ago. His nearest neighbors, a mile and a half down the road, the Marrow family consisted of a widowed father and his thirteen-year-old son, Nick. Around six months ago, Ethan had come upon the kid on one of the trails behind his house; he was bent over a tree stump, poking at wires in a busted CD player with a screw driver. Frustrated and close to tears, Nick threw the CD player against another tree, and Ethan had picked it up. He'd offered to show Nick how to fix it, and the kid let loose for twenty minutes about how his dad used to do stuff like that with him until his mother died almost a year ago, and how now his father mostly sat in the leather recliner in their living room and watched *Law and Order* reruns.

Ethan had begun fixing the CD player on that stump in the woods, Nick scowling nearby for a while until he finally came over and watched, asking questions, asking Ethan to undo what he just did so that Nick could try it himself. The next day, Nick had stopped by the cabin on the way to school, beaming with the news that his dad had been so impressed by Nick's hidden talent that he'd gotten off the recliner and driven Nick to Home Depot to set up a "fix it" shop in their garage. Nick hadn't mentioned that Ethan had actually fixed the CD player, so now Nick needed Ethan to teach him how to fix other small appliances. Every week or so he turned up with something new. Last week it had been an electric shaver. He'd shown the boy how to fix it, then took it apart again and had the kid take a crack at it. It had taken Nick Marrow an entire week of afternoons after school, but he'd done it.

Early this morning, when Ethan arrived home from his six-mile run, he found Nick sitting on the top step of the cabin's porch, slumped over a silver toaster. With tears in his eyes, Nick explained that his mother had bought the toaster a few years ago and had their names engraved on it, something she'd had done after seeing it on an episode of *Everybody Loves Raymond.* The toaster suddenly didn't work that morning while his dad was making frozen waffles, and his father burst into tears and left the room and hadn't said a word since.

"I can't fix it," Nick said, tears pooling in his eyes. "I tried for hours in our garage. I can't even deal with trying anymore."

"This one's on me," Ethan assured the kid. "I'll have it ready for you after school. How's that?"

Nick's bony shoulders had slumped with relief and then he ran off toward home.

Poor kid. Grief was something Ethan knew about all too well.

Ethan turned the toaster upside down and was about to reach for a screwdriver when the rapping intensified. Ethan glanced up and almost jumped. A young man in his early twenties was knocking on the window and waving frantically at Ethan. His cheeks were almost as red as his hair.

*Who the hell is that?* Ethan wondered, rushing over to the door to save the guy from frostbite. It was difficult to get lost in Ethan's neck of the woods, which really was the woods. If you came down this way, you most likely meant to.

The moment Ethan opened the door, the guy burst in.

"Man, it is freaking freezing here!" the guy said. "Hey, can I hang by that fireplace for a minute? I can't even feel my nose."

Ethan nodded, and when the guy darted over to the fireplace, hopping up and down to warm himself, Ethan could plainly see a huge SUV parked in the dirt driveway.

The SUV had New York plates. Which meant it wasn't anyone Ethan wanted to see.

"You're Ethan Black?" the guy asked, rubbing his hands together.

"Who wants to know?"

He gestured to the messenger bag slung across his navy blue down jacket. Stitched in black script across the flap of the bag was the name of his company.

"The law firm of Harris, Pinker and Swift," said the guy.

Three years ago, a messenger delivering a lawsuit or subpoena was as commonplace to Ethan as breathing. Not anymore.

*Man, whatever this is, I don't want to know,* he thought. Ethan wanted to run his miles and fix Nick's houseful of broken appliances and be left the hell alone. The last thing he wanted—the very last thing—was anyone from New York City coming to call.

"George Harris asked me to personally deliver this package to you," the messenger said, opening his bag and pulling out a plain manila envelope. "He said to tell you it concerned William Sedgwick."

William Sedgwick? The name changed everything.

Ethan nodded and took the package, which he set on the wood table in front of the fireplace. Then he poured some coffee into a thermos, added milk and sugar, and handed it to the messenger, who gave him a surprised thanks. Ethan then pulled a fifty from his wallet and tucked it into the messenger's still-cold hands, and told him to scram before he developed frostbite.

From the window, Ethan watched the SUV make its way slowly up the half-mile-long drive and then turn onto the main road. When the car disappeared from view, Ethan eyed the package on the table. It was a simple manila envelope with Ethan's name and address handwritten across the front.

What could this be about? It had been three years since Ethan had contact with William. And they'd met only once. What could the man want with him now?

He wondered what would have happened if he hadn't met William Sedgwick on that fateful evening three years ago.

*You know what would have happened,* he reminded himself.

Ethan threw another piece of wood in the coal stove, stoked the fire in the massive stone fireplace, brewed a fresh pot of coffee, fixed the Marrows' toaster, watched the fresh powdery snow start to swirl down and around in the wind outside, and even washed his breakfast dishes, all in the name of procrastinating. He didn't want to open that envelope. Not yet.

*"One day, Ethan Black,"* William Sedgwick had said, *"I might just call in that favor you promised me . . . "*

The day must have come. Yet what could a man of William Sedgwick's wealth and power possibly need from Ethan? William had known that Ethan had completely given up his old life, knew that he'd taken his advice and built himself the cabin up here. Ethan had once sent him a postcard from the general store in town.

Curiosity got the better of Ethan. He slit open the envelope and peered inside. Two letters and two five-by-seven photographs were the entire contents. One letter was on the lawyer's stationery; the other was from William Sedgwick, handwritten in black ink.

*Dear Ethan,*

*Once you told me that if I ever needed a favor, I should just say the word. I'm saying it. I have complete faith that you will do what I am asking of you, which is a great comfort to me.*

*If you're reading this, I have passed on . . .*

"Damn," Ethan said, shaking his head.

He slid the letter back into the envelope and placed it gently on the table.

He'd read enough for the moment.

"What do you mean you're not going to the reading of the will?" Jenny Coles asked, pouring two cups of tea from the pot on the coffee table.

"I mean I'm not going," Amanda repeated. She leaned back against the sofa in her small living room and wrapped her hands around the warm mug, breathing in the comforting aroma of Irish Breakfast tea.

Jenny put her feet up on the coffee table and flipped her long auburn hair behind her shoulders. "Amanda, let's go over your situation, shall we? One: You were fired from your job yesterday. Two: Your health insurance will be terminated at the end of the month. Three: You have to pay your rent in three weeks. Four: Diapers don't grow on trees. Need I go on?"

Jenny was Amanda's best friend and had been since high school, when Jenny moved to Queens from Brooklyn. The women were complete opposites and always had been, but for some reason, that worked for them. Jenny was outgoing and daring and trendy; at the moment she wore a long black mohair sweater coat, a white satin camisole, and sexy low-rise jeans, with knee-high black leather boots. In contrast, Amanda wore a long sleeve pink T-shirt with jeans and sneakers and a burp cloth tossed over her shoulder. "Mom clothes," Jenny called them.

Jenny sipped her tea. "I'll sit on this sofa for as long as it takes to convince you that it's not wrong to accept whatever your father left you in his will."

Amanda let out a deep breath. "But Jenny, it is wrong. How can it not be wrong to suddenly take money from a man who didn't care that I was his daughter when he was alive? What does that say about me?"

"It says you're not an idiot," Jenny insisted. "It says you need the money. It says you won't let pride stand in the way of surviving. It says that until you find a new job with benefits, not easy to do at the start of the holiday season, you're screwed."

"Even if you're right," Amanda said, "I—"

*I don't want his money. I wanted* him. *I wanted a father.*

"Sweetheart," Jenny said. "I know your dream was

for your father to be a dad to you. But that never happened and now it never will. It's time to stop. To let go of that and look to the future. And the future requires the money he may have left you."

Amanda crossed her arms over her chest. "I don't want his money. It would make me feel dirty to use his money when it has no meaning behind it."

"Oh, Amanda," Jenny said. "Integrity is not going to pay your rent."

She was right, Amanda knew. But how could she do it? What would her mother think? Her mom hadn't taken a dime from William Sedgwick her entire life.

*Mom? I need some guidance here.* Amanda directed her thoughts toward the ceiling.

"How about if you just go to the reading," Jenny suggested. "Just go and listen. Maybe he didn't leave you money. Maybe he left you a beautiful letter, saying how much he regrets what a crappy father he was."

"That's possible," Amanda said, brightening. "Perhaps he did write me a letter or left a memento of who he was. I'd like that. And it would be nice to be able to see Olivia and Ivy, offer my condolences to them."

Suddenly it occurred to Amanda that she had seen one of her sisters, by complete coincidence, on the very day their father had died. It seemed like divine intervention had placed Amanda and Olivia in each other's paths yesterday. Even if Olivia hadn't seen her.

"You're right," Amanda told her friend and took a sip of her tea. "I'll definitely go."

Jenny smiled, grabbed a chocolate chip cookie off the tray on the coffee table and bit into it with a satisfied sigh. "I knew I'd say the right thing eventually. That almost feels as good as this cookie tastes."

Ethan stood by the window of his cabin, alternately glancing at his watch and looking for a flash of Nick Marrow's royal blue down jacket to appear in his driveway.

*Come on, kid.*

It was four o'clock, and with a six hour drive to New York City ahead of him and the storm coming, Ethan wanted to hit the road now.

Finally, the bright blue turned up against the dusting of white snow outside.

"Going somewhere?" Nick asked, gesturing at Ethan's suitcase by the door.

"New York City," Ethan said.

"Wow! Really? That's so cool! I'm dying to go to New York. You know people there?"

"I used to," Ethan said. "Now, just some business."

"I didn't think you had any business," Nick said, pulling off his hood and gloves. "My dad and I figured you were either a reclusive millionaire who didn't have to work or a bounty hunter maybe, or even an escaped convict."

Ethan laughed. "None of the above. I'm just a regular guy who likes living a simple life, that's all. Your toaster's all fixed. Works like new."

Usually a whirlwind of motion, Nick froze. His gaze shot to the toaster on the kitchen table and at the plate of two chocolate-frosted Pop Tarts next to it, and he burst into tears.

Usually when the boy was on the verge of tears, which was often, he blinked back the tears hard. A thirteen-year-old boy didn't want to be caught crying. But this time, the tears fell down his cheeks, and he didn't try to stop them.

"Nick? What's wrong?" Ethan asked, placing a hand on the boy's shoulder. "The toaster works great. The Pop Tarts are proof."

Nick sniffled. "I don't know. I thought maybe . . . I don't know," he said, covering his face with his hands.

"You thought maybe what?" Ethan asked.

"I thought if the toaster didn't work, then maybe that would almost be a good thing." His face crumpled and he slid down to the floor on his butt, the tears streaming down his face. Sobs wracked his thin body.

Ethan grabbed a box of tissues from the counter, then slid down next to Nick. "It would be a good thing because you could maybe start to forget a little? Not forget your mom, I mean, but forget that she's gone?"

Nick turned to Ethan in surprise. "Yeah. That's exactly what I mean." Fresh tears welled up in his hazel eyes. "How'd you know?"

Ethan leaned his head back against the wall and stared up at the ceiling. "I lost someone close to me once. I know."

"Your mom?" Nick asked.

"My wife," Ethan told him.

*And our unborn child.*

"When was that?" Nick asked.

"Three years ago."

The boy thought for a moment. "Hey, that's when you moved here. Three years ago."

Ethan nodded. "That's right. Something about all this land, all this green—well, when it's not covered in snow—all these trees and lakes and trails, is good for getting over hard stuff."

Nick chewed on his lower lip. "Are you over losing your wife?"

Ethan thought of the wallet-sized photograph he kept of Katherine, three months pregnant and not yet showing, except for the tell-tale glow on her face, the joy in her smile.

"No, Nick. I'm not over it. But there are ways to help a person find peace with a terrible loss."

"What ways?" the teenager asked.

"Like hiking. Like jogging. Like taking things apart and putting them back together. Like talking to those close to you."

Not that Ethan talked to anyone.

Nick let out a frustrated breath. "I can't talk to my dad. Every time I bring up Mom, he looks like he's going to cry."

"You know what, Nick? I think if you bring that toaster home to your dad, and whip up some of his favorite frozen waffles, he might take it as a sign."

"A sign of what?" Nick asked.

"That some things can be fixed."

The boy brightened. "You think so?"

"Yeah, I think so," Ethan said. "You and your dad are both still here. And though you'll always miss your mom, you can always find ways to honor her memory. Using that toaster that she loved is a fine way."

*Or planting a tree in the back yard.*

Katherine had loved trees. She'd been studying horticulture.

"Yeah, that's true," Nick said, getting to his feet. He picked up the toaster and looked at it with reverence, then headed for the door.

"Those Pop Tarts are for you," Ethan told him.

Nick smiled and chomped on one pastry and put the other in his jacket pocket.

"Look, Nick, I'm not sure when I'll be back. But if you need me, you call my cell phone, okay?"

Nick nodded. "I think I'm gonna be okay, though. I don't know, I just feel different. It's weird."

Ethan smiled. "Take care."

He watched the boy run through the falling snow toward home, the toaster in his arms.

It was time for Ethan to go home too. But for very different reasons.

# CHAPTER 4

At least ten times, Amanda had picked up the phone and put it back down again, undecided whether she should call her sisters to offer condolences for the loss of their father.

*This is insane,* she thought each time she put down the phone. How had their relationship come to this?

Because we have no relationship. We've never had a relationship.

In the end, Amanda decided to wait until the reading of the will, where she could speak to Olivia and Ivy in person. That would be warmer than a phone call anyway, she rationalized.

"Hey, that's not rationalizing," Jenny assured her when she arrived with a black pants suit draped over her arm. "It's the truth." She nuzzled Tommy with her nose. "Hi sweetie-pie! Guess who's going to babysit you while Mommy goes to the city! That's right! Auntie Jenny."

Amanda blew Jenny a kiss and disappeared into her bedroom with the pants suit Jenny was letting her borrow for the occasion. With a closet full of "mom clothes," Amanda didn't have much to choose from.

She tried the little leopard-print scarf Jenny had brought over, but it was both too trendy for her and seemed too whimsical for the occasion. Amanda put on the diamond stud earrings her mother had left her and her one pair of nice black pumps.

"You'll be fine," Jenny assured her when Amanda came into the living room. "Just remember that no matter what, you have Tommy. Okay? He'll keep you focused on what's important."

Amanda smiled and nodded and squeezed her friend's hand, giving Tommy one last kiss on the forehead before putting on her black wool coat and heading out.

She walked to the subway on the corner, trying not to think too much, and in the train station she bought a newspaper to keep her mind occupied. As the train rumbled into the station, she thought about turning around, dashing back upstairs and into her apartment building, but then the doors to the train opened and she made herself get on.

She flipped through the newspaper, unable to concentrate. She read her horoscope, which promised good news today, and then Tommy's, which assured strange news.

*Why am I reading this?* she asked herself, folding the paper and staring out the darkened windows of the train. *Just breathe and remember what Jenny said: No matter what happens, you always have Tommy.*

Forty minutes later, Amanda stood in front of

the skyscraper office building in which Harris, Pinker and Swift was located.

This was it, she thought. In more ways than one.

She headed to the elevator bank and waited, then rode up to the nineteenth floor, and didn't feel the slightest fluttering of butterflies until the doors slid open and she stepped out. At the end of the carpeted hallway were two glass doors and a huge gold sign engraved with the firm's name.

She pulled the ornate gold handle and stepped inside, and she suddenly felt lightheaded. She felt as though she'd stepped over a threshold and that her life wouldn't be the same after today.

"Just head right through that door," the receptionist told Amanda, pointing at a wood door to the left of her desk.

The moment Amanda entered the large rectangular room she could feel the tension.

Olivia Sedgwick sat ramrod straight at a long polished wood table, looking over a large leather appointment book. She wore a stylish, fitted black suit and a short, netted black veil over her honey blond hair, which was pinned up in an elegant bun.

Olivia's mother, a tall, thin, regal-looking woman in her late fifties, sat beside her daughter, staring from her watch to the round clock on the wall. When the door had opened, Olivia's mother's head jerked up expectantly. The woman seemed disappointed that it was only Amanda.

Ivy Sedgwick was across from Olivia. With her short, straight brown hair, fringe of bangs, and warm, expressive green eyes, Ivy always appeared friendly, which gave Amanda a false sense of security about the youngest Sedgwick sister. Ivy was as complex and as complicated as Olivia. On one side of Ivy was her mother, also tall, also thin and also regal-looking.

William Sedgwick definitely had had a thing for tall, thin, regal-looking women, since Amanda's mother had also fit that description.

What Amanda would give to have her own mother in this room, sitting beside her!

On Ivy's right and holding her hand, grasping her hand, really, atop the table was a good-looking man in his thirties. Amanda had never seen him before.

Ah. A diamond gleamed on the ring finger of Ivy's left hand. The man must be her fiancé.

*And I didn't even know she was engaged,* Amanda thought sadly. *We might as well be strangers.*

Amanda smiled inwardly at the sight of Ivy and her handsome husband-to-be. When they were teenagers, Amanda had found Ivy crying more than once in their father's summer home during their two-week vacations together. Once, Ivy had opened up to Amanda, sobbing that she was a plain-Jane who would never have a boyfriend, never be kissed, never get married. Apparently, Olivia had tried to set up Ivy on a blind date with a friend of the guy she was dating, and when the blind date glimpsed Ivy, he suddenly came down with the flu.

Or so he said.

Olivia was the oldest Sedgwick sister; Ivy the youngest. And at fifteen, Olivia Sedgwick, who pored over beauty and fashion magazines and transformed herself into a style maven, had more requests for dates than there were summer nights. Ivy, on the other hand, had spent so many summer nights watching television, especially cop shows, that she developed a huge interest in police procedure and forensic science and subsequently spent her days in the local police precinct as a volunteer, filing and doing data entry.

And Amanda, the middle sister, who had dark blue eyes like Olivia and silky chestnut brown hair like Ivy, spent her summer weeks with her sisters observing them, trying to find a way in. Amanda had turned down a date with a local boy in order to spend an evening watching *NYPD Blue* with Ivy, hoping a common interest would create a bond. But it never really did. And Amanda had read *Seventeen* and *Glamour* and *Vogue* until she knew the supermodels by name, but that too didn't make Amanda and Olivia any closer.

And then Olivia turned eighteen and stopped coming for the summer vacations, and the tradition simply dissolved. Looking back, Amanda wondered what the point had been since William Sedgwick was hardly around during the two weeks he arranged for the four of them to spend together. In all her times at the house in Maine, Amanda had only even managed to develop a friendly relationship with Clara, William's housekeeper and cook.

Now, as Amanda sat down next to Olivia, the beautiful blonde glanced at her and offered a solemn smile. Amanda smiled back, and then looked over at Ivy, who also smiled somberly. It was something. If not spoken condolence, then at least a sympathetic connection.

Amanda felt other eyes on her; both sisters' mothers were looking at her with contempt.

As usual. Not that both mothers had it in for only Amanda; Olivia's mother glanced with disgust at both Amanda and Ivy; Ivy's mother glanced with the same scorn at both Amanda and Olivia. That had been going on since the girls were little.

Amanda's mother had rarely seen the other Sedgwick sisters, since she hadn't felt the need to hover over her daughter while in the presence of William or the girls. Amanda's mom hadn't wanted to even lay eyes on the man who'd terribly hurt and abandoned her, but she had nothing but kind words for his other daughters, whom she felt were innocent children caught in a lot of anger.

Olivia's and Ivy's mothers now turned their scorn on each other. An argument might have broken out had the door not opened just then.

An imposing man of sixty-something entered, holding a briefcase, which he set down at the head of the table.

"Good morning, ladies, gentleman. My name is George Harris, and I am William Sedgwick's attorney. William was a long-time friend as well as a client, and I am deeply sorry for your loss." He waited a moment, then sat and opened the briefcase. "I am about to explain the pertinent sections of William Sedgwick's last will and testament, which is uncontestable."

"We'll see about that," Olivia's mother muttered under her breath.

Olivia sent her mother a sharp glance.

"William has left each of his three daughters an envelope dated as to when it is to be handed out and opened," the lawyer said. On that date, each daughter may come to our office to pick up her envelope from our safe."

"When does Olivia get hers?" Olivia's mother asked.

The lawyer cleared his throat. "On December tenth, Amanda Sedgwick may pick up her envelope. On January thirtieth, Olivia Sedgwick may pick up her envelope. On March twentieth, Ivy Sedgwick—"

Ivy's mother shot up. "March twentieth is Ivy's wedding date! William was up to something! I demand to know what's going on!"

"You will sit down please, Mrs. Sedgwick," the lawyer stated calmly, "or you will be escorted out of the building. You are here at my discretion only."

Ivy's mother glared at the lawyer, but sat. Ivy's fiancé patted Ivy's hand.

"Amanda, dear," Olivia's mother said, "why don't you open your envelope right now? What's a few days? Especially when we're all so curious!"

The lawyer stood. "Any departure from the terms of the will shall render null and void the contents of the envelope or any claim whatsoever to William's estate."

"Why does Amanda get her envelope first?" Olivia's mother demanded to know. "She's not the oldest."

"Why don't you mind your own business?" Ivy's mother snapped.

"How dare you—" Olivia's mother snarled back.

"I'll tell you how I dare," Ivy's mother shouted. "As Ivy is William's only legitimate daughter, she is the only one who should inherit anything!"

"Mom!" Ivy said, her cheeks turning red. "Stop it right now!"

"Dear, I'm only trying to look out for your best interests. You're planning a very expensive wedding in three months. Surely your father intended to help with the arrangements, so—"

"I doubt that," Ivy's fiancé suddenly said, his expression glum. "Why would he help plan a wedding that he never wanted to see take place? He didn't think I was good enough for Ivy."

"Oh, Declan," Ivy said. "My father was just being a snob. He thought only a Wharton MBA investment banker who plays golf would be good enough."

"And what it is you do?" Olivia's mother asked Declan.

"I happen to be studying for my MBA at NYU," Declan responded. "William thought a thirty-year-old should be firmly established in business, not going to school."

"Well I think education and the pursuit of professional advancement is the most important thing," Ivy's mother said, patting Declan's hand. "You'll be a huge success one day. Declan is the son of an old friend of mine," Ivy's mother added. "I'm thrilled that he and my baby girl are getting married."

"I think it's nice that William would leave us anything at all," Ivy said, "considering how little he was involved in our lives."

"I wouldn't be so appreciative yet," Olivia's mother retorted. "You don't know what's in your envelope. Perhaps it's a bill for those summers you spent at his house in Maine."

"Mother," Olivia said through gritted teeth. "*Enough.*"

"Yes, enough," Ivy's mother seconded, staring down Olivia's mother.

Olivia and Ivy shook their heads and let out deep breaths in unison.

The lawyer stood. "Good day, ladies."

Both mothers shot up. "What? That's it?"

"That's it," Mr. Harris said. He turned to Amanda. "I'll see you on the tenth, Amanda. You can come any time during the day to pick up your envelope."

The tenth was Friday, two days from now.

"Once again, ladies," Mr. Harris said. "I can't stress enough that any deviation from the terms of the will shall disqualify that person. Once again, please accept my deepest sympathy for your loss." With that, he clicked shut his briefcase and left the room.

As there was nothing left to say or do, the mothers stood, hugged their respective daughters, and left.

Amanda, Olivia and Ivy remained seated.

"I can't believe he's really gone," Amanda said, staring down at her trembling hands.

"I know," said Ivy.

Olivia nodded.

And the three women sat there in silence, not exactly companionable but not unfriendly either, until the receptionist came in to let them know the room was needed for a partners' meeting.

"Well, I have to get back to the magazine," Olivia said.

"And I'd better get back to the precinct," Ivy said. "Declan," she added, glancing at her watch. "You'd better hop in a cab if you want to make your ten o'clock class."

Declan glanced at the clock on the wall and nodded. "You'll be all right?"

Ivy smiled and nodded. Declan kissed her and left.

"Nine forty-five," Amanda said, eying the clock.

"Tommy is probably just about ready for his morning nap."

Olivia and Ivy glanced at her.

"How old is he now?" Olivia asked as they all gathered their belongings and headed to the elevator bank.

"He'll be a year next month," Amanda responded.

"He's a beautiful baby," Ivy said.

"He definitely has the Sedgwick eyes," Olivia added as the elevator came.

And when the three women said awkward goodbyes on the street and then went their separate ways, Amanda realized her sisters must have looked at the baby pictures Amanda had sent along with Tommy's birth announcement.

She smiled. Perhaps her sisters did care about their nephew, after all.

Ethan stood in the shadows of a doorway across the street from the Manhattan law offices of Harris, Pinker and Swift, reading the *New York Times* obituary of William Sedgwick as he waited for the Sedgwick sisters to appear.

*. . . survived by his three daughters, Ivy Sedgwick of New Jersey, Amanda Sedgwick of Queens, and Olivia Sedgwick of Manhattan.*

And suddenly, he saw her, Amanda, exiting the building with two women, whom he assumed were her half sisters, Ivy and Olivia. They stood in front of the building, moving aside when a group of office workers congregated near them to smoke cigarettes. Ivy, Amanda, and Olivia stood talking, their expression serious. Somber.

He studied Amanda, the one with the long brown hair. It was strange to suddenly see her in person after looking at her photograph for two days. When he'd finally read the rest of William's letter and then glanced at the photograph of Amanda, he'd been unable to stop gazing at it.

It was more than just her beauty, but he couldn't pinpoint what it was about her face that affected him so much. Some men might even consider her plain. She wore no make-up, and her hair was the hair of a teenaged girl—long and untouched by glop or dye or hairspray. It was her eyes, Ethan thought. Dark blue and searching, thinking.

Amanda Sedgwick was smart. He could see that.

What he knew of Amanda he could write down on the palm of his hand. He knew she was a single mother, but nothing of her relationship with the baby's father. He knew she lived in a dumpy apartment building in Queens. He knew she worked for a hotel, but in what capacity, he had no idea.

William's letter left Ethan wanting to know more. Sure, the letter from the attorney gave detailed instructions, including some pertinent dates and times, such as this morning's reading of the will, and the tenth, when Amanda would receive her envelope. But something was still missing. Though Ethan knew exactly what he was supposed to do, what he didn't know was why.

Ethan reached into his inside coat pocket for the manila envelope from William and pulled out the photograph of Amanda. He was careful not to slide out the other photograph. The baby's photograph.

Her hair was a bit longer now. She wore a plain

black wool coat, and a plain back wool hat was pulled down over her ears. She was rubbing her hands from the cold.

*Well, Amanda, you might soon be able to afford gloves,* he thought.

*Unless you screw up.*

The women went their separate ways, and he watched Amanda head for the subway. He thought about following her, checking her out a little, but he'd had enough of this city and it was barely ten o'clock in the morning.

Last night, when Ethan had finally arrived in New York, the sight of the Manhattan skyline caused every muscle in his body to tense. He'd had to pull over on the highway.

"Why did you make me come back, William?" he'd screamed at the top of his lungs in his car, thousands of glittering lights from apartment building windows and car lights decorating the night sky. "You know why I left. You know what happened here."

Now, he took a deep breath. *How the hell am I going to survive here another day, let alone a full month?* he wondered, turning his collar up against the biting wind.

As Amanda disappeared down the steps of the subway station, Ethan headed the opposite way, keeping his head down, lest anyone recognize him. This neighborhood had been one of his old stomping grounds, and the thought of running into someone he knew—someone he used to know—was unbearable.

The cards and phone calls and concerned expressions had all been unbearable. *I'm so sorry for your loss, Ethan. . . .* Over and over and over. And some *I didn't even know you were married, Ethan. You lived, ate, and breathed the company. . . .*

He stopped dead in the middle of Sixth Avenue and stared up at the bright blue December sky, willing himself to shake away the thoughts, the memories. And then he continued on toward his hotel, where he could hole up until it was time to officially start the clock on the favor he owed William. His hotel had an Internet café, which meant he could drink a lot of strong, bracing coffee while doing a little digging for information on the mysterious Sedgwick family.

# CHAPTER 5

Amanda couldn't sleep. Again. She glanced at her bedside table. Five o'clock.

Five AM on Friday, December tenth.

Envelope Day.

Since leaving the lawyer's office, Amanda had been able to think of nothing else. What would be in the envelope? And what kind of envelope? Legal-size? Manila?

Would there be a letter inside? A check? A memento?

"Whatever it is," Jenny had said yesterday as the two friends took turns pushing Tommy on a park swing, "accept it."

Amanda flopped over onto her back and pulled the blankets up to her chin. *Accept it.*

She'd spent her entire life "accepting it." Accepting that she didn't have a father. Accepting that her son didn't have a father or a grandfather. Accepting that she had sisters from whom she was almost completely estranged.

When you couldn't do anything about your situation, she reminded herself, sometimes you did just have to accept it. You couldn't control other people; you could only control *yourself.*

And so when it came to the contents of the envelope, Amanda had no idea what she would do.

She didn't want to cut off her nose to spite her face, she thought, flopping onto her stomach. But she didn't want to live off her father's money when he was barely her father in the first place. William Sedgwick and Paul Swinwood had both proved to Amanda that blood alone didn't a father make.

Love. Concern. Togetherness. That was what made a family.

"How much do you have in your bank account?" Jenny had asked yesterday. "Enough to cover another couple of months' rent and some bills, right? What about after that?"

"I'll find another job," Amanda had retorted, not wanting to tell her friend how dire things really were. "I have eight months' experience as a high-end hotel front desk clerk. There are countless hotels in New York. I'm sure I'll find another job."

It had taken two months to find the job at the Metropolitan.

"Oh yes," Jenny had said, "I'm sure your former boss will give you a glowing reference."

Jenny had her there.

Amanda sat up in bed and leaned back against the headboard. "Mom," she said, glancing outside at dark morning sky, "Give me the strength to do the right thing, whatever that is."

Her mother would tell her that Tommy was the most important thing and that if she needed the money her father left her she should accept it with gratitude and think of it as someone up there looking out for her when she needed help most.

Her mother would tell her that she hadn't needed William's money only because she had a small inheritance from her own parents that had enabled enough security, should she lose her job. Her cancer battle had eaten up that money. And Tommy's neo-natal bills had used up her mother's life insurance.

She was getting ahead of herself, anyway. There could very well be a lump of coal in the envelope. Directions to William's grave site.

*Nothing like bitter sarcasm first thing in the morning.*

Perhaps there *would* be a letter in the envelope. A long, handwritten letter from her father, explaining *why*. Explaining that he did love her, did love Olivia and Ivy, that he wished he had been a different kind of father.

*Just find another job,* Amanda thought, watching the dawn break outside her window. Any kind of job to bring in enough money to cover the rent and bills. She could do that.

*What's in that envelope is out of my control.*

*Please be a letter,* she thought as Tommy began stirring in his crib across the small bedroom. *That's all I want.*

"Right this way, Ms. Sedgwick," said George Harris's secretary.

Amanda steadied her shoulders and followed the woman through a door marked PRIVATE. Inside the room was a polished wood desk and a chair.

"Mr. Harris will join you momentarily," the secretary said and then closed the door.

Amanda paced the room, then sat down, then paced, then sat down and stared at the door.

She glanced at her watch. It was a little after nine AM. She'd paced her apartment, wondering, worrying, chewing a fingernail until Lettie had knocked on the door to babysit Tommy. And then it had been time to go, but Amanda's feet had stopped listening to her brain.

"It'll be okay," Lettie had assured her. "No matter what, honey, you'll be okay. You always have been. Just remember that."

*Remember that now,* Amanda told herself as the door opened and George Harris entered, a safety-deposit box in his hand.

With a cordial hello and a good morning, the lawyer set the box on the desk in front of Amanda. He withdrew a set of keys from his pocket, and opened the box, and Amanda closed her eyes.

"Are you all right?" the attorney asked.

"Nervous, but all right," Amanda said.

He offered an empathetic smile, and then removed a plain, white, legal-sized envelope from the box. "Here is your envelope," he said. "You are required to open it before midnight tonight. The contents of the envelope are self-explanatory, but should you have any questions, please don't hesitate to call."

"Thank you, Mr. Harris," she said, hoping he'd say something else, something assuring. But he said nothing before picking up the box and leaving the room.

When the door closed behind him, Amanda

turned back to the desk and stared at the envelope in front of her. Typed in plain black letters across the front was: TO BE OPENED BY AMANDA SEDGWICK ON DECEMBER TENTH.

Amanda picked it up. Practically weightless. There couldn't be more than one sheet of paper inside. Or a check.

She gnawed her lower lip and turned over the envelope. There was nothing written on the back.

She flipped it over in her hands, willing herself to open it, to just get it over with already.

She slipped her thumb along the back edge, but then shook her head and stuck the envelope in the inside pocket of her purse.

She'd rather be in her own home when she opened it. Who knew what was inside? A check for a penny? A check for a million dollars? A letter explaining why her father had decided not to be her father?

*Ugh. Just go home,* she told herself. *Go home, relieve Lettie, and open it.*

*Perhaps it will settle things for you once and for all.*

"Did you open it?" Jenny asked.

Amanda twisted the phone cord around her finger and stared at the envelope on her kitchen table. This was the third time Jenny had called since Amanda had gotten home from the lawyer's office two hours ago.

"Not yet."

Jenny let out a disappointed screech. "Amanda, how can you stand the suspense? It's killing *me*!"

*I can stand it,* she thought. She'd stood it for

twenty-eight years, and this was the very last opportunity to have some kind of understanding of the man who gave her life.

"You know what they say about ignorance being bliss," Amanda said. "I feel like when I open it, my entire world is going to change . . . or not, which is almost as bad." She sat down on a kitchen chair and stared out the window. "I'm scared, Jen. I'm scared of what's in this stupid plain envelope that weighs next to nothing."

"I know," Jenny said. "But you've been facing your fears head on for a long time, Amanda. Whatever is in there, you'll handle it fine. I know it."

"Thanks, Jenny."

"Call me as soon as you open it," Jenny said.

*Which may be never,* Amanda thought.

*You're required to open the envelope before midnight tonight,* the lawyer had told her.

The ringing of a buzzer startled Amanda. She wondered who it could be. Jenny was at work, and Lettie lived in the building and had no reason to ring the buzzer at the door downstairs.

"Yes?" Amanda said into the intercom.

"Amanda, it's Olivia."

Olivia?

Amanda pressed the buzzer that opened the downstairs door, then unlocked her apartment door and waited for her sister to make the trek up to the fifth floor.

Olivia was probably surprised by the shabby five-story brick apartment building in which Amanda lived—that she lived in this run-down neighborhood, a long subway ride and river crossing away from the glittering lights and riches of Manhattan.

"No elevator?" Olivia commented when she reached the top step on Amanda's floor. "Good thing I work out every day."

Amanda smiled. "Keeps me in shape." *Which is a good thing, because I can't afford the time or money for a gym.* "Come in."

Olivia came inside and removed her hat, gloves, and coat, which Amanda took and hung up in the hall closet. Olivia glanced around, clearly surprised that Amanda lived so simply.

"I won't beat around the bush," Olivia said, pushing a lock of long blond hair from her face. "I'm dying of curiosity about the envelope."

Amanda smiled. "I haven't opened it yet."

"Not curious?" Olivia asked.

"Oh, I am. I'm just more nervous."

Olivia nodded. "I think I will be too when it's my turn. But there's another reason I'm here too. Did you see this?"

Olivia held up *New York Now*, a daily tabloid newspaper that was full of gossip about wealthy and celebrity New Yorkers. She flipped some pages, folded the paper and handed it to Amanda.

> *Word has it that the daughters of William Sedgwick, one of New York's wealthiest businessmen and greatest philanthropists, were invited to the reading of his will only to receive cryptic information regarding their inheritances. Each daughter is to receive an envelope on a specific day, the contents of which no one knows. How exciting! Today, Amanda Sedgwick, 28, of Queens, is to receive her envelope. Let's hope our trusty informant can get a peek inside. We're dying to know!*

Before Amanda could even register her own shock, the doorbell rang again. This time, though, Amanda had a feeling she knew exactly who it was.

She was right.

Ivy.

At the sight of Olivia, Ivy laughed. "Okay, so I guess we're all curious about what's inside that envelope."

Olivia smiled. "My mother won't get off my back about it. She must have asked me a hundred times if I found out anything yet."

Ivy laughed and pulled off her gloves. "Mine too—though I'm sure you didn't need me to tell you that. Ah," she said, pointing at *New York Now.* "I read that garbage too. The partners of Harris, Pinker and Swift must be furious, trying to figure out who among their hundreds of employees, from lawyers to support staff, is on the *New York Now* payroll. Their celebrity clients especially don't appreciate reading about their confidential business in a daily gossip rag."

Olivia nodded. "I called in a favor to an executive at the paper to stop printing rumors about me and my family. I think this will be the end of it."

"Good," Ivy said. "And it's ridiculously premature and stupid for the paper to assume we're inheriting anything."

Once Olivia and Ivy were sitting down in the living room, in front of them a tray of hot tea and some cinnamon chip scones Lettie had brought over that morning, Amanda picked up the envelope from the kitchen table.

She brought it into the living room and sat down in an easy chair across from Olivia and Ivy.

"I'm a nervous wreck," Amanda said. "I feel like once I open this, there's no turning back. From what, I don't even know."

"I know what you mean," Olivia said. "There's a lot I don't like to think about concerning our father. I feel like these envelopes will force us to think."

"I guess that'll be a good thing, though," Ivy said, sipping her tea. Steam swirled up from the mug. "Right?"

Amanda smiled and shrugged. "I'm glad you're both here, in any case. I don't think I could have opened this alone. And who better would understand whatever's inside than the two of you?"

Olivia and Ivy both nodded.

"Okay," Amanda said. "Here goes." She slit open the envelope, took a deep breath and withdrew a simple piece of white paper, upon which seemed to be a long list of instructions. Amanda turned over the paper. The instructions continued on the back of the page. She looked inside the envelope to see if she missed anything. No, there was only the piece of paper.

"What does it say?" Olivia asked.

"I'll just read it aloud," Amanda said. She cleared her throat. "Amanda Sedgwick, my middle daughter, is to inherit my brownstone apartment building, located just off Central Park West on West Seventy-fourth Street, if she follows the enclosed instructions to a T."

Olivia gasped. "The brownstone is worth millions!"

"My mother is going to go ape," Ivy said. "As far as I know, William owns only three properties—

the brownstone, the Maine house, and a small country inn in central New Jersey. Real estate wasn't his thing. The brownstone is worth the most. Olivia is right—it's worth a fortune."

Amanda glanced at her sisters. Neither seemed particularly upset by the news; their expressions were more . . . curious.

"Read on," Olivia said.

"As stated by my lawyer, George Harris," Amanda read, "Amanda must follow the instructions exactly or her inheritance will become null and void."

"Whatever the instructions are, who'd know if she followed them or not?" Ivy asked.

Amanda read on. "Someone will be watching Amanda at all times to ensure she fulfills the terms of the will."

Spooked, Amanda dropped the letter as though it were a dead mouse. The paper fluttered out of her hands and landed on the area rug.

"Someone will be watching me?" Amanda repeated. "At all times?"

Olivia and Ivy glanced at each other. "That sounds really weird," Olivia said.

"Yeah," Ivy seconded. "I don't like it. Especially as a cop, I don't like it."

"Read on," Olivia suggested. "Maybe there's some explanation of who will be your supposed watchdog."

Amanda took a deep breath, picked up the paper and continued reading aloud. "Amanda will be allowed two slip-ups. Upon the third, her inheritance will be null and void."

"Slip-ups?" Ivy repeated. "What on earth . . . ?"

"Amanda is to move into the brownstone next

Saturday," Amanda read. "She is to use the red bedroom, and her son's nursery will be the blue room. She is never to enter the white room unless she is married."

"This sounds crazy!" Olivia said. "And what's this nonsense about the white room?"

Amanda took a deep breath. "I don't like any of this. Listen to the rest: 'Amanda is to live in the brownstone for at least one month. During each of the first thirty days, Amanda must sit in the formal parlor, on the brown leather sofa for one hour, twice a day."

Olivia and Ivy looked at each other. "I've only been in the brownstone a couple of times," Olivia said, "But I've sat on that sofa. It's directly across from the fireplace, above which is a portrait of the four of us in Maine."

"I remember when we took the picture for that portrait!" Ivy said. "It was the summer I was fifteen. The height of my gawky period."

Amanda and Olivia laughed.

"I always thought it was strange that he kept that portrait in his house in the room he used so regularly," Olivia said. "Why have a portrait of his daughters whom he had no interest in?"

"Who can figure out anything about William Sedgwick?" Amanda responded, shaking her head.

Amanda looked over the rest of the letter; there were more inane instructions about what not to touch and where not to look and then some legalities and the name and address of William's lawyer. She put down the letter and sat back against her chair, wrapping her hands around her mug of tea. She eyed her sisters, chatting about their father's eccentricities as though this were a common occurrence, three sisters having tea, talking.

A comraderie was developing among them. If anything, this crazy letter and the terms of the will was making new relationships possible. And for that Amanda was grateful.

Suddenly a cry came from Amanda's bedroom, and Olivia and Ivy jumped up.

"I hope we didn't wake him," Ivy said.

"No," Amanda responded with a smile. "It's time for him to wake up. She headed inside the bedroom to bring Tommy out to meet his aunts, lest they make excuses about having to be somewhere and run out the door.

"Awww," Olivia said, her features softening at the sight of the baby. "He's so beautiful."

"Just perfect," Ivy cooed, trailing a gentle finger along his cheek.

"Well, I'd better get going," Olivia said, taking her coat from the hall closet. "I have crazy deadlines and my publisher is sending me to Paris for a fashion show next week. I'll be gone for almost a month."

*The entire time I'll be tested in the brownstone,* Amanda thought, surprised by her disappointment. So much for developing a relationship.

"Hey, I'm going away for a few weeks too," Ivy said, smiling. "Declan and I are going to Ireland, where his parents still live, to visit his friends and relatives who won't be able to come here for the wedding. I'm so excited!" But a cloud passed over Ivy's expression. "I just wish our father had liked him—approved of him," Ivy said. "At least before there was time to try to change his mind, but now . . . "

"The most important thing is how *you* feel," Amanda told Ivy.

"That's right," Olivia said, pulling her black knit hat over her hair. "And remember something. No one was good enough for William. Not even his own daughters."

"That's harsh, but unfortunately very true," Ivy said, slipping on her coat.

Amanda nodded. "Well, maybe these envelopes and their contents will shed some light on the mysterious William Sedgwick, the father we barely knew."

Olivia and Ivy nodded. There was little left to say on the subject.

"Well, good luck with your move to the brownstone," Ivy said to Amanda. "I still don't like that bit about someone watching you, but perhaps it's just a ruse to deter you from not following his instructions."

"I'm sure it's exactly that," Olivia added. "I mean, it's not like he could have hired someone to spy on you from inside the house."

"That's true," Amanda said, feeling a bit better about that part of the letter. "Anyway, I haven't decided that I'm going to go through with this bizarre thing," Amanda said. "I don't know that I even want our father's brownstone. I never spent a single day in his home. I'm not sure I'd be comfortable inheriting it when he's gone. It has no meaning to me whatsoever."

"Maybe he's trying to change that," Ivy offered.

"From the grave," Olivia added.

Amanda shrugged. "I guess I need to give this all some thought."

Olivia nodded. "Well, if you do decide to fulfill the terms of the letter, I'd keep that piece of paper with you at all times—you don't want to forget any of the instructions about what rooms you are and aren't allowed to go in."

"Who knows—maybe there are trip wires or hidden cameras or something." Ivy rolled her eyes.

Amanda smiled. And then with a few more complements about Tommy and good-byes, Olivia and Ivy were gone.

Amanda waited a moment for them to make their way downstairs, then looked out the window. A man stood under the awning of the building across the street, his hands shoved inside his pockets. Amanda couldn't see him clearly in the dim lighting, but he seemed to be looking up in her direction.

Amanda gasped and stepped back. Was she truly being watched? Already?

She stood on the side of the window and glanced out again, careful to stay hidden. She saw Ivy get into her squad car, parked right in front of her building, and she saw Olivia get into the back seat of a black sedan that was waiting for her.

The man across the street still stood there.

Amanda squinted to see him, but his face was hidden in shadow. He was tall and well built but she couldn't judge his age. He wore a hat so she couldn't see the color of his hair.

*He could be anyone,* Amanda told herself. *Don't let this crazy letter make you paranoid.*

Amanda peered outside again. The man was gone.

* * *

*Well, well,* Ethan thought, watching the glamourpuss and the cop exit Amanda's dumpy apartment building. They were chatting like old pals, like sisters, thick as thieves.

He wondered if that were a fitting cliché. Were the Sedgwick sisters bursting with resentment over the way they'd been treated by their father? Had they been waiting for the day Daddy Dearest would keel over so they could get their hands on his millions?

Or were they grieving the loss of the father they'd never really known? A man who'd spent only a handful of weeks with them since they were born.

Ethan had done his research. He'd taken everything he'd read online about William Sedgwick and his family with a grain of salt. First of all, there wasn't much. Second of all, it was mostly gossip rag filler. Apparently, William preferred a new girlfriend every few months to any type of long-term relationship, including those with his children. Ethan couldn't quite reconcile that with the man he'd met in the middle of the night three years ago, a man whose affirmation for life, for people, for family, had saved Ethan's life.

He glanced up at Amanda's window just as the curtain parted. She stood there in the soft glow of a lamp. He couldn't make out her features; he was too far away and dusk had fallen, but again he was struck by the sight of her.

*You won't be living here for long,* he thought as he turned and headed for his car, which he'd parked a couple of blocks away. *Soon, you'll be trading this dump for a luxury brownstone.*

He was surprised that she lived so humbly. It

wasn't that the neighborhood was bad or dangerous; it was perfectly fine, perfectly nice. But it wasn't Manhattan. It wasn't hot or hip or anything remotely superficial, which was what he'd expected.

As if he knew what to expect of Amanda Sedgwick. There was very little written about her. A simple online search had brought a wealth of unimportant information on the magazine editor and the cop because of their work, but Amanda Sedgwick warranted only a handful of Google references—all recent ones in which her name appeared in connection with obituaries or gossip about the inheritances.

*I know nothing about you, and I don't want to know anything about you,* he thought, glancing up again at her slight figure in the window. *I just want you to slip up fast at the brownstone so I can get the hell out of this city, get the hell away from the memories, the images. Get the hell away from the truth.*

He saw Amanda dart away from the window. She must have noticed him standing there, watching her.

*It's only the beginning, honey.*

# CHAPTER 6

The next day, as Amanda was cooking dinner for herself and Tommy, who sat munching his appetizer of Cheerios in his high chair, there was a knock at the door. She jumped and almost dropped the pan of chicken on the peeling linoleum floor.

She slid the pan into the oven, took off her apron, and padded to the door. She listened for a moment, then looked through the peep hole. No one was there.

Which didn't mean someone wasn't lurking underneath or to the side of the door.

Amanda eyed the chain lock and the deadbolt. There was no way someone could get inside. Between the locks and the "burglar bars" on her fire escape window, she was safe.

She glanced out the living room window. A man stood in the shadows of a courtyard across the street. He appeared to be looking up—at Amanda's window. At Amanda. She looked at her son, so happy in his high-chair. This was no way for her to live—for Tommy to live—jumping out of her skin. The brownstone offered a potential new life. For Tommy's sake, she'd take it.

It didn't take long to pack. Amanda wished it had taken much, much longer. That's how unprepared she was to move into her father's brownstone. But she really had no choice but to go now. The letter had been clear about the date and she had decided to follow the rules unless or until they became intolerable.

Jenny and Lettie were over to help. Amanda had decided she couldn't afford the apartment without a job anyway, and she'd just figure it out when the time at her dad's was up. Lettie was packing Amanda's small bookcase, mostly cherished books and photo albums. She opened Tommy's very first album, with at least a hundred pictures of him the first few weeks of his life.

"Who's this hunk?" Lettie asked, holding up a Polaroid picture that had been tucked inside the album.

Paul Swinwood.

Tommy's father.

Amanda couldn't bear to put the one photograph she had in the album as though it belonged there; nor she could bear not to include it, somehow. It was the only photograph she had of Paul, and one day, Tommy would surely want to see a picture of his father.

"That's Tommy's dad," Jenny answered for Amanda when it was clear Amanda couldn't answer.

Lettie put the photograph back. "Ah. I hope I didn't upset you, dear. I don't know much about your personal life, but I do know I've never seen a man in this apartment."

"It's all right, Lettie," Amanda said. "The thought or sight of Paul lost the power to hurt me a long time ago." How she wanted that to be true, and how it wasn't. "He disappeared into thin air when I told him I was pregnant."

*And took with him my heart and my trust. . . .*

Tommy had his father's glossy, thick dark blond hair, but other than that, he looked like Amanda. She was grateful for that.

"I'm sorry, sweetheart," Lettie said.

"I have Tommy," Amanda said. "That's what matters."

Lettie squeezed her hand.

"I'm going to miss living down the hall from you, Lettie," Amanda said. "You've been so wonderful to me, such a good friend. I don't know what I would have done without you to watch Tommy. I can't tell you how much I appreciate all you've done for me."

"It's been my pleasure," Lettie said. "And now I'll get to come visit you in a fancy schmancy townhouse off Central Park West!"

Amanda smiled. "I do hope you will come, Lettie. Especially because all of my father's crazy instructions will make it almost impossible for me to venture too far from the brownstone."

Jenny wrapped the last glass in newspaper and put it in a box. She marked it where it was going and taped up the box. "Your life is about to change, Amanda, for the much, much better. I'm so proud of you for agreeing to fulfill the terms of the will!"

*I'd wait on that pride for at least a month,* Amanda thought, her stomach flip-flopping.

Bright and early Saturday morning, Amanda stood on West Seventy-fourth Street, one hand on Tommy's stroller and the other clutching his overstuffed diaper bag. The taxi driver placed her two suitcases on the curb, smiled and left, and she stared up at the stunning brownstone that would be her home.

If she didn't screw up William's crazy rules.

The building was tucked between other beautiful brownstones on a tree-lined street. Central Park was, literally, a stone's throw away.

"What a difference from our old home," she said to Tommy, kneeling down next to him. He was bundled up in a stroller sleeping bag and a blue wool hat with the Yankees insignia—a gift from Lettie's husband. His round apple cheeks were slightly red from the fresh cold December air. "Isn't it beautiful, Tom? You'll have your own room, too. For the first time, you'll have your very own nursery."

Without your very own crib. It would be strange to live without her furniture. When Amanda had picked up the keys from George Harris yesterday morning, the lawyer had explained that the brownstone was fully furnished, including the nursery, and that Amanda and Tommy would be in need of nothing, except personal clothing. The taxes and maintenance were paid for through the law firm, as were the services of a housekeeper and handyman. Even the cabinets and the refrigerator were stacked with enough food for at least the first week.

Amanda had put her furniture, which didn't add up to much, into storage. Once she had a chance to breathe, to think, to plan, she'd start looking for an apartment for her and Tommy. She wouldn't rely on this brownstone being her home. There had to be a catch even beyond the silly rules in the letter. She'd make sure she had a new apartment lined up so that she'd have options.

"You know I hate to be a parade rainer," Jenny had said yesterday, "but how are you going to look for an apartment when you don't have a job to list on the application? How are you going to prove you can pay your rent?"

*Good questions*, Amanda had thought.

"Honey, *accept*," her dear friend had said. "Do what you have to do. Which is to live in that brownstone exactly as instructed for a month. Big whoop. Once it's yours, you can sell it for a more modest place and invest the rest in Tommy's future."

Jenny was right, Amanda knew that. There was a time for pride and there was a time for reality.

Right now, it had to be about reality.

"Okay, Tommy, time to go inside," she whispered, bracing herself.

There were three entrances. One was a stately black door at the top of six graceful stone stairs; the other was a red door two steps down that was covered by an ornate wrought-iron gate. There was another entrance through the small back garden, which she'd been told about by day. Amanda opted for the red door. She hoisted Tommy in her arms, pushed open the gate, and wheeled the stroller with her foot until it was behind the gate.

She'd have to come back for the suitcases in a moment and with any luck they'd still be there.

The new keys she'd received from Mr. Harris worked effortlessly. She pushed open the door, stepped across the threshold, took a deep breath, closed the door behind her, and entered into a large foyer with pale red walls covered with small paintings, lovely watercolors, and lithographs.

"You're early."

Amanda jumped at the unexpected voice. A woman in her fifties, wearing a plain gray dress and an apron, held a sponge in one hand, and a small bucket with cleaning supplies in the other.

"You startled me," Amanda said, catching her breath.

"You're early," the woman repeated. "My name is Clara Mott. I am Mr. Sedgwick's master housekeeper."

"Of course!" Amanda said, smiling. "Clara! It's me, Amanda Sedgwick." She well remembered Clara from their summers at the house in Maine. It was many years since she'd last seen the woman, and Clara had aged, but the most dramatic change was in her manner.

"You remember me, don't you?" Amanda asked.

No response.

"William Sedgwick's daughter," Amanda added, confused by Clara's coldness.

"I know who you are," the woman said, her hazel eyes stopping on Amanda for just a moment. A disapproving moment.

"I have been retained by the estate of Mr. Sedgwick to continue cleaning the brownstone on a twice-weekly basis. Wednesdays and Saturdays."

Amanda waited for Clara to say something, anything, about her father's death, but the housekeeper said nothing else. Her eyes shifted from Amanda to the bucket in her hand.

"Wednesdays and Saturdays," Amanda repeated, nodding. "This is my son, Tommy," she added, nuzzling the baby's head.

"I have a lot of work to do," Clara said, her eyes roving over the baby for just a moment. She set down the bucket. "I'd rather not use harsh cleaning products while in the same room with the child," she added, eyes on her sponge.

*Yes ma'am,* Amanda thought. *Dismissed.*

Perhaps Clara was simply mourning the loss of her long-time employer. Or perhaps she was simply worried about the loss of her job now that William was gone.

"That's very thoughtful," Amanda said, careful to be polite. She well knew the truth behind the old cliché of catching more flies with honey, and perhaps Clara would be willing to answer some questions about William if Amanda remained civil.

"The staircase to the main level is there," Clara said, pointing across the marble foyer, which was bigger than the living room of Amanda's old apartment. "I'll get your suitcases."

"Thank you," Amanda said, and Clara stepped out, returning with both suitcases, one in each hand. For a woman in her fifties, she certainly was strong. Clara set the suitcases by the staircase, then immediately set to work, removing the many small antique figures from atop a beautiful antique wooden console table.

Clara did good work. The black-and-white marble floor gleamed, and overhead was a stunning chandelier with hundreds of tiny lights—not a dust mote in sight.

There were three closed doors and a staircase leading upstairs. Amanda glanced around to see what might be a danger to Tommy, determined there was nothing, and set down the baby on the long Persian runner, where he alternately crawled and cooed. She pulled a talking teddy bear from her diaper bag and handed it to him, then pulled out the letter of instruction from Mr. Harris.

From her father, really.

> *There are four floors in the brownstone. The lower level, a few steps down from street level, has a bathroom, spare bedroom, a laundry room, a small storage room, plus an entrance to the back patio. The main level has a kitchen, dining room, a formal living room, and a powder room. The upper level has a master bedroom and bath, two bedrooms, and a second full bathroom. The top level was originally maids' quarters but are not currently in use.*
>
> *Amanda is to sleep in the red bedroom. Tommy is to sleep in the blue nursery next door. Amanda is never to enter the master bedroom—the white room. She's never to use the powder room on the main level—not even to look in the mirror. She's never to open the window next to the cactus in the living room. She's never to open the cabinet above the oven . . .*

*Why in the world can't I open a kitchen cabinet?* she wondered. These rules seemed silly.

Amanda felt eyes on her. She turned around,

but Clara was busy polishing the legs of the console.

*Are you the spy?* Amanda wondered of Clara. No, how could she possibly know if Amanda followed the rules if she only came twice a week for a few hours?

She scooped up Tommy and headed upstairs to the main level. As Amanda reached the top step, she sucked in her breath.

Wow. She stood there, taking in the exquisitely decorated living room. A Persian rug of soothing and subtle blues and golds lay across the expanse of hardwood floor. A rich brown leather sofa dominated one side of the sitting area; across from it in front of the fireplace were two lighter blue antique chairs made cozy with throw pillows. Incongruously, next to the sofa was a playpen with two stuffed animals.

A baby grand piano sat in the alcove of the front bay window. Paintings graced the walls and sculptures defined the corners. There was only one plant, a large cactus by the window flanking one side of the bay that Amanda was never to open.

It looked like an ordinary window, she thought, eyeing the luxurious velvet drapes.

And above the fireplace was the portrait of William, Amanda and her sisters.

Amanda held Tommy close, breathing in the clean, fresh scent of his hair. "Look, sweetie," she said. "There's your mommy when she was a teenager. Just sixteen years old. And there's your aunt Olivia and your aunt Ivy. And there's your grandfather."

Tears unexpectedly stung the back of her eyes. *But you'll never get the chance to know him.*

*I'll never get the chance to know him.*

The painting was obviously commissioned by William from a photograph. Amanda remembered that day, a rare day in which William actually spent time with his daughters. The girls had been about to sit down to lunch when William had come outside, commented on the nice weather, and asked Clara to snap a photo of the four of them. Olivia, who'd been a budding photographer, positioned them in front of a lilac tree, then nodded at Clara to take the picture.

No one was touching. No one had an arm around one of the others. No one was quite smiling. But the four of them were together.

With one last look at the painting, Amanda headed down the pale yellow hall toward the back of the house and found herself in a sunny kitchen, complete with breakfast nook. A high chair was in position at the table, and on a nearby hook were several bibs.

Beside the kitchen was a small formal dining room, with deep red walls and beautiful built-ins, in which china and glasses were stored. Above the polished dark wood table was an ornate chandelier. Amanda couldn't imagine what cause she'd ever have to enjoy a meal in this room, but it was beautiful.

Back down the hall, Amanda found a small library, lined with bookshelves from the floor to the twelve-foot-high ceiling and filled with books on every topic imaginable. There were even four rows of books for babies and children and another playpen near a comfortable-looking easy chair.

With Tommy still in her arms, Amanda headed

up another short round of stairs to the upper level. There were four doors off the landing. Amanda assumed the one painted white was the master bedroom she was not to enter. An ornate silver key hung from a ribbon on the doorknob.

There was also a red door, a baby blue door, and a pale yellow door. The yellow door opened to a large, cheerful bathroom with large soft towels and decorative soaps lining the counter. The red door led to Amanda's bedroom. Painted a paler red than the door, the room was dominated by a darkwood four-poster bed with a beautiful quilt and several pillows. There was an antique dresser with a huge round mirror, complete with a silver brush and comb set, and next to the dresser was a walk-in closet.

A gorgeous round throw rug filled the middle of the floor. Amanda set Tommy down on the center of the rug; he sat happily, chewing on a teether she'd pulled out of her bag.

For a moment Amanda just stood and watched her son. He'd woken up this morning without a sneeze or a cough or a fever, and his cheeks were a healthy shade of peach instead of flushed.

So far, so good, Amanda thought, sitting down on the edge of the bed that would be hers for an entire month.

Ahh, she thought, sinking down on the plush mattress. The baby bear bed. Very comfortable.

A small gold picture frame on the bedside table caught her attention. Amanda reached for it and gasped in surprise.

It was a picture of her mother.

She held the photograph to her chest for a moment, then looked at her mother's beautiful face. Her mother was very young in the photo, in her early twenties. Amanda wondered if the photograph was always on this table, in this room.

No, that couldn't be. William and Amanda's mother had known each other twenty-nine years ago, for a very brief period. He'd had many other women in his life since Amanda's mother. Amanda didn't even want to guess how many. He must have had the photo and instructed someone, Clara most likely, to place the photo in the room Amanda would occupy, plus do all the ridiculous color-coding and add the baby things to the house.

Tommy began to fuss; it was getting to be his nap time.

"Time to see your room, sweetie," she cooed. She took one more look at her mother, returned the photograph, and headed next door.

She gasped. The nursery was exactly what she'd always dreamed of creating for Tommy. She'd never had the money for all the extras, little details that delighted the eye and sparked the imagination, like the mural of tiny dancing monkeys with long tails on one wall, and the pale yellow shelves holding antique blue cars and trains. On the floor, leaning against one entire wall were at least a hundred stuffed animals, small and huge, all looking new and clean and adorable. A train set sat on a toddler table under the window.

The walls were painted a soothing pale blue, and the name Tommy was spelled out in white block letters over the crib, a beautiful wood sleigh model with a firm mattress and soft coordinating sheets. There was a changing table stocked with everything

Amanda would need, a diaper pail, a small armoire and a closet.

For a man who never wanted to meet his grandchild, he went to great lengths to make sure Tommy had a dream room. It only deepened her confusion and she felt a twinge of apprehension. What was William up to?

Amanda changed Tommy's diaper and dressed him in a pair of comfy jammies from the armoire, then set him down in the crib and waited for her son to fuss due to the unfamiliar bed. He didn't. He closed his eyes and pressed one little hand against his temple. In moments, he was asleep.

Amanda looked at her son, so comfortable in his new crib, and felt her first sense of ease. Maybe she was worrying over nothing. She let out a deep breath.

She had no idea what to do with herself now. She could unpack or take another look around the rooms . . . or see if Clara would like a tea or coffee break, she thought, eager to ask questions about her father.

With a last look at Tommy, Amanda tiptoed out of the nursery, leaving the door ajar. She headed downstairs, surprised by the silence. Had Clara left already?

No, she found the housekeeper dusting the piano. "Clara, I'm about to make a pot of tea. Could I interest you in sitting down for some?"

"I'm on duty, Miss Sedgwick," Clara said, stressing the *Miss.* "I don't take breaks while I'm working."

"Of course," Amanda said. "So, how long have you worked for my father?"

She saw the woman visibly stiffen at the words *my father.*

"I'd really better not dawdle," Clara said. "Once I get to chatting, suddenly an hour's gone by."

Amanda nodded. Cracking Clara wouldn't be easy. Perhaps the woman didn't know much about William anyway. She wasn't a live-in housekeeper and had never been, except for the summer vacations in Maine, when her father had been mostly absent.

*Have it your way, Clara,* she thought. *For now. I'll open you up eventually.*

Amanda glanced around the large, unfamiliar room. Tommy was asleep, there was no job to go to, and Clara was doing the housework. There wasn't much for Amanda to do, and she wasn't used to so much free time. She wondered how she'd cope for an entire month.

# CHAPTER 7

Two hours later, Amanda had unpacked, familiarized herself with the house, and re-read the ridiculous instructions three times. Clara had left a few minutes ago, as unwilling to talk as when Amanda had arrived.

While Tommy played with a talking stuffed mouse in his playpen, Amanda stood by a window in the living room—not the one with the cactus, of course—and glanced out at the brilliantly sunny day. It was another mild day for December, in the low fifties, and suddenly Amanda wanted to be outside, exploring her new neighborhood. Although she'd worked in Manhattan for several years, she'd never spent much time just wandering around. After work she'd rush home, needing to care for her mother and later longing to see Tommy. And there were always groceries to pick up and laundry to do.

Now, for a month anyway, she was sort of on vacation.

Very sort of. Per the instructions, she had to sit on the leather sofa—not either of the chairs—for one hour at ten-thirty and again at three-thirty.

It was now ten twenty-five.

She sat. And sat. For a good long while she looked at the portrait of her father and sisters. It was so strange how the painting managed to make them look like a real family. It was a moment captured, but a moment that wasn't representative of the truth.

Photographs do lie, she thought.

The three girls looked nothing alike then, yet there was something similar in all of their expressions—a Sedgwick expression passed down from William, who had it too.

A bit overwhelmed by the portrait, Amanda decided to stare at the grandfather clock and watch the hand slowly tick. The instructions said she wasn't to do anything while she sat, including reading. She was, however, permitted to talk to Tommy or read to him, so she pulled his favorite book from her diaper bag and began reading about a talking cow.

There were ten minutes to go of the hour when Tommy began fussing like crazy. Nothing she said would soothe him.

He wanted to be taken out of the playpen but Amanda wasn't permitted to stand.

*This is so ridiculous,* she thought. *I won't follow these stupid, arbitrary rules at Tommy's expense.*

*Someone will be watching at all times . . .*

Amanda jumped up. She comforted Tommy then went to the window to see if someone was standing out there, watching her through the center bay that was only covered in sheer drapes. The very idea gave Amanda goosebumps.

At the side window she peered out, hiding herself behind the velvet curtains. There were some people walking on the sidewalks, delivery men across the street, a messenger on a bike. Was someone watching her right now?

*Creepy! I'm not doing this for a month,* Amanda told herself. *There's no way.*

*Where are you going to go, then?* she was forced to ask herself.

*How about out of this house for starters?* She needed air and she needed to think.

It was now eleven-thirty. At least the hour was up.

She dressed Tommy in his jacket and hat, made up a fresh bottle for him, cut up a banana, grabbed a yogurt, and headed outside. She was so glad to be out of the brownstone.

The air felt so good on her face. She wheeled Tommy to the corner, then waited for the light to turn green so that she could cross Central Park West.

As they neared the entrance to the park, Tommy began crying and fussing, so she decided to stop at a vacant bench near a hot dog vendor rather than deal with the crowd that was teeming in and out of the park. Teens on skateboards, mothers pushing strollers, businessmen, kids, people walking dogs, people of all shapes and sizes, nationalities and colors, were coming and going. And pigeons. Lots of pigeons.

"That's one strike," said a deep male voice. "Two more and you're out on the street."

Amanda whirled around to her left. Sitting on the bench next to hers was a very good-looking man, dark-haired and dark-eyed. He appeared to be in his early thirties.

He was holding a sheet of paper that looked remarkably like the instructions she'd received from William.

"Paragraph two, line two," the man said without looking at her. "'Amanda Sedgwick is to sit on the leather sofa in the living room for one hour twice a day, at ten-thirty and at three-thirty.' You got up early."

Amanda jumped up, gripping Tommy's stroller. "Who are you?" she demanded. "How do you know my name? How did you know I got up early?"

*Someone will be watching you . . .*

"It's my job to know," he said, replacing the paper inside his leather jacket.

"Tell me who you—" she shouted at the man, but she only ended up frightening Tommy, who started crying again.

Amanda bent down to soothe her son, hoping to calm herself down in the process. When she looked back, the stranger was gone.

As a chilly wind crept into the early afternoon air, Ethan pulled his gray wool scarf tighter around his neck and continued up Columbus Avenue, trying to shut out the image of the baby in the stroller.

And of Amanda.

Why did she have to be so beautiful? Why did there have to be a baby involved? Why did he have to do this?

*You don't have to,* he reminded himself. William called in a favor. Ethan could have said no. He could still say no. Get in his truck and head home and see what Nick Morrow had that needed fixing.

*You need fixing,* he muttered at himself.

He knew that was why William Sedgwick had called in this particular favor. William had fixed Ethan once, and now, he was playing Good Samaritan once again, sending Ethan "home" to a woman and a baby.

But why this woman and this baby? And for God's sake, why Ethan? Why the hell would William Sedgwick want a bitter, soulless recluse anywhere near his beautiful daughter and his baby grandson?

*Damn!* he thought, picking up his pace. He was walking fast and heading nowhere in particular.

*Nowhere in particular.*

There was a time when a phrase like that would have made no sense to Ethan. Once upon a time, every second of his day had been accounted for, every stride he took purposeful. There had been no time—or interest—in aimless walks. Or in random thought. No time for anything unless it was about business.

Ethan Black, former corporate raider, one of the most respected and reviled businessmen in New York City, hadn't become a multi-millionaire by wasting time.

In his mind's eye, he saw Amanda's baby, bundled into a blue fleece jacket and a matching hat, and he squeezed shut his eyes and willed away the image.

Thomas Sedgwick, age eleven months.

Sedgwick. Amanda had given the baby her name. William Sedgwick's name. For the money train, most likely. The dossier he'd received from William's lawyers said the father of Thomas Sedgwick was out of the picture and always had been.

Out of the picture. Ethan wondered what kind of father he would have been to his own child. No, he didn't have to wonder. He knew. He would have been up there with the crappiest. Ethan would rarely have seen his child, or listened to the child's gurgles and coos. He or she would have been pulled out for appearances when it suited Ethan. Like Katherine had been.

Another image invaded Ethan's mind. This time a woman's, a beautiful woman with soft, long blond hair, intelligent blue eyes, a Playboy Bunny's figure, and a Seven Sisters education.

The week before she died, Katherine had publicly announced her pregnancy. *Mr. and Mrs. Ethan Black are expecting their first child . . .*

Since Katherine's death, the sight of a child, a baby, especially up close, sucked the air out of Ethan's lungs. He would wonder if his own child would have had his straight dark hair or his wife's—his late wife's—wavy blond tresses. His dark brown eyes or her blue.

His inability to protect those he loved, or her fight to the end to keep her family together.

Her fight to the end. Ethan would never know exactly how Katherine had spent those final seconds, and perhaps he should be grateful. Based on the medical examiner's report and the crime scene investigator's, Katherine had been shot at far range, as if by a sniper. She hadn't known the bullet was coming. And she'd died very quickly, if not instantly.

The baby booties she'd been knitting had been found by her feet. A pale yellow, since they hadn't yet known whether the baby she was carrying was a boy or a girl. It was too early to tell, and besides, Katherine hadn't wanted to know.

Perhaps that was for the best as well.

Katherine was three months pregnant when she died.

And the deaths had been his fault.

"It wasn't your fault!" William Sedgwick had said. The police had said. The shrinks had said. But Katherine's family had said otherwise. Then they demanded to bury Katherine in their family plot in Pennsylvania, where she'd grown up and where they lived, and Ethan had said of course.

It was enough that her life, and her unborn baby's life, had been taken here. Katherine didn't have to rest here without peace for all eternity.

Ethan gulped in the cold winter air. There were people all around him, thousands of people whizzing by, but he might as well be in his remote Maine cabin, and for that he was grateful. That was the thing about New York City. With eight million people all around you, no one was going to notice a grown man with tears in his eyes.

Or a murderer who'd shot a pregnant woman knitting baby booties in broad daylight.

Ethan had no idea what he would have done if Amanda had actually gone inside the park. There was no way he could have followed her; he would never step foot in that park. And the idea of watching her disappear into the crowd, no idea if she was all right, would be too much to bear.

The park was perfectly safe, he told himself. Unless you were the wife of Ethan Black.

It shouldn't matter anymore; he wasn't the Ethan Black he'd been three years ago. But it did.

# CHAPTER 8

Amanda was out of breath by the time she reached the corner of Seventy-fourth Street. She couldn't wait to get inside the house, lock the doors and draw the curtains.

*It's my job to watch . . .*

My God, she already had one strike. How had she messed up so badly after being in the brownstone for only a few hours? Why had she gotten up early? Tommy would have survived for a few more minutes.

Two more and you're out . . .

And where to? she thought, panic rising in her stomach. She couldn't make any more mistakes. Not until she had everything figured out and a plan. And a job.

"Amanda!"

Amanda whirled around at the familiar voice. It was Paul Swinwood. Tommy's father.

*Whoa. Whoa. Whoa. Whoa.*

He was standing in the middle of Seventy-fourth Street, staring at her with what she assumed was the same expression on her own face: absolute surprise.

"It really is you," he said. "Oh my God, Amanda."

He rushed toward her, and in her numb state of shock, all she could think was that he was even better looking than she remembered, if that was possible. Tall—six foot one—and broad-shouldered, with dark blond silky hair, warm brown eyes, and one dimple in his left cheek.

"Amanda, I can't tell you how good it is to see you," he said, his expression gentle. She could tell he was measuring her reaction, trying to figure out if she hated his guts, if she would speak to him. He turned his attention to the stroller, where Tommy sat, contentedly chewing his teether. He pressed his hand to his heart and gasped. "My son?" he asked, his voice breaking. "Oh, God, Amanda—is this our child?"

Amanda nodded, unable to speak, unable to breathe.

She hadn't seen Paul since the day she told him she was pregnant, about eighteen months ago. The fury in her warred with something else—something she didn't think she wanted to admit.

"I wasn't sure if you'd—" he began. "I mean, I didn't know—" He shook his head and took a deep breath. "I guess I didn't want to know for sure. Then. Oh God, I don't even know what I'm saying."

Amanda had no idea what to say. She was still in shock at actually seeing him. For so long after that final day, the day she told Paul she was pregnant, she thought about him, his face, the way he held her, the way he kissed her, the way he made he love to her, the way he talked about his dreams for the future. Never had those dreams included marriage or family, but Amanda had only known him a few months.

"He's so beautiful," Paul said, his gaze, reverent, on Tommy. "He looks exactly like you." He took a deep breath. "I am so sorry, Amanda. So, so sorry. It must have been very tough, raising him alone all these months."

Amanda also took a deep breath. His words revived her anger and helped steady her. "It's been a challenge," she said calmly. "But I've loved every second of it."

A couple wheeling a baby stroller was trying to pass them, and Amanda wheeled her own stroller out of the way. She peered down the street at the man and woman, the man pushing the stroller, the woman's arm linked through his.

The reality of what she once dreamed made a stark contrast to where she found herself now. She whirled around for a moment to see if the man from the park had followed her. Was he watching her right now? Central Park West was full of people walking or waiting for buses or taxis. Perhaps he was standing at the park's entrance, hidden from view, watching her the whole time?

*You're not in the brownstone and don't have to be right now, she reminded herself. Therefore, he has no business spying on you.* Two policemen were walking slowly by on Central Park West. There was a huge police presence in this neighborhood, and that calmed her a bit. Running into her ex was the least of her problems, though she did wonder why he'd shown up on this exact block.

"What's his name?" Paul asked, gently reaching a gloved hand to Tommy's hair, so much like his own.

She froze, uncomfortable with Paul touching her child. She pulled the stroller back a bit and Paul straightened up.

"Thomas. Tommy. It was my mother's father's name."

"It's a good name," Paul said.

For a moment, they stood there, on the street corner, and again Amanda was struck by the lie of the moment. If someone snapped their photograph just then, the mother and the father and the almost-one-year-old baby, who would guess that this was the first time the father had actually seen the baby? Or that the mother was still as raw inside as the day he'd walked out of her life?

"Can I take you for lunch?" Paul asked, his blond hair ruffling in the wind. "I'd do anything to just sit down and talk with you, find out how you've been, how Tommy has been, what his infancy was like. I have so many questions."

Paul looked so hopeful, his expression so tender, that for a moment Amanda felt the urge to touch him, to reach for his hand.

*Don't be ridiculous!* she mentally yelled at herself. He abandoned you when you told him you were pregnant. He never answered your calls and hasn't cared a whit about you or Tommy since.

"What I'd give to just look at that little face for an hour," Paul added, his expression full of wonder as he gazed at Tommy. "Please, Amanda," he said. "I know I hurt you terribly. I know I treated you like—" He glanced down at the street. "Just give me half an hour, just to be in your company and Tommy's. Please."

An hour for the explanation she'd always wanted. An hour that she didn't have to be a prisoner in that brownstone, following rules, being watched by a stranger with contempt in his eyes.

She nodded at Paul and relief flooded his face.

After Amanda settled Tommy's stroller on the side of their little round table in a charming Italian restaurant, she took a seat and a moment to study Paul. His expression was hopeful, eager, excited. His gaze, as he looked at Tommy was full of awe and reverence. Each tiny movement brought a smile to Paul's face, each little frown or cough, worry.

A waiter quickly placed menus, glasses of ice water, and a basket of hot rolls on the table and hastened away.

"Thank you for agreeing to lunch," Paul said. "I know you must hate me."

"I don't hate you, Paul," she said. "I don't think I could ever hate my child's father."

She could hardly believe she was even with her child's father, sitting across from him in a restaurant, as though sharing a meal with Paul Swinwood was a common occurrence.

But she didn't hate him. She meant that. He was Tommy's father. And for Tommy's sake, she wouldn't let her anger, her rage, her pain, all the tears and sleepless nights—not to mention going through pregnancy and childbirth and raising Tommy alone—control her. If she could possibly help it, that was.

He held up the bread basket for her. "I remember how much you loved garlic knots."

"I still do," she said, taking one and biting into the delicious roll.

He added another to her plate, then took one for himself. "You don't know how relieved I am to hear you don't hate me. That there's a chance for a fresh start."

A fresh start? Not hating him was one thing. Starting over in any capacity was quite another.

"You hurt me more than I could even express," she told him. "And you deprived Tommy of a father. He'll be a year old next month, Paul."

"Will you let me try to explain why I did what I did?" he asked. "I know there's no excuse, no explanation that could ever make up for how I handled things, but can I at least try to tell you?"

Amanda glanced at Tommy, bit her lip, and nodded.

The waiter interrupted them to take their order, and Amanda was relieved. What could Paul really say? And did she even want to hear it?

Paul took a deep breath. "You knew that my relationship with my father is non-existent, right?"

"Yes, of course," she said. She well remembered his brief references to his father and their terrible relationship. Once, when Paul had been telling her about his father, he broke down in tears. It was the first time she'd ever seen a man cry. The tears were sudden and fast and he'd gotten embarrassed and had blinked them back hard, but the sheer force of emotion had been visceral.

His relationship with his father was one of the reasons she'd felt so close to him so fast. So many nights, they talked about whether it was worse to have a father you fought with daily and never got along with, or a father you didn't fight with but didn't know either. They'd never been able to come to a decision on that one.

"Well, the night before you told me you were pregnant," Paul said, "my father's sister, my aunt Leslie, called to tell me my father had died, that his years of smoking had done in him. Lung cancer."

"Oh, Paul, I'm so sorry."

"He was only fifty-two-years old." Paul said, gripping the white cloth napkin on his lap. He shook his head and hung his head back for a moment. Tears came to his eyes, and Amanda could see him struggling to blink them back. "When you told me you were pregnant, all I could think about was my father, who, even on his deathbed, couldn't forgive me for not being the son he wanted. All because I didn't want to go to law school like him, and his father, and his father. He never forgave me for embarrassing the family and becoming the first Swinwood to be blue collar."

"I've never understood that. Especially since you're a success," Amanda said. "You own your own construction company!"

"Construction wasn't my father's idea of a profession," Paul said. "It's not something an 'educated man' does, according to him. What a snob. He thought I was an embarrassment, coming around to see my mother in a pickup truck with dirt and grime on my jeans."

Amanda shook her head. "I wish people would just let people be themselves."

He nodded. "All I've ever felt, most of my life, was my father's disappointment in me, Amanda. I was never good enough from the time I was six or seven years old. And when you told me you were pregnant, I just went numb at the responsibility of what that meant. Of being a failure to my own child. Not being good enough. Not being what I'm supposed to be."

For a moment she wondered if her own father might have felt that way. She couldn't reconcile those kinds of feelings with a man as powerful and confident as William Sedgwick. And it was difficult to understand those feelings in Paul, as well. He'd seemed so loving, so full of confidence, so full of life.

"I'm still not even sure I understand how a family is supposed to work," Paul continued. "God, this is all so stupid. I hear myself talk and I sound like a whiney kid. 'Poor me, my daddy didn't love me.' It's no excuse for running away from you and our child."

Amanda didn't know what to say.

And then Paul covered her hand with his. She pulled it away.

"I'm sorry," he said. "I just—"

*Wanted to touch you,* she silently finished the thought for him. She had the same urge.

*Don't be stupid. Don't be stupid. Don't be stupid. This man abandoned you, abandoned his own child.*

"I know it's not a good excuse, but I was already overwhelmed with my father's death and then I got your news. And I blew it. I did the wrong thing.

I don't expect you to forgive me. But I want you to know how sorry I am. And if there's anything I can do, I will. My company has made some profit this year, and I've got some savings. I'll write you a check right now," he said, pulling out his wallet.

"Paul," she said, putting her hand on his arm. "I don't need your money. And I'm very sorry to hear about your father."

*I know what it feels like now.*

"Raising a child on a sales clerk's salary can't be easy," he said, shaking his head.

A sales clerk. How long ago that felt now. She'd been working in the women's clothing section of a department store when she'd met Paul, shopping for a birthday gift for his grandmother.

"It's okay, Paul," she said. "Let's just start from square one."

He glanced at her hopefully, and she realized she shouldn't have said that. She didn't even mean it, not the way it sounded anyway. It would be a long, long time before she could ever, would ever forgive Paul Swinwood for the way he'd treated her.

But he was her child's father, and for Tommy, she would try to start fresh so that Tommy could have his father in his life.

Their lunch was served, and they ate mostly in silence. It was painful to be with him, to be sitting so close to the man who'd broken her heart. There'd been a time when ridiculous little things, such as the way his dimple appeared when he smiled or the way he pushed his silky hair out of his eyes, used to enthrall her. But now the sight of these gestures just made her feel sad. And lonely for the woman she used to be—a woman who trusted easily and loved easily.

"I need to get home," she said. "Thank you for lunch."

"Are you living in Manhattan now?" Paul asked.

She nodded. "Let's just take this new aquaintanceship slowly. Okay? Not too much too soon." She wasn't ready to tell him anything about herself. That he knew her—their—son's name suddenly seemed like too much information. Although chance meetings happened on the streets of Manhattan all the time, she couldn't help but feel suspicious that he'd resurfaced precisely when her fortunes changed. Did he know about the inheritance and want a part of it?

"I understand completely," he said. "Can I give you my number? I'm living in Manhattan now too. Not too far from here. Will you call me when you're ready to see me again? I'd love to get to know Tommy. To have the chance to be a father to him."

She nodded, accepting his card. "I'll call."

He smiled, so warmly, that she smiled back.

And then she stood and wheeled Tommy away, afraid to look back.

The moment Amanda was safely inside the brownstone, she raced for the telephone and called George Harris.

"I'm sorry, Miss Sedgwick, but Mr. Harris is in a meeting."

"Please tell him it's an emergency," Amanda pleaded.

"One moment," the woman said in as bored a tone as possible.

Amanda closed her eyes and sat on a chair in the parlor.

*Please come to the phone,* she silently chanted, gripping the phone to her ear.

"Amanda, is everything okay?" the attorney asked.

Thank goodness.

"No, everything is not okay," Amanda said. "I will not put my son in danger, Mr. Harris. And whoever this man is who's supposed to be watching me is more interested in unsettling me. He accosted me near the park today. When I was with Tommy. I won't—"

"Amanda, calm down," Mr. Harris said. "Take a deep breath."

*You try that with that stranger staring up at your windows and following you.*

"I don't know if I can do this," Amanda said, her voice breaking. "I can't deal with having someone watching me, spying on me!"

"It's entirely up to you, Amanda," the lawyer said. "But if you do choose to veer from the terms of your father's will, you will not receive your inheritance."

"Do you know who this man is?" Amanda asked. "The one who's watching me?"

"I'm very sorry, Amanda, but I can't reveal that information. Now I must return to my meeting," Mr. Harris said.

*Thanks for your concern,* Amanda thought bitterly, clicking off the phone.

Tommy began crying and rubbing his sleepy eyes.

"Oh, Tommy," Amanda said, rushing up to his nursery and cradling him in her arms. "It's okay, sweetie. Mama's here. Mommy wishes she could make your life better." She rocked Tommy in her arms until he settled down, closing his eyes. Once he was asleep, Amanda put him in the crib and traced a finger along his smooth cheek.

It's a roof over our heads, she told herself. A very nice roof. A very nice free roof. And living here for just one month could allow me to live comfortably forever. Maybe I can stay home with Tommy. I could even look into nursing school. Or medical school, for that matter.

She only had to hang tight for twenty-nine more days. If she followed the rules, she wouldn't have any more run-ins with her spy.

*Just do what you have to,* she told herself, heading for her hour on the sofa. *And then everything will be all right.*

For the rest of the day, Amanda played with Tommy, looking for any physical signs of Paul in his face, in his expression. Nothing. Except for the hair.

Could she give him a second chance? Did she even want to? She couldn't deny her child a father—not when that father actually wanted to be part of his life.

She'd start there and see what happened.

As Amanda was getting ready for bed, Jenny called, and Amanda was never so grateful to hear her friend's voice. She told Jenny about the man in the park, and though Jenny thought it was odd, her take was that the guy probably worked in the security department of Sedgwick Enterprises and had been hired to do this silly freelance assignment. He probably didn't like it any more than Amanda did.

Feeling much better and finally allowing herself to think about Paul, how it was when they'd met, Amanda felt herself drifting off to sleep when she heard a noise.

She listened hard. Perhaps it was Tommy, turning over in his crib and hitting the bumpered side rails?

Silence.

She'd have to get used to this place, she thought. Its sounds and smells. Her old apartment was incredibly noisy. The radiator clanked (when there was heat). The refrigerator buzzed. And the sounds of city life outside constantly made their way through the windows, even when they were closed.

The brownstone must have had very expensive, thick windows because she barely heard anything. There was the ticking of the grandfather clock and that was it.

And to the soothing tick tock, Amanda finally drifted off to sleep.

# CHAPTER 9

*Can't breathe,* Amanda thought, trying to push away the pillow from her face. *Can't breathe . . .*

At first, she thought it was a dream. A nightmare. But then she realized she *couldn't* breathe. Panic and adrenaline overtook her and she struggled against whatever was pressing against her face. It felt like a pillow. Pressing harder. Harder.

She batted wildly, fruitlessly with her arms.

*I can't breathe. I can't breathe. I can't breathe.*

*No!*

*Tommy!* The face of her little boy swept through her mind, and Amanda felt a surge of adrenaline helping her fight.

But she was getting weaker. Weaker.

Weaker.

*Help me!* she thought desperately, her arms flailing. *Help me!*

It was no use.

Weaker. Weaker . . .

Just as suddenly, the pillow was removed from her face, and she sucked in air, gasping. She bolted up, pulling in the air in raspy gulps.

And then she froze, her hand braced along the edge of the headboard of the bed.

Two figures—she could barely make them out in the darkness—were struggling just feet from the footboard. As one of them turned, an arm striking out to hit the other, she could see a dark ski mask. A deep voice let out an expletive, and then one of the figures bolted from the room, followed by the other in pursuit.

Her heart racing a mile a minute, Amanda rushed into Tommy's room, praying for his safety. Her son lay sleeping peacefully in his crib as though nothing out of the ordinary had happened.

*Thank you,* she prayed heavenward, clutching him to her chest, her gaze darting around in the dark room for anything she could use to protect herself. There! She grabbed a heavy paperweight snowglobe off the dresser and then ducked down.

The snowglobe wasn't much of a weapon, but it was all she had.

"Amanda?"

A man's voice. Deep. Out of breath. Not particularly full of concern . . .

Amanda squeezed her eyes shut for a second, tightened her grip on Tommy with one hand and the snowglobe with the other, and crouched down farther.

"Amanda, I can see you there by the dresser. Are you all right? Is the baby all right?"

*How do you know about my baby!* she wanted to scream. *Who the hell are you? Get out of my house!*

But she was scared silent.

She heard the man fumble for the light switch. She held the snowglobe slightly aloft, ready to strike.

The room flooded with light.

She gasped; it was the man from the park. With a jagged, bleeding cut on his face.

"Stay back or I'll—" she warned. *I'll what?* Amanda thought, panicked. *I'll hurl this snowglobe at you?*

"I'm not the one who just tried to smother you with a pillow," he said.

She stared at him, afraid to take her eyes off him for one second lest he lunge for her or for Tommy. He would overpower her, anyway. He was tall, a bit over six feet, and leanly muscular. Amanda was five foot six and on the willowy side. But she would fight to the end to protect herself and Tommy.

"What the hell are you doing in my house?" she demanded. "How did you get in here?"

"I was hired by your father to make sure you followed his instructions during your stay here," he said matter-of-factly. "Hired by your father's estate, I should say. I have a key to the brownstone."

Her eyes widened. "*What?*" she spat. "You have a key to my home?"

He reached into the pocket of his black leather jacket and pulled out a silver key and held it up. As he did so, his jacket lapels parted a bit and she could see the trickle of blood on his gray wool scarf and on his neck.

"Put the key on the dresser and then get the hell out of here," she said through gritted teeth.

"Can't do either," he said. "The key comes with

the job. And I don't think you want me to leave before I make sure whoever tried to kill you didn't come back through a window."

*Whoever tried to kill you . . .*

Amanda's legs gave out, and she fell forward on her knees. She clutched Tommy against her chest, and thankfully he didn't even stir.

The man started, as though he was going to either lunge for her in her moment of weakness or try to help her. But when he saw the baby was fine, he leaned back against the bedroom door.

Amanda crouched back against the wall, suddenly aware that all she wore was a long, thin white night gown. At least it was long. She didn't have a free hand to grip the V-neck tighter or pull down the hem.

The man took a deep, wincing breath, and Amanda remembered he'd been hurt in the struggle. Tall and muscular notwithstanding, if he was hurt, she could possibly streak past him and get downstairs and outside before he could catch her.

Or not.

If he was lying about who he was, Amanda would have no chance against him. There was anger in his eyes, not concern. That didn't exactly make her feel safer.

He ran a hand through his dark brown hair. "I was doing a final surveillance when I saw a figure creeping up the stairs from the hall window."

*A final surveillance.*

"How can I be sure it wasn't you who tried to suffocate me?" she asked.

"If it were me," he said, his dark brown eyes glinting, "you'd be dead."

*How reassuring*, Amanda thought, anger coursing through her. "Is that supposed to make me feel better?" she asked him, slowly rising to her feet. She stayed where she was, beside the dresser. "And what do you mean, *surveillance*? Are there cameras in this brownstone? Are you watching my every move?"

He shook his head. "There are two—" he began, then stopped as he eyed the baby in her arms. "Do you want to put him down?"

"No, I don't."

"There are two cameras," he said without missing a beat, "and I can view your activities through my wristwatch screen. One camera is in the living room. So I can make sure you do your time on the sofa. Another is pointed at the door to the white room. If it is opened, other than at a specific time when the housekeeper attends it, a silent alarm will go off and I'll be alerted."

"Who are you?" she asked for the second time. "What's your connection to my father? Did you work for him?"

He shook his head. "I met him only once. I owed him a favor and he called it in."

"What favor?"

He glanced at her, then away. "It's not relevant."

"Well I deserve to know something about the man who's spying on me!" she said, her voice rising.

"Fine. Know this: I'd appreciate if you spent your remaining days here as uneventfully as possible. If you don't veer from the rules, I won't have to be in your face. If you do what you're supposed to, you can collect your undeserved fortune, and I can go back to my life."

Amanda froze. "My undeserved fortune? What is that supposed to mean?"

"Are we going to stand here and argue?" he asked. "Or are we going to try to figure out who just tried to kill you by pressing a pillow over your face?"

*Oh God. Oh God. Oh God.* Amanda closed her eyes for a moment. Her hands began shaking; to steady them she shifted Tommy into a more comfortable position in her arms.

"Are you all right?" he asked.

"No, I'm not," she snapped. Tommy stirred. "I'm not okay at all."

# CHAPTER 10

After calling the police, which seemed to assure Amanda that Ethan wasn't her would-be killer, Ethan instructed her to barricade herself and the baby inside the nursery and not open the door to anyone but the detectives. He'd never seen a woman move faster. She rushed inside and closed the door behind her. Ethan heard her dragging a chair over to the door and then the click as she secured it under the doorknob.

He then checked the entire brownstone, every room, every closet, every possible hiding spot. When Ethan first arrived in New York, the lawyer, Harris, had given him keys to the brownstone and a floorplan and requested that he familiarize himself with the house. He had. The brownstone was definitely empty now. The intruder had left the way he'd come, in through a back window facing the small yard.

Before Ethan could even get back upstairs, two policeman had arrived. They took statements, dusted for prints, and took the pillow into evidence.

"Could be anyone," one policeman said, slipping his notepad into his pocket. "Even I read about you in the papers, Ms. Sedgwick. Heiress moves into multi-million-dollar brownstone. Friends, enemies, strangers come out of the woodwork. We'll do what we can."

"I'm hardly an heiress," Amanda said.

The policeman glanced around at the beautifully decorated living room, the antiques and paintings, the baby grand piano, and nodded. "You are to a lot of greedy psychos."

"Everyone is so reassuring tonight," Amanda snapped, dropping down on the leather couch..

"We just don't want to give you a false sense of security, Ms. Sedgwick," the policeman said. He and his partner then left, promising to call with any information.

"How about some coffee?" Ethan asked her, surprising himself. He wasn't exactly known for his hospitality. Especially in someone else's house. But she looked so terrified and tired and so completely shot.

He wanted her to look as she did in the photo he'd been given. Self-assured. Mysterious. Intelligent. That Amanda Sedgwick he could deal with, handle. This terrified, angry one was a different story altogether.

She wore a thin, white terry robe, tied tightly around her waist, but he could see the top of her white cotton nightgown. Her weariness coupled with her slight figure made him feel protective of her. She took a deep breath, and he forced his gaze from her breasts, which were outlined through the thin robe.

"Why don't you sit down in the kitchen, and I'll put on some coffee?" he suggested. It felt too weird to sit in the living room; it was too cozy.

She nodded and slowly rose, gripping the lapels of her robe. She should have gripped the bottom of the robe instead. As she got up, the robe parted, outlining one long leg and a bit of her thigh.

He followed her into the kitchen, forcing himself to stare at the floor, at her bare heels instead of her backside.

She pulled a chair from the table and dropped down onto it, resting her face in her palms. "I can't believe this," she said. "I can't believe any of this. I feel like I'm watching a *Law and Order* episode, but it's my own life."

"I've never seen *Law and Order.* I don't even have a television," he said.

She glanced at him, but said nothing. There were faint shadows under her blue eyes, and he looked at the clock on the wall. Two-thirty-five A.M.

He opened cabinets until he found a canister of ground coffee, filters, and two mugs. He brewed a full pot in the coffee maker that was on the counter, then grabbed a bag of Milano cookies from the cabinet.

He glanced at her, her face pale as she just sat there, slightly shaking her head. He set down the bag of cookies. "You could probably use a rush of sugar."

She slumped over the table, dropping her head on top of her arms.

"Are you all right?" he asked, rushing over to her. He kneeled beside her.

Her head shot up, and she jumped out of the chair.

"I'm sorry," he said. "I didn't mean to startle you. I just wanted to make sure you didn't pass out."

"I'm fine," she said. She rolled her eyes upward and let out a harsh breath. "*Fine.* That's a joke. I'm anything but fine."

He stood and headed back to the coffee maker, poured two mugs full of the steaming brew and handed her one. "Have some coffee. Cream and sugar?" She nodded, and he got out the milk and found the sugar and placed it on the table.

"Someone tried to kill me," she said slowly, as though she were trying to wrap her mind around it. "Someone broke into my house—my father's house—and tried to suffocate me." She shook her head. She seemed about to say something else but then just closed her eyes. She took a sip of the coffee.

"Every window and door and possible entry into this brownstone has been locked and double-checked," Ethan told her, leaning back against the sink.

"Whoever tried to kill me got in once," she said. "They'll get in again." She picked up the mug, her hand trembling. "And you have a key! Who else did my father hand keys to? There's no way I can stay here."

"You'd be forfeiting a lot of money," he reminded her.

She whirled to face him. "Which I'll enjoy from my grave?"

He decided to take that as the rhetorical question it was.

"How do I know for sure that you didn't try to kill me?" she asked him.

"I told you how you know."

She glared at him. "And I told you that the fact that I'm alive isn't reassuring."

But it clearly was. "If you think I'm the one who tried to kill you, why didn't you tell the police that you suspect me? Why are you here alone with me?"

She burst into tears, surprising him. He stared at her.

"I'm overwhelmed," she said, wiping angrily at her eyes. "I don't know what the hell to do, what to think."

"I have no reason to want to hurt you," he told her. "I was hired to make sure you followed your father's rules for thirty days. That's it."

She shredded a napkin on the table. "Well, hopefully you've got something else lined up because I'm not staying here. I won't risk my son's life for a house that doesn't even mean anything to me."

He glanced at her. The house meant nothing to her? Her father's house? Her *dead* father's house?

What Ethan would give to know his own father. His mother had been young, and his father had skipped out on her when he heard the news. He and his mother had never seen or heard from the man again.

"I never stepped foot in this house until yesterday," she continued. "That's how close my father and I were."

"Ah," he said, taking a sip of his coffee. "I don't know the details. I don't know anything about you or your relationship with your father."

She raised an eyebrow. "Then why you? Why were you hired to spy on me?"

Ethan shrugged. "I don't know."

"You don't know? What did he tell you?"

"Your father didn't tell me anything," Ethan explained. "I met him only once, three years ago. We talked for five, ten minutes, tops. That's it."

She stared at him. "You met him *once.* One time only? And you only talked for five or ten minutes?"

Ethan nodded.

"And you'd never met before that?" she said.

"Nope."

"Yet he entrusted you to watch his daughter's every move for a month?" she asked.

"Clearly," Ethan said, taking a bite of a cookie. It was delicious.

"Why?"

"As I said, I owed him a favor, and he called it in," Ethan explained.

She looked exasperated. "What favor? Why can't you tell me?"

"Because it doesn't matter," Ethan said. "I owed him, and I told him if he ever needed anything, I was his man. For three years I didn't hear from him."

"Until he died?" she asked.

Ethan nodded. "I received a letter from him and his lawyer by messenger." He shook his head and looked up at the ceiling, an architectural masterpiece of beams. "It's still hard to believe he's actually gone. He seemed so vital. Powerful. There was a life force in him."

"You got all that from meeting him *once*?" she asked. "For five or ten minutes?"

He nodded.

She waited for him to elaborate. When he didn't, she said, "What happened during those five or ten minutes? What was the meeting about?"

"It wasn't a meeting in the way you think," he said. "But forget it. It's not relevant, and I'm not going to talk about it." He stood up. "More coffee?"

She eyed him, then nodded. "So you owed him a favor, and he called it in for this. To watch my every move for a month."

"Not your every move," he said, refilling their mugs. "Just the ones pertaining to his rules of obtaining your inheritance."

"So there are no cameras in the bedroom or bathroom?" she asked, her eyes narrowed.

"No," he said. "I'm just supposed to make sure you do your time on the sofa and don't go into the white room and don't do seven other things."

"What's the significance of these rules?" she asked. "Why can't I go in the white room? What's so special about the window by the cactus?"

He shrugged. "I have no idea."

"I guess he had his reasons," she said. She stood and shook her head. "What the hell am I doing? I'm sitting here talking about his stupid rules when I don't even plan to spend another night in this place!"

"Amanda, if you break the rules, you forfeit your future," he reminded her again, "Tommy's future."

Her eyes filled with tears, but she shrugged, then sank down on the chair. "I've managed to deal with every problem thrown my way, but I just don't understand what's happening here."

"What's happening is you're going to inherit a brownstone apartment building worth millions of dollars," he pointed out.

She carried on as if she hadn't heard him. "I can't go to a hotel because I'm practically broke. I can't go to my parents because they're both gone, and my sisters, who I barely know anyway, are away. I can't impose on friends—not with a baby. I have to figure something out."

Ethan took a deep breath. "I'll tell you what," he said, trying to rush it out before he could stop himself, which was what he wanted to do. "I'll act as your security guard for the night. That way, you won't have to make any decisions about staying or not when you're under this kind of stress."

She eyed him. "*You'll* be my security? I don't even know you. I know nothing about you. You think I'm going to allow a total stranger to stay here, overnight, with me and my child? Thanks, but no."

*You think I want to?* he felt like yelling. *You think I want to be here for one more second, let alone the hours until daybreak?* So why the hell was he trying to help her out?

*Because her father saved my life. And I owe him. And if I learned anything from the past three years, it's that my word needs to mean something.*

He sat down and tried for his most gentle tone. "Look, your father helped me out once, and now I'm going to help him by helping you. Period."

She looked toward the ceiling. "Well, you won't tell me anything about your relationship with my father, so I have no idea what to think. I'm leaving. I'm taking my son and leaving and going somewhere safe for the night. I can stay with a girlfriend for tonight at least."

"Suit yourself," he said. "If you want to make it this easy on me by leaving now, go ahead."

"Easy on you? What are you talking about?"

He took a sip of coffee. "I live hundreds of miles away from here, and that's where I want to be. I hate this city. I hate being here. But I promised William I'd do anything for him if he needed my help, and he called it in, so I'm here. That I'll get to go home after just a few days is great. So if you want to end this game now, go ahead."

Her eyes flashed with anger. "How dare you? This is my life, not a game."

"Fine, leave," he said. "But where are you going to go tomorrow night? Or the next?"

"I don't know!" she said, covering her face with her hands. "I'll figure it out. I always do."

"I've already figured it out for you," he said. "You're going upstairs right now and getting as good a night's sleep as you can under the circumstances."

She stared at him, trying to take the measure of him, he knew.

"Can I see the letter my father wrote to you?" she asked.

He nodded and reached for his leather bomber jacket and pulled out a manila envelope.

A letter and two photographs slid onto the table.

Amanda picked up the photographs. "It's so unnerving—all of this," she said.

"I can imagine," he responded.

Amanda scanned the short letter, then looked at Ethan.

"That's it?" Amanda asked.

"That's it."

Her shoulders sagged. "He didn't explain why he left the 'bulk of his estate' to his daughters—daughters he never even wanted to know?"

Ethan shook his head.

"And he didn't explain why he wanted you to be my watchdog?"

"No again," Ethan said.

"I don't understand him!" she said. "I don't understand any of this!"

"We might not be able to get to the bottom of his intentions," Ethan said, "but we can try to figure out who broke in here tonight." He was about to grab his notebook when he saw her hand tremble. "And I think we should get started on that first thing in the morning. Right now, you need some rest."

"I doubt I'll be able to close my eyes for a second."

"I'll be close by in the white room," he said. "If that's all right."

She studied him for a moment. "My father handpicked you, for whatever reason, to make sure I followed his rules. I need—want—to believe that my own father wouldn't put my life in danger."

"You really didn't know your father at all, did you?" Ethan asked.

She shook her head. "No, I didn't." She took a deep breath. "I want to bring Tommy's crib into my room tonight. If I can't do that, I'm willing to forfeit everything right now."

"The rules don't specify that you can't bring his crib into your bedroom," Ethan said.

"Good."

"Do you need help wheeling the crib in?" he asked.

*Please say no.*

She nodded.

*Damn.* She wished she had a burglar alarm system but that would make Ethan's presence and job as her "security" unnecessary. And for some important reason, her father wanted him there.

# CHAPTER 11

Ethan followed behind Amanda as she opened the door to the nursery and stepped inside the room.

A cold sweat broke out on his forehead, and he felt dizzy enough for a moment to have to grip the edge of the changing table along the wall.

*Get yourself together, man,* he told himself. *Just breathe. Don't look at anything. Don't think about anything. Just push the crib into the bedroom and get the hell of the nursery.*

But he was rooted to the floor, suddenly unable to move. In the soft glow of the night light, he could see the baby blue walls, the block letters spelling out *Tommy*, the lamp on the dresser with the antique carousel base. Three wooden trains on the window sill.

And the crib itself. This one was nothing like the one in his former house. Katherine had chosen a white crib, with spindles. He could even remember the little sheets, pale yellow with tiny farm animals, even though he'd only gone in the room once, when Katherine had shown it off after it was all decorated.

From the first day she found out she was pregnant she'd started working on the baby's room. She'd also carried around a pregnancy book that explained the stages of development, what was going on in her body that week.

"He has knees now!" she'd once said, beaming, as she'd passed by his study.

Ethan had barely looked up from his computer. How he wished he'd been more interested. How he wished he'd been a different person.

"He's such a sound sleeper," Amanda said. "I'm sure we won't wake him up."

Ethan was about to say, *Katherine, he's not even born yet,* when he remembered where he was.

He closed his eyes for a second and brought a halt to the memories.

And then he heard the strains of Brahms' Lullaby, so softly playing from the rotating mobile hanging over the crib.

The day before Katherine died, he'd brought home a CD of the same lullaby. She'd been so surprised, so incredibly pleased by such a simple gesture that he accepted her thanks and didn't tell her that his secretary's assistant had given it to him for a Secret Santa gift. His secretary had opened it for him, of course, wrote a thank-you card in his name to the assistant, then immediately rewrapped it, and placed it in his in-box with a memo noting all of that and her suggestion to give it to Katherine as a gift.

The music was beautiful. He'd played it over and over again after her death.

"Ethan? Are you all right? Your hands are trembling."

He glanced down at his hands, at his ringless fingers and steadied them on Tommy Sedgwick's crib.

*You can do this,* he told himself. *Once, you could do anything. You can do this.*

He forced himself to think of Maine, of his cabin, of chopping firewood. Of Nicky Marrow needing his help and companionship. Once his former life was gone from his mind, he began pushing the crib slowly across the room.

Afterward, all he wanted to do was crash. Amanda asked him to check and recheck the doors and windows, and he did.

He paused in the living room and looked at the portrait of William with his daughters. "I'll do everything in my power to keep Amanda and Tommy safe," he whispered to the lifelike oil version of William Sedgwick. And then he stood by the tall windows and looked out at the night sky. The buildings blocked the moon and most of the stars. He could just make out the trees in Central Park.

Katherine had been killed in Central Park.

That was a painful time and tragic event that he didn't want to think about tonight.

He squeezed his eyes shut and stepped back from the window. With a final glance at the painting of the Sedgwicks, he headed into the kitchen and was about to clean up, but Amanda had beat him to it. The mugs were washed and were upside in the dish drain. The coffee maker sparkling. The bag of Milanos back in the cabinet. He eyed the high chair, its blue-and-white plaid vinyl seat, the white tray.

Someone had sent a similar one as a gift right after Katherine had announced her pregnancy. Or perhaps all high chairs looked alike. Ethan didn't really know. He hadn't paid attention.

He took a gulp of air and then turned off the lights and headed upstairs. He found Amanda waiting for him on the landing.

"Everything's locked up tight," he assured her.

She nodded and looked him in the eye. "Guess I'll head in then."

"See you in the morning," he said, his hand on the doorknob to the white bedroom. He paused. "Amanda."

She turned around. "Yes?"

"I just want you to know that for tonight you're safe. Your son is safe. I assure you of that."

She stared at him for a moment, her blue eyes less guarded. "Thank you," she said in a low voice. And then she disappeared into her room, closing the door and locking it.

He opened the door to the white room, which was off-limits to her. Why? he wondered, as he stepped inside. The room was as plain as a room could get, much like his bedroom in the Maine cabin. It was the master bedroom, though, and quite large, with its own bathroom, which oddly enough, was fully stocked with both men's and women's toiletries.

A queen-sized bed with white sheets and a white

down comforter dominated the room. On either side were two white end-tables, each topped by a lamp. A plain white wooden dresser with a mirror above it was against one wall, and there was a low-pile white rectangular area rug on the floor by the bed. There were no paintings on the walls.

Everything was white, but it wasn't the white of purity or beauty, and it certainly wasn't bridal. It was more austere. Plain.

He walked over to the two windows on the wall and glanced out. The view was of the row of brownstones across the street, and if he craned his neck he could just make out the tall, leafless trees in Central Park.

*What the hell am I doing back here?* he wondered, running a hand through his hair and down over his tired eyes. *Why the hell did you bring me back here, Sedgwick?* he asked silently toward the dark night sky. *What are these arbitrary rules all about? And why would you ask this of me? Why would you make me—*

Ah. Suddenly it made sense. William Sedgwick was not only forcing Ethan out of isolation and literally forcing him back to the scene of the crime, he was also adding a woman and child to the mix.

A woman and her baby.

*Nice bit of psychology, William, but it's not going to work. I'm not going to fall for Amanda. I'm not going to get all googly-eyed over her baby.*

*I didn't even do that for my own wife and unborn child.*

The thought sobered him. Ethan took a final glance out the window using his micro binoculars. There were two couples walking toward the park, and several people walking along Central Park West.

A car started. A car alarm blared. But there was no one lurking in a doorway or behind a tree—as far as Ethan could see.

He turned from the window and dropped down on the bed, exhausted.

Even if Sedgwick was trying to "save his life" again by setting up this scenario, what would Amanda get out of it? An embittered recluse who lived in a one-room cabin in rural Maine, where it was minus five degrees today?

And how could William Sedgwick have forseen that he and Amanda would have much contact, anyway?

Ah again. William Sedgwick was no idiot. The man had left his daughter a multi-million dollar property. He had anticipated the greedy and the ruthless would come out of their lairs—just as the policeman said.

*I'll do all I can to protect your daughter, William, but that's it,* he said, looking out through the window at the night sky just before sleep overtook him.

# CHAPTER 12

Amanda awoke to the delicious aroma of bacon frying. She heard eggs cracking against a bowl, then the sizzle as they were poured into a hot pan.

*He cooks too,* she thought out of nowhere.

And then panic gripped her, and she threw off the heavy down comforter and rushed over across the room to Tommy's crib. Relief flooded through her as she gazed at her sleeping baby. He looked so peaceful, so healthy.

"Sleep little baby," she sang softly, glancing at the antique clock on her bedside table. It was just after 7:00.

Her eyes stopped on the photograph of her mother. "Thanks for watching out for me, Mom," she whispered. "We made it through the night."

She'd finally fallen asleep around four A.M. For two hours, she'd tossed and turned, unable to stop staring at the door handle, sure it would start slowly turning. Before she'd turned in, she'd gotten a steak knife from the kitchen and placed it on her bedside table. It was better than a snowglobe, but still she'd had a hard time falling asleep.

She glanced at herself in the mirror over the dresser. There were faint shadows under her eyes, and she was pale. She quickly dressed in jeans and a cream-colored sweater and her black leather boots. She put on the delicate silver necklace that had been her mother's. The chain and its cultured pearl pendant always made her feel protected, as though her mother were with her.

Tommy began stirring and slowly opened his big blue eyes, so much like her own. She scooped him up. "You're Mommy's big boy," she said, kissing him on the forehead and cheek and stroking his dark blond hair. Paul's hair.

She thought of him suddenly, then put him out of her mind again. It was all too much—Paul wanting to re-enter her life, her father's death, the inheritance, Ethan, the . . . intruder.

She preferred *intruder* over *psychopath intent on suffocating her.* She wanted to think the break-in and attempt on her life was random, that someone had simply noticed the brownstone had been unoccupied for a week, thought to rob it, then found her.

*Heiress . . .*

Could someone she knew want to kill her for this brownstone? she wondered, goosebumps rising along the nape of her neck. But it made no sense, unless it was one of her sisters, which was absurd. . . .

Tommy began fussing, and Amanda forced her thoughts to the moment, which included a diaper that needed changing and a stranger in her kitchen.

* * *

With Tommy in her arms, Amanda came downstairs to find Ethan setting a platter of scrambled eggs, a plate of bacon, both rye and wheat toast, and two mugs of coffee on the dining room table. Though he wore the same clothes he had on last night—worn jeans and a white button-down shirt, he was freshly shaven . . . and a lot less menacing looking.

"Morning," he said, not even glancing her way. He set the table for two, then sat down and began heaping eggs and bacon on his plate.

"Morning," she tossed back.

He sipped his coffee. "I'm glad you're up early. Let's get right to work." He flipped open a notebook on the table and tapped his pen against it. "Let's list—"

"Can we wait until I have Tommy settled in his high chair?" she asked.

He paused for a second, then nodded. "Does Tommy like his eggs scrambled?"

"Scrambled is perfect," she said. "Thanks for all this." She was surprised. Very surprised. A man had never made breakfast for her before. Under any circumstances, let alone these.

"No problem."

"Meeeee," Tommy said, pointing at the coffee mugs.

Amanda smiled at her son. "Tommy takes his coffee with milk and sugar," she said to Ethan.

"Oh. I didn't realize babies drank coffee. I'll pour him a cup—"

She laughed, surprising herself. "I was just kidding."

"Oh," he said again.

She smiled. "You don't have kids, huh?"

His face paled as his expression darkened. Uh oh. Had she put her foot in her mouth?

"I—" she began, not quite sure how to rectify what she'd said.

"Why don't you get him settled, and we'll start on making our list of suspects," he said.

*Yes, sir.*

She placed Tommy in his high chair. "How about some delicious scrambled eggs, Tom?"

"Ess! Ess!" Tommy said, clapping his hands. He ate the few forkfuls Amanda put on his tray and then pointed to the platter for more.

"You're quite the chef," Amanda said, putting eggs on her own plate. "Tommy is pretty particular."

"I wasn't always," he said. "I learned when I had to."

"Which was when?"

He froze for a second. "Do you know where the salt is?"

*Okay*, she thought. *A little too personal.* "Is that like, 'How about those Mets?' "

He smiled, for the first time since she'd met him, and it transformed his face. She had to stop herself from staring. "That's exactly what it means."

The ice somewhat broken, she waited for him to ask how old Tommy was or what his middle name was, the small-talk questions everyone asked about a baby. But he didn't.

"What's so special about the white bedroom?" she asked. "Why is it off-limits?"

He shrugged. "I have no idea. It's as ordinary and plain as a room gets."

"So my father's rules are completely arbitrary?" she asked, frustrated. "What's the point of that?"

"I really wouldn't know," he said. "Are you ready to get started?" he asked.

She let out a deep breath. "I guess so."

"Was last night the first time that someone has attacked you?"

Amanda felt her stomach tighten. She nodded.

"So it's possible, and likely even, that whoever tried to kill you last night wants to make sure you don't inherit this brownstone."

"I really don't know what to think," she said. "Maybe it was just a random break-in."

He glanced at her. "One day you stand to inherit a multi-million dollar property, you move in, and almost immediately someone tries to kill you . . . so we can assume that the attack is connected to your sudden inheritance—but that's *all* we can assume."

She pushed her plate of eggs away.

"What about them?" Ethan asked, pointing with his pen at the portrait of the Sedgwick sisters, just visible from where they sat.

"What about them?"

"It stands to reason that one or both of them could inherit the brownstone if you don't," Ethan said.

Amanda bristled. "They're my *sisters.*"

"But you're not close," he pointed out. "You said that last night."

"But—"

He eyed her. "Would you say you know them well?"

"No, but—"

He jotted down their names. "Then they go on the list. I'm sure the person I fought off last night was a man, but that doesn't mean he wasn't hired by them."

Tears pricked at the backs of Amanda's eyes and she blinked them away. "Under the most terrible circumstances, I got my sisters back," she said. "Because our father died, the three of us were actually in the same room together, two different times, actually talking." She stood up and paced. "No, I don't claim to know Olivia and Ivy well, but I'd bet anything they had nothing to do with this."

"I'm putting them on the list anyway," he said. "Amanda, I'm sorry, but they're the most obvious suspects. No one else would inherit by killing you. Let's just put them down and then eliminate them when we're absolutely able to."

"Why can't we just let the police do this?" she asked.

He sipped his coffee and sat back. "Because we need to be prepared."

"Prepared? For what?"

"For anything, Amanda. You need to know who you need to be wary of, who you need to be careful around. Everyone in your life is suspect now."

She looked him in the eye. "Even you?"

He put down his mug. "Amanda, I know you've been through quite a lot. But if you can keep your eye on the prize, you'll come out of this with your future, your security."

He was right. Very right.

She stopped pacing and sat back down. After a moment she nodded and wrapped her hands around her mug.

"We need to find out from Harris who your share forfeits to," he said.

"Good luck," she told him. "Harris hasn't exactly been forthcoming with information."

"We'll ask anyway. We'll let him know your life may depend on the answer."

She paled and closed her eyes, then stood again suddenly. "Forget it. Forget all of this." She glanced at Tommy. "I'm his mother. I'm all he has. I can't risk my life for a house. I'm a strong, resourceful person, I'll find something else. So write me up, Ethan. Tell Harris I broke too many rules. I'm not staying here. I'm not risking my life or my son's."

"Amanda, I know you don't know me. I know you have no reason to trust me. But you don't have to walk away from all this. We can figure out who tried to hurt you. Don't let whoever it is win."

"Why do you even care?" she asked, sitting back down. "What's it to you?"

"I told you—"

"Yes, you told me. You owe my father a favor. But I'm allowing you to repay that favor early, which is, according to what you said last night, exactly what you want. To get out of this city that you hate. So why are you trying to get me to stay?"

"I have my reasons," he said.

"That answer is getting a little old."

"Then I suggest you stop asking me questions," he retorted. "Let's narrow down who would benefit from you being out of the picture," he said. "What about Tommy's father?"

"What about him?" Amanda asked, Paul's face immediately coming to mind.

"What's the story?"

"The story?"

Ethan glanced at her. "Who is he? Where is he?"

"He hasn't been in our lives since the day I told him I was pregnant," Amanda admitted. "Well, until yesterday afternoon. I ran into him right after we met near the park."

Met near the park. Ha. That was a nice way of putting it.

"You ran into him for the first time in over a year and a half? That's a bit coincidental, don't you think?"

"Paul doesn't even know about the inheritance. He doesn't even know my father died."

"Maybe he does know," Ethan said. "There was an obituary in every major New York City newspaper."

The *New York Now* column popped into her mind. *Survived by his three daughters . . . sole heirs to his vast estate . . .*

"What's his full name?" Ethan asked.

Amanda hesitated. "Swinwood. Paul Swinwood." She watched him jot that down. "But he was so—" She stopped, realizing how foolish she sounded, even to herself. Paul Swinwood had been "so this" and "so that" when they were dating too. It didn't stop him from abandoning her and leaving her to raise their child completely alone.

She took a deep breath and poured herself another cup of coffee. "It's just that he was so reverent, so full of awe at just the sight of Tommy. I've never seen him with that expression before. He wants to be in Tommy's life."

"And how do you feel about that?"

"I want it for Tommy," she said. "Beyond that I

don't know how I feel. He really did a number on me."

Ethan glanced at Tommy. "I'm sorry to hear that. I was raised by a single mother. It was hard on her."

"Did you ever know your father?"

He shook his head. "He took off when he found out my mother was pregnant."

"How could a man do that?" she asked. "I don't understand it. Even if he's scared of whatever . . . the responsibility, I guess. How can he just run away as though it's not happening?"

"So he can pretend it isn't happening," Ethan said. "What I don't get is how they stay away. When you know you've got a five-year-old child, a ten-year-old, a twenty-year-old. How do you just put that out of your mind?"

"Do you know anything about your dad?" Amanda asked.

He shook his head. "He was some guy my mother dated for only a short while. Her home life wasn't too great and she looked for love wherever she could find it, I think."

"Is your mom still living?"

He shook his head. "Car accident a long time ago."

He seemed lost in thought for a second, his expression fond, tender. Then he glanced at Tommy in his high chair, wacking his spoon onto the tray. "For Tommy's sake, I'd like to believe that his father is sincere. But for your sake, I'm very suspicious about the timing."

She nodded, unable to form words, unable to even form a thought. This was all too much. And a very strange part of it was how much she was appreciating it all being dumped on someone else's shoulders for a little while. Someone's strong shoulders.

"Tommy looks exactly like you," Ethan said in practically a whisper.

"I'm always glad for that. For the past year, I haven't had to look into the mini face of the man who broke my heart."

He glanced at her then and nodded. "I can understand that. My mother always used to say I looked a lot like my father."

She felt her cheeks burn. "Oh . . . I . . . I'm sorry. I stuck my foot in my mouth there."

"Not at all," he told her, helping himself to another slice of bacon. "My mother often told me she'd loved my father very much, even though they'd only dated a short while. That he was an irresponsible jerk who abandoned her didn't take away from her memories of loving him before she knew he was an asshole."

Amanda looked at him and smiled. "You were conceived in love." She glanced at Tommy. "I never really looked at it that way. I wish I had. Tommy was conceived in love too. Even if I was the only one in love. Thinking that way would have helped me a lot through my pregnancy and these past eleven months." She took a deep, fortifying breath, surprised at how much better she felt. She placed her hand on Ethan's arm, and he started, slightly jerking it away. "Thank you."

He nodded, but kept his gaze on his notebook. "I think we'd better get back to this," he said, tapping the list he'd made.

Amanda nodded.

"There's also the possibility that—" He paused, eyeing her for a moment.

"The possibility that what?"

"That William fathered other children, children he didn't claim as his own," he finished.

She felt herself bristling. "I have no idea about that."

"That's why I said it's a possibility. And a possibility that we should check out. Perhaps someone out there got very angry at being left out of the will."

Amanda glanced down at the table. "I'm trying to decide which would be worse—having him acknowledge me as his child and then neglect his role as a father, or not acknowledging me at all." Again she felt her cheeks burning and silently cursed herself for not thinking before she spoke.

"Well, I'd say both suck equally."

Amanda smiled, then laughed.

He smiled back, and she was struck again by how good-looking he was. His dark, thick hair was slightly too long, and she had an impulse to push the heavy locks off his forehead. His dark brown eyes were intense, sharp, probing. He had a strong, masculine nose and a slight cleft in his chin.

"So William wasn't interested in fatherhood, period?" Ethan asked. "From the beginning? And with both your sisters, too?"

Amanda nodded. He offered child support, which my mother refused. And he invited me and my sisters to spend two weeks with him in his house in Maine every summer."

"What was that like?" he asked.

"It was wonderful and weird at the same time," she said. "Wonderful because for those two weeks, I had a father. Like every other kid, I had a father. If I saw him in the hall or around the grounds, I could call out 'Dad,' and someone would actually turn around in response. I can't tell you what that meant to me. To be able to call someone Dad. To have a father. Even for just two weeks every summer."

"I can definitely understand," Ethan said.

And again she felt like an idiot. Why did she keep putting her foot in her big mouth? Why was she blathering on about poor little her, when he never even knew his father?

"I'm sorry," she said. "I keep—"

"You're entitled to your own feelings, Amanda," he said. "My own circumstances don't have anything to do with yours. I've never been one to believe in feeling better about something just because someone else seems worse off."

She looked at him for a moment, unable to speak. Tears pricked the backs of her eyes. "You're a very generous person," she finally said.

He looked back at her, holding her gaze for just a few seconds. "Generous." He shook his head. "I think that's a first."

"Well surely the people in your life think so," she said. "I'm sure they're the beneficiaries of that generosity on a daily basis."

"There are no people in my life," he said, and suddenly something shifted in his eyes. The sparkle that had been there in their intense brown depths was gone, replaced by that same coldness she'd seen in them when they'd met in the park, when he'd surprised her in her bedroom, and when she'd come downstairs this morning. He tapped his notebook with his pen. "Back to business. Another possibility is that someone feels you don't deserve this. Someone offended by your lack of grief."

"How would anyone know how I feel?" Amanda snapped. "I'm grieving plenty."

"For yourself," he said. "For the father you never had and the father you'll never get to have. You're not crying your eyes out for William Sedgwick himself."

Anger boiled in her gut and she stood up. "How dare you? You don't know anything about how I feel! No one does! Well except for my sisters, maybe, because they probably feel exactly the same way."

"Okay," he said, holding up a hand. "I'm sorry. So let's say it's not about anger, but more calculated. Someone trying to scare you into leaving before your time," he said. "Perhaps the intruder wasn't planning on killing you, but just *scaring* you."

"I don't know," Amanda said. "That pillow was pressed against my face hard enough and long enough to kill me in a few more seconds had you not come." She dropped down into her chair. "Oh my God, Ethan. You saved my life. You saved my life, and I haven't even thanked you."

She looked in his eyes for any flicker of warmth but there was only the coldness. He didn't say *you're welcome.* He didn't say *no problem.* He didn't say anything.

"Who are Tommy's godparents?" he asked suddenly.

"He doesn't have godparents," Amanda said.

Ethan took a deep breath. "What I'm asking is,

if something should happen to you, who will get custody?"

Amanda stiffened. *Don't get defensive. It's a reasonable question.* "My best friend from high school, Jenny. If you're suggesting that my oldest friend tried to kill me so that she could get custody of Tommy and his big inheritance at my death, then we can end this stupid exercise right now."

"Amanda, I wasn't suggesting any such thing. I just asked the question. I wanted to know if one of your sisters was his godmother."

"No," she said curtly.

She took a deep breath. Soon after her son's birth, Amanda had asked both of her half sisters if they would be her son's godmothers. Both said their jobs and lifestyles—Olivia's constant traveling and Ivy's dangerous profession—would make them terrible godmothers, but both said they would as a last resort. In the end, Amanda had decided on neither. It had been clear that her sisters were uncomfortable about being asked; to be fair to them, it was really as though a stranger were asking them to take care of her child should something happen.

"Amanda?"

She started and blinked and realized Ethan had asked her another question. "I'm sorry, what?"

"Are you all right?" he asked.

"Was that your original question?"

He smiled. "No."

"I'm fine. I hate this, but I'm fine. I'll be fine."

He eyed her for a few seconds and gave her what she took as a reassuring nod. "What are your sisters' mothers like? I did some research online, but a lot of what I found was gossip rag material. I do know that Ivy Segwick's mother was the only one married to William and that Olivia's mother sued him for a staggering sum of child support."

"I don't know their mothers well," Amanda said. "But they did both attend the reading of the will and both were particularly interested in their daughters' inheritances. There's definitely no love lost between them. And there were no tears shed over William."

"So let's add Ivy's mother, Dana Sedgwick, and Olivia's mother, Candace Hearn," he said, jotting down their names.

"Good Lord, Ethan, why not add Ivy's fiancé to the mix? And how about everyone we've ever known in our entire lives?

"I'll settle for those with any kind of a motive," he retorted. "Who's this fiancé?"

Amanda crossed her arms over her chest. "Declan Something. Apparently, William didn't approve of him. He didn't think he was good enough for Ivy because he's not established in business yet."

"Have you met him?"

"At the reading of the will," Amanda said. "I didn't even know she was engaged before then," she added in a low voice.

Ethan glanced at her. "What was your take on him?"

"He seemed very much in love with her. They seemed very much in love. Ivy's mother was worried that William was 'up to something' by setting the opening of her inheritance letter on the day of her wedding."

Ethan seemed to be letting all this sink in.

"Perhaps the fiancé is worried too. Worried that if Ivy goes through with the wedding, she'll get nothing. Maybe he wants to get you out of the way now so that the brownstone can be split between Ivy and Olivia."

"That sounds pretty far-reaching, Ethan."

"Everything we're talking about is only speculation. We need to explore all possible angles. Your sisters might be furious that you're set to inherit the brownstone. And their mothers might be furious that their daughters have to wait for whatever's coming to them, which may not be as good. And considering that William owned only a house in Maine and a cottage in New Jersey, it's possible that your sisters and their mothers and this Declan guy feel more than a little threatened."

She felt a chill run up her spine and shivered. "You've got my sisters on your list, their mothers, Ivy's fiancé, and the father of my child."

He glanced at her, waiting.

Tears came to her eyes. "I don't want any of them to be the one who tried to hurt me last night. I can't tell you how much I don't want it to be any of them."

As tears streamed down her cheeks, Amanda just sat there, numbly grateful that Tommy was absorbed by making a tower of two blocks over and over again. Suddenly, she felt Ethan's hand atop her own. Surprised, she glanced up at him, and he took his hand away.

*No,* she wanted to say. *Please put it back. Your hand is warm and comforting and strong. . . .*

*Don't be a fool,* she cautioned herself. *You don't know this man. And you know better than to be lulled into a false sense of security.*

"You know, it's not really fair to focus on my sisters or their mothers or Ivy's fiancé or Paul Swinwood," she said. "There could be any number of unclaimed heirs. Like you said, his obituary was in all the major papers. And then there's the housekeeper—"

Ethan glanced up at her. "What?"

Amanda sat up straight. "The housekeeper! Clara Mott. She was here yesterday when I arrived. She has her own key! How the hell did I forget about her?"

He jotted down her name. "Harris didn't mention the housekeeper. Perhaps he didn't think it was relevant to my job. She must have come well before your couch sentence."

"My couch sentence," Amanda repeated. "That's a good way to put it. And you're right—I arrived just before nine in the morning, and she was already there, apparently almost finished. She remarked that I was early. She was long gone before ten-thirty

"How did she strike you?"

Amanda thought about Clara, her cool demeanor. "She was a bit cold. Unfriendly. Wouldn't make small talk, didn't even acknowledge my father's death. Just all business. I guess I was a little surprised because I thought she'd remember me more fondly from our two-week visits in Maine."

"Well perhaps she's angry that she wasn't left anything in the will," Ethan said. "Perhaps she was in love with William. Perhaps a thousand things. We'll check her out. In fact, she may be the perfect person to start with for investigating William's personal life and the women in his life."

"There are phone books for every borough in

the cabinet under the telephone," Amanda said. "We could look up her address."

"Let's do it."

Ethan took the Manhattan White Pages; Amanda took Queens. And it turned out they didn't have to worry about checking Brooklyn, the Bronx, or Staten Island.

Clara Mott lived only a few blocks away.

"Expensive neighborhood for a housekeeper," Ethan pointed out. He glanced at the bright yellow clock on the wall. "It's barely eight o'clock. Let's wait until nine and give our Ms. Mott a call. We can use the time to come up with careful questions."

Amanda nodded, relieved to think of dour Clara Mott as a ruthless, greedy bitch and would-be killer instead of her sisters or Paul.

# CHAPTER 13

At exactly eleven, the doorbell rang.

"She's very punctual, isn't she?" Ethan said to Amanda as he glanced at the grandfather clock on the wall in the living room.

He had a feeling Clara Mott would be as precise with her answers. She'd been curt on the phone. Ethan had told her he had been retained by William's estate to investigate a break-in at the brownstone last night, and he might as well have told her that it was December for all it seemed to register as out of the ordinary. Ethan explained that with her familiarity with the brownstone, she might be able to shed light on access points or perhaps even secret doors or tunnels leading outside.

"Since I'm stuck here for another thirty minutes, you'll have to open the door," Amanda reminded him. He glanced at her and was struck by how sexy she looked on the sofa, which had an ornate dark wood frame around the buttery brown leather upholstery.

He suddenly envisioned her lying down across the pillows, her cream-colored sweater rising to show an expanse of stomach, her large breasts rising and falling with her breath, her long, silky brown hair spilling over the side . . .

"Ethan?" she said.

He started, shaking himself out of his very inappropriate fantasy, glad it hadn't gone further. He wouldn't have been in any position to walk to the door, let alone conduct a sharp investigation of Clara Mott.

"Sorry," he said as the doorbell pealed again. He headed to the front door, relieved that someone else, even the sour housekeeper, would be between him and Amanda. Things had gotten a little too personal a little too quickly for his tastes. Amanda had a way of getting him to talk, something that only teenaged Nicky Marrow had been able to do in the past three years. Amendment: he had to add William Sedgwick to that short list. He'd gotten Ethan to talk plenty, to spill his guts to the point where he felt his despair, whereas all he'd felt before William had come along was emptiness. Coldness. Nothingness. After William, Ethan had *felt.* And he hadn't wanted to. But once the dam burst, he couldn't close it up again. The only thing to do at the time was to go into seclusion, far, far away from here, from New York City.

And yet here he was.

Fantasizing about making love to a woman when he hadn't had much of a sexual thought in three years. His despair over Katherine, over their unborn child, had taken over his mind, soul and body. He hadn't had sex in three years.

*Concentrate, Black,* he cautioned himself. *Concentrate and open the damn door.*

He cleared his throat and pulled open the door to find a prim, sour-faced woman wearing a dark gray wool coat.

"I was about to leave," she snapped.

"Sorry about that," he said. He gestured for her to come in, and she stepped over the threshold and into the foyer. "Thank you for coming, Ms. Mott. I appreciate it. May I take your coat?"

"I'm sure I won't be here long enough to justify that," Clara responded.

He led the woman into the living room. "Please sit down," he said. "Make yourself comfortable. Can I get you some coffee or tea?"

"Nothing, thank you," she said, taking one of the antique chairs across from the sofa.

Ethan noticed she didn't even so much as glance at Amanda. He sat down on the matching antique chair instead of the sofa, careful to give the impression that he was on Clara's side, not Amanda's. If Clara was the attempted murderer, if she did have a major axe to grind against Amanda, he wanted to make sure he seemed neutral like someone Clara could call back with information. He had to make the woman feel that he was an ally.

"Before we begin," he said to Clara, flipping open his notebook, "I just need to ask Miss Sedgwick to remind me of the exact time she was attacked last night." He shifted slightly, so that he could address Amanda yet still see every one of Clara's facial movements. "Ms. Sedgwick, can you remind me of the exact time of the incident." He surreptitiously eyed Clara for any change in her expression—fear, surprise, worry—anything, but again, she was poker-faced.

"The *incident?*" Amanda repeated with the perfect touch of haughtiness. "I wouldn't call someone trying to suffocate me with a pillow an *incident.*"

He pretended to be absorbed with his notes. "Yes, right. What was the exact time?"

"It was just after ten," Amanda said.

He jotted that down in his notebook. "Mrs. Mott—"

"It's Miss," Clara corrected.

"Miss," Ethan repeated. "Miss Mott, I understand that you have keys to this brownstone. Who besides yourself and Miss Sedgewick has a set?"

"How would I know?" Clara asked.

"Well, perhaps while you were here sometime, someone let themselves in," he said. "Can you recall anyone ever letting themselves in?"

"No, just William himself and Miss Sedgwick, yesterday."

"Miss Mott," Ethan began, "would you say that William entertained often?"

"I'm not paid to discuss my employer's private business," she responded.

Ethan nodded. "I understand and appreciate your discretion, Miss Mott. I'm in no way inquiring in a personal sense, but simply to ascertain if there were a large number of people familiar with this house or only a small number."

Clara pursed her lips. "I would say a large number. There was generally a party each quarter to celebrate the success of his company."

Ethan made a show of jotting down that information. "I'd like to ascertain whether or not William gave a key to a friend, perhaps. A lady friend, maybe. Do you recall if William was involved in a relationship—"

Bingo.

Clara's cheeks flushed, just slightly. She regained her composure quickly, though. "It's my business to look after his home, not his personal life," Clara snapped.

"Of course," Ethan said. "I'm very sorry to have to even ask such a question. The estate is hoping to get to the bottom of the incident here last night, and I'm looking for any information, anything that might lead me to who tried to murder Miss Sedgwick."

"From incident to attempted murder," Amanda threw in, right on cue. "I'd appreciate it if you stopped calling it an *incident.*"

"I apologize Miss Sedgwick," he said, barely looking at her. He turned his attention back to Clara, who seemed pleased by his inattention to Amanda, a beautiful young woman and heiress, and the daughter of her employer. He paused for a moment to give Clara an opportunity to address Amanda, to express shock or outrage or the least bit of concern for what happened last night. But the woman remained silent, sitting straight-backed. There were no questions as to how Amanda was doing or feeling. If she was all right. If she'd been hurt, if her son was all right.

In fact, Clara hadn't so much as eyed the

playpen where Tommy sat cheerfully playing with a board book.

"I'm afraid I don't have any information that could help you," Clara said. She glanced at her watch. "I'd better be going. I have an appointment."

"Thank you so much for coming," Ethan said as she stood.

"Yes, thank you," Amanda seconded.

Clara primly nodded. "I'll see myself out."

And so she did. The moment the door was closed, Ethan said, "Damn. I want to follow her. But I don't want to leave you here alone."

"And I don't want to be here alone," she said. "But it's just a couple more minutes till my time is up here. Go ahead. I have a cell phone. You can call me to tell me where you are, and I'll come meet you."

"No, it's not worth it," he said. "We won't lose sight of Clara just because we can't track her right now. And there's no way I'm leaving you and Tommy here alone. Not even for two minutes."

She glanced at him, something shifting in her expression. *You care,* her expression said. *Thank you.*

*Don't get used to this,* he wanted to warn her. *Because in just a few weeks I'll be hundreds of miles away.*

"Ethan, can I ask you to change Tommy's diaper? He's really starting to fuss. . . ."

Ethan stiffened and looked at Tommy. "I can't," he said in such a low voice he wasn't sure she heard him.

She smiled. "Oh come on. I'll bet you can change a diaper. You must have nieces, nephews?"

"I told you there are no people in my life, didn't I?"

The smile left her face. "Well, changing a diaper is pretty easy."

He glanced at her and the coldness was back in his eyes.

That ended the issue.

Clara Mott was either a slow walker or she was doing some window shopping. Ethan knew she'd turned left out of the brownstone and then right onto Columbus Avenue, so they rushed out of the brownstone, Amanda wheeling a very quickly-changed-and-dressed Tommy, in the direction Clara had gone.

They spotted her several blocks up and across the street, and then she turned onto Eighty-sixth Street.

And disappeared among the crowds.

"Damn," Ethan said, catching his breath. "We lost her. She could have gotten on a bus, or gone into any of these stores or buildings."

"Ethan," Amanda said, gnawing her lower lip. "Do you think Clara could be the one? Did she try to kill me last night?"

He looked at her, then back out at the crowded intersection where Clara had disappeared. "I don't know, Amanda. The attacker was wearing a ski mask, but I'm quite sure it was a man. He could be working for her, though. She's certainly not trying to hide her animosity toward you. Were she guilty, I would have expected her to feign concern and surprise."

"Maybe she's too smart for that. Reverse psychology?"

Ethan nodded. "Well, we'll keep tabs on her. At least we know where to find her every Wednesday and Saturday."

"She was very protective of my father's privacy," Amanda said. "Perhaps she just takes me for a spoiled daughter who never had much to do with William except for those summer weekends."

"Or perhaps she was in love with William. Or perhaps she feels that her compensation for continuing to clean your father's house after his death isn't enough."

"Well getting rid of me wouldn't get her anything," Amanda said. "It's not like she'd inherit the brownstone if I didn't. So what could her motive be?"

Ethan shrugged. "Her motive might have nothing to do with money. She could be motivated by rage or her unrequited love for William—who knows? Perhaps she just wants to ensure you don't inherit the brownstone."

"By killing me," Amanda said. "Great."

"Or scaring you to keep you from lasting the thirty days," Ethan reminded her.

"How did this become my life?" she asked, shaking her head.

"I know what you mean," he said. "One day everything's the same, and then in an instant, everything changes, and you don't even recognize yourself."

"That's exactly it," she said, holding his gaze. "That's exactly how I feel."

"Let's take advantage of Tommy's nap time by paying a visit to someone else who might shed some light on William's personal life."

"Who?" Amanda asked.

"His secretary," Ethan said. "She'd been with William only for the past six months, so there won't be a loyalty issue. And I'll bet she'll be able to tell us quite a bit."

"What happened to Sally?" Amanda asked. "I remember her being very pleasant on the phone the few times I called as a teenager. She was the one who always made the arrangements every summer, sending me my train tickets, that sort of thing."

"I did some research," Ethan said. "Sally was with William for twenty-one years. But she died last year in a car accident."

"My father must have been so upset," Amanda said. "And I didn't know a thing about it." She shook her head. "I wish he would have let me into his life. Tommy could have brought him so much joy, but my father wasn't even interested in seeing him."

"Your father sounds like a complicated man," Ethan said gently. "Maybe his secretary will be able to shed some light—at least on the last six months of his life.

"I hope so," Amanda said. "I really hope so."

# CHAPTER 14

While Ethan waited downstairs in the lobby of the building where Sedgwick Enterprises had its offices, Amanda headed for the elevator. The doors were about to close, and naturally, no one in the elevator thought to hold open the doors for the woman with the baby stroller.

"Thanks!" she called out sarcastically to the businessmen who'd rushed in and watched the doors close right in her face.

She pressed the up button and waited. The doors slid open and a group of people exited, and Amanda quickly pushed the stroller in. Two women actually gave her dirty looks when they had to squeeze in to fit around the stroller.

Finally, the doors pinged open to the tenth floor. *Sedgwick Enterprises: We Build Business* was written across the ornate double doors in gold block letters. Amanda had never been entirely sure what her father actually did. He'd once said he bought and sold corporations, but that was a field Amanda knew little about.

She took a deep breath and pulled open the doors. A very attractive receptionist sat behind a polished redwood station. When the woman learned who she was, she immediately dialed Nora Corey's extension.

"Nora, Amanda Sedgwick is here to see you. Mr. Sedgwick's daughter." She listened for a moment. "All right." She replaced the receiver and turned to Amanda. "She'll be right out."

Amanda sat down on the leather chair across from the reception desk.

"I'm so sorry for your loss," the receptionist said.

Amanda smiled. "Thank you very much."

A couple of minutes later, the inside door opened and a very pretty redhead in her twenties appeared.

"Amanda Sedgwick?" she asked. "I'm Nora Corey."

Amanda stood. "Pleasure to meet you."

The woman nodded and extended her hand. "I'm so sorry about your dad. I lost my father a few years ago, so I totally understand."

Amanda smiled and thanked her. "Miss Co—"

"Nora, please."

"Nora, I'm hoping you might—"

"And who is this little sleeping cherub?" Nora interrupted, kneeling down in front of Tommy's stroller. "Is he your son?"

Amanda nodded. "He'll be a year next month."

"He's so beautiful," Nora said. "I can't wait to have a baby. Well, first I have to find a boyfriend, huh?" She laughed. "Hi little guy," she whispered at Tommy.

*Thank you,* Amanda said silently up to the heavens. *I think this woman is going to be a big help.*

"Nora, I know this is last minute, but I'm hoping you'll allow me to take you out to lunch today. I have so many questions and—"

"Can we go to Fishers?" Nora asked, her green eyes twinkling. "It's this really great fish and chips restaurant around the corner."

"Sounds good to me," Amanda said.

Nora beamed. "Great. I am so premenstrual and when I'm getting my period I crave fish and chips. The greasier the better. Can you give me five minutes to finish an email?"

Surprised, Amanda smiled. "Thanks. Take as much time as you need."

Nora smiled and disappeared. Less than five minutes later, she was back, coat and purse in hand. And fifteen minutes later, they were seated inside Fishers, handed menus with over ten variations of fish and chips, from baskets to sandwiches to entrees. Tommy lay sleeping in his stroller next to their table.

"Ooh la la," Nora said. "Now that is what I'm talking about."

Amanda glanced up in time to see Ethan approaching the table directly next to theirs. Nora's eyes were now feasting on him instead of the menu.

"Hot, hot, hot," Nora whispered, tilting her head in Ethan's direction before he was close enough to hear. "Doesn't he remind you of that actor who used to be on ER?"

Amanda never watched ER, but she thought she knew who Nora was talking about, and yes, he sort of did look like that actor. She knew, intellectually, that Ethan was a very good-looking man, but she hadn't really looked at him that way. Now that she saw him through Nora's eyes in a public place, she could objectively see that he was, indeed, hot.

"Omigod," Nora said. "I can't believe I'm going on and on about some guy when you're in grief over your dad. I'm sorry."

Amanda touched Nora's hand. "No, no—it's okay, really. You're making me smile."

"Good," Nora said. "Oh great, here comes our waitress." Their orders taken and sodas delivered, Nora said, "I liked your dad a lot. I only worked for him for six months, but he was really nice."

"Nora, I want you to know that this conversation will be completely confidential. I don't want you to worry about your job," Amanda said.

"Oh, I'm not worried. I already have a new boss. At first I wasn't sure if I'd be fired or transferred, but apparently your dad had left a glowing performance review for me, and so one of the senior vice presidents snapped me up. I'm cleaning up your dad's office this week, and then I start my new job on Monday."

"So what was my dad like to work for?" Amanda asked.

Nora leaned in. "Don't tell anyone I told you this, but he was the easiest boss I ever had. And he owned the entire company! All the other secretaries on my floor had killer bosses."

"What made him so easy to work for?" Amanda asked.

"Well," she lowered her voice, "this is the part you should keep to yourself. He didn't exactly work very hard, at least not since I joined the company six months ago. His second in command was pretty much running the corporation. Your dad was more like the figurehead. He wasn't involved with the daily running of the company."

"So what was his schedule?" Amanda asked.

Nora pulled out a day planner from her tote bag and flipped to a page. "Here's a random day:

9 a.m.: Get shoes shined.
9:30: Coffee with head of Acquisitions.
10:30: Bloody Marys with head of PR.
Noon: Lunch with Mimi. Order dozen roses to precede her to table. Make sure 'trinket' is in coat pocket.
3pm: Meeting with—"

"Can we go back to lunch for a sec?" Amanda asked. "Who's Mimi?"

Nora puckered and laughed. "His lady friend. Mimi Farthwell."

Amanda darted a glance at Ethan, who subtly nodded. Amanda knew he was telling her to keep pressing for more information. "Nora, and this will be totally confidential: did my dad have many lady friends?"

"Actually, only two. Mimi for weekdays and another woman for weekends. Her name is Lara O'Hara, which I always remember because it rhymes. Omigod. I can't believe I just told you that your dad had two girlfriends! You're his daughter! Is it okay that I'm telling you this, right? I always stick my foot in my mouth!"

"It's okay, Nora," Amanda said with a smile. "Your forthrightness is incredibly refreshing. But you know, I'm curious. Usually secretaries of executives have to be incredibly discreet. Have you gotten into trouble for being forthright?"

"Nope," she said. "My uncle is a bigwig at Sedgwick Enterprises, so he got me the job. I think the reason they matched me with Mr. Sedgwick is because he was not very active these last months. It's not like I was privy to any confidential business matters. The executives under your father all knew he was ailing, so when Mr. Sedgwick asked to step down to a figurehead position, his exes were thrilled to get the power."

Ailing? Her father was ailing—was suffering from cancer—and she didn't even know about it.

"I was told he had cancer but . . .?" Amanda shook her head.

"Yes," Nora said, "Apparently he didn't want anyone to know."

Amanda's head was spinning with information. Mimi. Another woman. Cancer. Stepping down . . . She was grateful when the waiter interrupted them to serve their lunch, yet she had little appetite for her basket of fried cod and French fries. She waited until Nora had finished slathering tarter sauce on her own basket of fried fish and then tasted it before asking her next question.

"Nora, do you know why he chose to step down? And why six months ago? Was his cancer becoming more aggressive and unresponsive?"

"Oh God, is this scrumptious or what?" Nora said, savoring her mouthful of fish. "I know this is the most fattening thing in the world, but I don't care. I have it at least once a month."

Amanda smiled. "It is good. And I really appreciate that you're taking the time to have lunch with me."

Nora waved her hand dismissively. "My pleasure."

Amanda could feel Ethan's eyes on her, telling her to keep going.

"So do you know why he stepped down?" Amanda asked again. "Was it only because of his cancer?" She hoped it didn't seem odd that she didn't know much about her own father.

Nora popped a French fry into her mouth. "Not that I knew of. Well, I mean, sort of. I heard—and this is totally gossip—that his heart actually broke when Sally died, so I guess he just gave up and gave in to death to join her."

"Sally? His former secretary?"

Nora nodded. "According to gossip, they were involved for years. I guess she looked the other way when it came to his other women, considering that she would have made all the arrangements."

Amanda was disgusted. "So she had an appointment book like yours, full of his romantic lunches and notes to order flowers and 'trinkets' and whatever else? That's horrible!"

Nora shrugged. "From what I heard, Sally and Mr. Sedgwick had an understanding. Sally enjoyed the special treatment of being his lover. I mean, can you imagine the job perks? And she probably was able to use her position as his secretary to her advantage. She could probably hold things over his head since she was privy to everything."

"Are you saying she did hold things over his head?" Amanda asked.

"I really don't know . . . actually, I doubt it. I didn't know Sally, but I've heard she was one of the sweetest women on earth. I think she truly loved him and decided it was worth being one of many. At least as far as the company went, she was his number one. I did hear that he had many affairs with some of the best-looking women in the company."

Amanda pushed her practically untouched plate away. "Was Sally married? Did she have children?"

"Um, are you going to eat that?" Nora asked, gesturing at Amanda's basket. "I'd love to try yours."

Amanda smiled. "It's all yours."

Nora forked a piece of fish from Amanda's basket into her own. "Sally was never married. I think she has a son, though, a teenager . . . Hey, maybe by your father! Oops! I'm so sorry . . ."

Amanda glanced at Ethan; he surreptitiously raised an eyebrow that said: *Bingo.*

As Ethan threw some bills on the table to pay for his own fish and chips, he watched Amanda and Nora slipping on their coats at the front door of the restaurant. He could hear Amanda thanking Nora and then extending her hand, but Nora pulled Amanda into a hug. Nora said something about needing to hit the drugstore before heading back up, so while Amanda feigned having left her gloves at the table, they said their good-byes at the door, and Nora headed out. Amanda waited for Ethan to join her and they exited the restaurant together.

"Let's take the bus back to to the brownstone,"

he told her, gesturing at the bus stop just before the corner. "We'll discuss what we just learned."

Amanda nodded and wheeled Tommy's stroller over to the short line. She kneeled down to unstrap Tommy, and his eyes opened. His face crumpled, and Amanda soothed him with a reassuring caress on his forehead. Ethan folded up the stroller and held onto it, and Amanda boosted Tommy up into her arms.

"Wow, I can't tell you how many times I've gotten on a bus by myself, trying to lug the stroller and carry Tommy at the same time. It feels so good to have help."

"It must be very hard to be a single mother," he said. "A lot of work all on you."

Amanda nodded. "It is hard. It's hard to be a parent even when there are two of you, but shouldering everything is tough. At least I know I'm capable right? Sometimes I feel like I could handle anything." She paused. "Yeah right. Like I handled what happened the other night."

The bus rumbled to a stop at the curb, and Amanda and Ethan got on, taking seats in the back.

"You handled that exceptionally well, Amanda," Ethan said. "You're a very strong woman."

"Sometimes I wish I didn't have to be," she said in a very low voice. "I know that's not exactly a feminist thing to say, but sometimes I just wish I could relax."

"That has nothing to do with feminism and everything to do with need. You're human, period."

She offered him a bit of a smile and stared out the window. Ethan felt eyes on him and glanced around and found himself looking into Tommy Sedgwick's round blue eyes. The baby smiled and then grabbed one of Ethan's fingers.

"Whoa there, little guy," Ethan said, his chest constricting.

"He's got some grip, huh?" Amanda said, laughing. "Sometimes I can't pry his hold off."

Suddenly Ethan felt his air supply dwindling. The eyes staring at him, the chubby fist around his finger.

"Ethan, are you okay?" Amanda asked. "You look pale all of a sudden." She removed Tommy's hand from his finger. "Was he cutting off your circulation?" she said, half-jokingly.

Ethan smiled and shook his head, but the truth was that the baby had done just that, figuratively if not literally.

# CHAPTER 15

As Amanda wheeled Tommy in his stroller up Seventy-fourth Street toward the brownstone, Ethan tapped the little spiral notebook he held. "We have a lot to go over," Ethan said.

"I don't even know where to begin. If I even want to begin," Amanda said. "Do I really want to dig into my father's past? His affairs? His many affairs? His possible children? My possible half brothers or sisters?"

"I know it must be hard on you, Amanda," he said. "But we're not looking into his private life for salacious reasons. We're just trying to find out who tried to hurt you so that it doesn't ever happen again."

"I know. You're right. I just have to keep remembering that."

"So you're in?" he said. "You're staying?"

"Oh God," she said. "My head was so full of what Nora told me that I didn't even think about the brownstone and the stupid rules. I definitely can't stay there alone."

"You don't have to," Ethan said, holding her gaze. "I think I've proven you can trust me."

She looked at him, wanting to believe him, needing to believe him, but how was she supposed to trust anyone?

*You can trust yourself,* a voice inside her said. *That's the only person you need to trust. And your gut says this guy is on the up and up. For whatever reasons—and they don't seem to have anything to do with you—he's willing to see this through.*

"Amanda!"

She whirled around to find Jenny and Lettie walking up the block, waving and beaming. "I am so glad to see you two!" she called. As the two women caught up, Amanda kneeled down next to Tommy's stroller. "Tommy, look who's here! It's Aunties Jenny and Lettie!" Tommy smiled and laughed and tried to grab the pompoms hanging off Jenny's coat's zipper. The two women eyed Ethan, gave each other knowing looks, and grinned at Amanda. She cleared her throat. "Um, this is Ethan Black. He was retained by my father. . . . Ethan, this is Jenny, who I've known since high school, and this is Lettie, who I used to live near. Lettie took great care of Tommy while I was at work."

Ethan smiled at the women. "Very nice to meet you."

Jenny and Lettie could barely contain their smiles and curiosity, and Amanda's cheeks colored in embarrassment. "We actually came by a little earlier," Jenny said, "but you weren't home. I stopped by Lettie's this afternoon to see if she wanted to join me in surprising you with a little visit."

"And you did!" Amanda said.

"From the outside, the brownstone is gorgeous," Jenny said. "I can't wait to see the inside, but I'm going to have to come back for a tour another time." She glanced at her watch. "I have to get to work. I just couldn't resist stopping by. We both had to see your face and our little munchkin!"

"I'm so glad you did," Amanda said, wrapping her two friends in hugs. "It's so good to see you."

"So everything's okay? You're settling in fine?" Jenny asked.

Amanda glanced at Ethan. "Um, yeah, I'm settling in." She wasn't about to frighten her best friend when there was nothing Jenny could do.

"Sweetheart," Lettie said, "I wanted to come with Jenny so that I could offer to take Tommy for a few hours. If you need some time to yourself, I'd love to babysit while my kids are with their father."

"Lettie that's so sweet," Amanda said. And if Lettie babysat Tommy, Amanda and Ethan could pay a visit to that Mimi person or Sally's son. "It actually would be a big help."

Lettie beamed. "Great. I'll take him to the Children's Museum. They have a wonderful play area for babies his age."

Jenny wrapped Amanda in a hug. "Call me soon," Jenny said. "Nice meeting you, Ethan," she added, winking at Amanda and completely mortifying her.

Ethan smiled back. "You too."

After Jenny headed up the block, Amanda explained Tommy's schedule, that he'd had his nap and was ready for lunch, and Lettie smiled. "You leave it to me. I'll bring him back when, say, six?"

"Perfect," Amanda said. "Thanks so much, Lettie. This will give me a chance to get some things done."

"My pleasure," Lettie said. And with kisses and hugs, Lettie was off, Tommy playing with his new miniature Big Bird that Jenny had brought.

"I assume you can absolutely trust her," Ethan said as they watched Lettie walk up Seventy-fourth Street toward Columbus Avenue.

Amanda nodded. "I've lived next door to her for a long time, and she's taken care of Tommy since I returned to work. She can definitely be trusted." That was the one thing, aside from Jenny's friendship, that she was absolutely sure of.

"Why don't we head in, then, and make a plan," Ethan said, aware she'd been fired recently.

Amanda nodded, and as she climbed the steps to the brownstone, she felt funny. Not humorous funny. Strange funny. As in something didn't feel right.

It was Tommy, she realized. It wasn't often that she left Tommy with his sitter, except for the times she was at work.

"Amanda?" Ethan asked.

She blinked and realized she was staring down the street, at the distant figure of Lettie. Amanda could just make out the stroller. He was in the best possible hands other than her own, Amanda reminded herself.

"I'm okay," she told him and for the moment, she meant it.

* * *

They decided to start with Mimi Farthwell, William's weekday lady friend. Her address and telephone number were listed, and when Amanda introduced herself over the phone, the woman insisted she come over before Amanda could even get a word out.

"I'd come to you, dear, but Pashmina doesn't travel well," she said cryptically before confirming Amanda had the right address.

When Ethan and Amanda arrived at Mimi's, they were surprised to discover that she lived in a modest apartment, not even a doorman building. Amanda had expected a luxury skyscraper, but Mimi's building was a five-story brick tenement between a deli and a cell phone shop. The one-bedroom apartment looked the part, though. The walls were painted gold, and luxurious touches were everywhere, from velvet settees to the gorgeous oriental rug in the living room to the huge sunflowers in a vase on the upright piano. And Mimi herself, a very attractive woman of forty-something, wore a flowing black silk outfit with a small black feather boa around her neck.

"I'm so glad to finally meet one of William's daughters," she said, her eyes brimming with tears as she gestured for Amanda and Ethan to come in. "And it's nice to meet you," she added to Ethan. "Are you married?"

Amanda felt her cheeks pinken. "No, Ethan is a friend."

"It's important to have those," Mimi said. "Ah, how rude of me. This is Pashmina," she said, kissing the head of a tiny white dog in her arms. "She doesn't like taxis."

Amanda smiled at the dog. Mimi set her on a red velvet pillow on the floor and the dog immediately put her head on her paws and closed her eyes.

Mimi insisted on serving tea and scones. When cups were poured and everyone was seated, Mimi started to cry. She dabbed at her eyes with a tissue. "I was madly in love with William," she said. "We were planning to marry."

"I didn't know," Amanda said. "I'm so sorry."

"He was a very private man," Mimi said. "Well," she added with a flourish. "I think I'm ready now."

Amanda glanced at Ethan. "Ready?" Amanda asked.

Mimi's nose wrinked. "Oops. You have to forgive me. I'm known for being forthright. It's one of the things William loved most about me."

*I have no idea what you're being forthright about,* Amanda thought. She figured if she waited, the woman would just say it.

Mimi leaned forward. "I hope it's not too indecent a sum," she whispered. "I always told William that his money didn't mean a thing to me, but he was always so generous."

"This indecent sum," Ethan said, "are you referring to what William left you in his will?"

"Is it terribly large?" Mimi asked. "Because just a small remembrance is all I really want."

"Mimi," Amanda said. "We have no idea what William might have left you in his will."

"Might?" she said. "You don't know if he left me something?"

Amanda shook her head. "I wouldn't have any idea."

"Then why are you here?" she asked.

"I do know that you and my father were . . . close," Amanda said. "And I was hoping you might be able to tell me more about him. We weren't as close as I wished we were when he was alive, and I guess I'm hoping to get to know him better now. I know that must sound strange."

The woman looked down her nose at Amanda. "Yes, it does."

"I didn't come here to judge you," Amanda said. "And I'd appreciate it if you didn't judge me."

"I'll do what I please," Mimi said. "It's your own fault if you weren't close to your father. Are you the one who got the brownstone?"

Amanda glanced at Ethan. Was Mimi pretending not to know who she was? "Yes."

"The reading of the will as far as his daughters were concerned was more than a week ago," Mimi all but hissed. "I've been waiting for a call from his lawyer about coming in to hear what I've been left—that's the real reason I don't like to leave the apartment—but the lawyer hasn't called. When you did, I was sure you were coming to give me my check."

"I'm sorry to have to disappoint you," Amanda said. "It is possible that William's will hasn't been entirely sorted through. He knew many people—"

"I read in *New York News* that his three daughters were his sole beneficiaries." Mimi said. "Of course, I still expected the phone to ring with news of what I was left. I mean, I didn't expect to read of my inheritance in the paper."

"Why?" Ethan said. "You were his girlfriend, weren't you?"

*Whoa there, Ethan,* Amanda thought. *Do you really want to make this woman angry enough to kick us out? We haven't even gotten to the attack yet!*

Mimi bristled. "William was a private man. He didn't flaunt our relationship."

"So he didn't tell anyone the two of you were engaged?" Ethan asked.

Mimi lifted her chin. "No, he wanted it to be a secret."

Amanda doubted there was any such engagement, except in Mimi's dreams.

"Mimi," Ethan said. "I think you're right. I think the fact that more than a week has passed since the reading of the will might mean that you were left nothing."

Mimi stood so abruptly that Pashmina jumped off her little pillow. "That cheap son of a bitch. I've known it in my gut for days now that I wouldn't be getting a call. Why would he leave anything to you selfish girls. You weren't even in his life! I was! I was in his godamn bed!"

"I wanted to be in his life," Amanda said. "He wasn't interested in being a father. He never was."

"I know," she said. "I tried for the past two years to get him to make me pregnant before my clock tick-tocked out of business, but he kept telling me he had a vasectomy and that he never wanted to have another child. I didn't believe him about the vasectomy, and I tried to trick him into knocking me up, but it never took."

Vasectomy. Amanda filed that piece of information away. And she tried to mentally erase any thought of how Mimi tried to trick her father into getting her pregnant. Poking holes in condoms?

"I'll bet that Prune Face was left something," Mimi said, pacing. "She was, wasn't she?"

"Prune Face?" Ethan asked.

"That sneaky housekeeper, Carol or whatever her name is."

"Clara," Amanda said.

"Whatever," Mimi said. "She had a good thing going there, I tell you. Did you ever see that episode of *Sex and the City*, when Samantha slept over at her lover's, and when the man went to work in the morning, the housekeeper flew into a jealous rage and dumped Samantha out of bed and called her a slut? Well that's Clara. She'd find me sleeping in William's bed and slam doors until I woke up. And then she'd come in and vacuum the bedroom when I was in there. She once even dusted a lamp on the bedside table right next to my face. And I'm allergic to dust. That crusty old bitch."

"Mimi," Amanda asked. "Do you have a key to the brownstone?"

Mimi shook her head. "I asked for one repeatedly, but William said I didn't need one, that his door was always open for me. Guess it's closed now," she all but spat.

"Mimi, did you love my father?" Amanda asked.

"He was thirty years older than I," Mimi said. "He could barely get it up half the time."

Ethan stood, his expression dark. "Mimi, I know this is your house, but I'd appreciate it if you'd consider the fact that you're talking to William's daughter."

Mimi snorted. "I wouldn't even have known he had a daughter, let alone three, except that one time I called him at work, and a temp mentioned that he wasn't in because he'd stepped out to buy a teddy bear for his newborn grandson. *Grandson.* I didn't even know he had a daughter! That's how close we were."

Amanda's stomach flopped. *Out picking a teddy bear for his grandson . . .*

So William had gone to a toy store himself? That brown teddy that had arrived a few days after Tommy was born was from William himself? He hadn't sent a secretary to pick it out? He had cared?

"Mimi, thanks for your time," Amanda said, standing. "I'm sorry for your loss."

"No need to be sarcastic, missy," Mimi said.

Ethan rolled his eyes. "We'd better be going, Amanda."

As the door closed behind them, Amanda could hear Mimi throwing things. "Do you believe their nerve, Pashie? All high and mighty. That son of a bitch didn't leave me a damned thing! Two years of fucking an old geezer for nothing!"

"Let's get out of here," Ethan said. "I feel like I'm covered in grime."

Amanda took a deep breath and let him lead the way down the stairs.

# CHAPTER 16

They stopped at Ethan's hotel so he could pack his duffel bag, which didn't contain much, despite the fact that he'd known he'd be staying in New York for a month.

"I travel light," he explained to Amanda when she raised her eyebrow at how little he'd packed. "And what did I need for the job? Some jeans, maybe a nice pair of pants just in case, a few shirts. A shaving kit."

She smiled and sat down on the chair at the small desk. When they'd first approached the hotel, she thought she might want to wait for Ethan in the lobby, but then the thought of being alone, even in a lobby crowded with desk clerks and porters and guests, made her uncomfortable. She knew all too well how invisible you could be to the hotel staff unless you were throwing a tantrum or running around naked.

And so she'd chosen to come upstairs with

Ethan to his room. His small room. Dominated by a king-sized bed.

"Since we have a good hour before we have to be back at the brownstone for your date with the sofa, I'd like to hop in the shower. Unless that would make you uncomfortable."

She could feel her cheeks turning pink. "No, not at all," she said.

He smiled and disappeared into the bathroom. She could hear the water running.

She'd lied. The answer to his question was *yes.* Yes, it would make her uncomfortable. Surprisingly uncomfortable. She suddenly pictured him naked, then blinked fast to shake the image from her mind. But it remained. Of Ethan Black, all six-feet plus of muscular man, damp and clean and half-naked under a small hotel towel.

*What the hell am I thinking?* she wondered, tapping her forehead with her palm. But the image was still there.

She stood and paced the room, then sat back down on the chair, then stood, then sat back down. Lord, what was wrong with her? She knew it's been a long time since she'd been with a man, but c'mon.

It had been a long time. Pre-pregnancy long. Paul Swinwood long.

Suddenly she imagined Ethan coming out of the bathroom, wrapped in the tiny towel, his body slick, his hair damp. The towel would fall, and he'd be naked, and they'd both reach for it at the same time, and then they'd play tug of war with the towel, but he'd win because he was so much stronger, so much bigger, and he'd tug and tug until she was pressed tight against him, her breasts crushed against his chest, her pelvis pressed against his erection. He'd undo her pants and slide them down, remove her panties with one finger, and then he'd—"

"Amanda?"

She started and blinked and looked up, and there he was, damp and half-naked under the tiny white hotel towel. "I-I—was just thinking about something."

Could he see her sweating? Could he hear her heart beating a million miles an hour?

What he could see were her breasts. He stared at them, then up at her eyes, then down at her parted lips. She glanced down and realized her nipples had hardened into peaks.

"I was going to ask you if you minded if I came out in just a towel," he said. "I forgot to take in clean clothes."

"I don't mind," she said.

And so he came out, in that tiny towel, and it dropped.

And when she stood to reach for it, he grabbed hold of it at the same time and suddenly they were playing tug of war, but she wasn't trying very hard.

He had her on the bed in a few seconds, her clothes off nearly as fast. "I've been fantasizing about this from the first moment I laid eyes on you," he said, his hands roaming, cupping, caressing, her breasts. His mouth took over and she moaned with pleasure, arching into him, and he grabbed her hips and pulled her up to him.

As in her fantasy, he peeled off her white cotton panties with one finger, and he kissed and suckled her body as he went, first her stomach, then her thighs, then between her legs.

She arched and moaned and reached for him. They kissed and fondled in wild and urgent abandon until they were breathless. She was unable to get enough of him, and when he withdrew she screamed and covered her mouth with her hand as his own fingers explored inside her, gently at first, softly, and then harder and more deeply. And then he slid his body down the length of her, his penis now pulsing with hot desire. She was dimly aware of his taut arms on either side of her, holding himself up over her. He kissed her again, passionately, his chest rubbing her nipples into peaks as his erection was inches from being inside her. Amanda was glad she was on hormone pills to stabilize her monthly periods so birth control wasn't a problem at this unexpected event.

"Oh, Ethan," she breathed into his ear, her hands in his hair. She ran her nails up his back and met his thrusts, moaning, purring, panting.

"This is too good," he said before flipping her over on top of him, guiding her onto him. They sat up; his mouth on her breasts, and he rocked her until she couldn't last another second.

And once she was sated, he grabbed her hips and rocked her up and down on top of him until he groaned and was then breathtakingly still.

She collapsed onto his chest and then rolled off him, lying flat on her back next to him.

Breathing hard, he looked over at her, his eyes still dark with desire, and he moved the hair out of her face. "You are so beautiful," he said.

"You too," was all she could manage back.

For quite a while they just lay there, not speaking, just listening to each other's breath.

"We'd better go," she said. "It's almost three-fifteen."

He nodded. "What I wouldn't give to just stay here for another couple of hours."

"I know," she said. "But we're transportable. What we can do here, we can do at the brownstone."

He grinned. "True."

They returned to the brownstone just in time. Ethan made himself comfortable across from Amanda, his notebook flipped open. He began writing.

"Notes about Mimi?" she asked.

*No, I'm writing you a love poem. No, I'm writing you a love letter. No, I'm writing you my deep thoughts and feelings about how intense things have been between us and how I had to have you back there in my hotel room, and it was an incredible experience, and things aren't going to be weird between us even though we barely know each other and just had mind-blowing sex . .*

Why did Amanda have a feeling he wasn't going to say any of those things?

He nodded. "Not that I could forget anything that came out of her mouth."

Oh God. He'd gone from what happened in his hotel room to business just like that?

Amanda had always felt she had a lot to learn about men, but some things should just be genderless, like not pretending something monumental didn't just happen between them. Or maybe that was a man thing.

Or an Ethan thing.

"Ethan, I—" She stopped, having no idea what to say, or what she even wanted to say. She didn't even know how *she* felt!

*So just leave it alone. Clearly he wants to do just that. And so do you.*

Amanda opened the can of soda Ethan brought her from the refrigerator. "I can't believe that woman. How could my father have been involved with someone with such an ugly heart?"

"He probably didn't know," Ethan said, putting his feet up on the coffee table. "Mimi was probably a great actress, and they both got what they thought they wanted."

"Which was?"

"Your father got an attractive younger woman as a weekday girlfriend," Ethan explained, "And Mimi got a rich older man and an even richer fantasy life about the fortune he'd leave her one day."

Amanda's stomach twisted. "I can't imagine being involved with someone just for his money."

"Money can definitely twist some people around," Ethan said. "I used to be guilty of being motivated by the almighty dollar."

She glanced at him, surprised. "Did Ethan Black actually say something of a personal nature?"

"I guess I did," he said, snapping open his own soda can.

She looked at him. "Tell me more."

"I'd rather talk about the case," he said. "While you're stuck on that sofa, let's put the time to good use."

"Talking about yourself isn't a good use of our time?" she asked.

"No."

End of story, according to the look on his face and the fact that his attention was fully on his notes.

"Ethan, is everything okay?" she asked. *All right, so I can't completely let it go.*

"Everything's fine," he said. "I just want to catch the psycho who tried to hurt you."

*So you can leave,* she thought. *So you can go on with your life.*

She still had several more weeks of him. She couldn't imagine that was anywhere near long enough to crack open his hard shell.

*What have I done?* Ethan thought as Amanda ran to the door to welcome in Lettie and Tommy.

*Why couldn't I just resist her as I have from the minute I met her?*

He waved at Lettie as she and Amanda passed by the kitchen. Amanda was giving her the grand tour.

*You shouldn't have made love to her,* he berated himself. *She was vulnerable, and you shouldn't have done it. Now she's going to expect—*

Expect what? He had no idea what she'd expect or want. Maybe she just needed what he'd needed. In that hotel room, he had to have her. Maybe that was how she'd felt. Good, hard sexual release.

When did a woman ever feel that way, though? Ethan knew in his heart that she was going to expect something from him and that he wouldn't be able to give it. It's going to get ugly, he thought.

*Just ignore it. Just get back to the business at hand of getting through the month without any harm coming to her or Tommy.*

# CHAPTER 17

The next morning, Amanda began to wonder if she'd fantasized the entire thing. Had she and Ethan not shared an incredible and incredibly intimate experience? Had she actually dreamed it? She lay in bed, the early morning sunshine streaming in through the windows. It was seven o'clock, and Tommy was still sleeping.

After bringing Tommy back home last night, Lettie had stayed for an hour or so. Then Amanda slid two chicken breasts in the oven, made garlic mashed potatoes (Tommy loved them) and asparagus, and invited Ethan to a home-cooked meal, which they'd eaten mostly in silence. He'd said he was "wiped" and then he'd disappeared into the white room, the door closing behind him.

*I didn't dream making love to Ethan. I can still feel the imprint of his lips on mine, of his . . .*

She traced a finger over her lips, remembering, feeling, and closed her eyes, but she was suddenly swallowed up by an intense loneliness. *Why do I keep making mistakes when it comes to men? Why do I keep giving myself to men who don't want me?*

*Why am I lying here feeling sorry for myself when I promised myself I'd never wallow in self-pity again?*

She sat up, threw the covers off, and took a deep breath. If Ethan Black wanted to forget that they'd made love in his hotel room, so be it. She couldn't forget, but she would push the memory out of her mind and move on.

*Fool me once, shame on you. Fool me twice, shame on me.*

She wouldn't let him have a second chance.

Ethan didn't seem the least interested in a second chance. The next day passed in a dull blur. They'd sat in the kitchen for both breakfast and lunch, making phone calls and finding no one home. Amanda had called Lara O'Hara, her father's "weekend lady friend," but no one answered and there'd been no answering machine.

Ethan had come to agree with Amanda that it was unlikely either of her sisters were involved. He figured if it were one of them, they'd stick around closer to home to protect their interests. Instead, both were out of the country.

The heaviness that had lifted off Amanda's chest was palpable. She'd known in her heart that her sisters weren't responsible, but to hear Ethan finally say it took a pressure off that she hadn't even known was squeezing her chest.

Ethan thought they should focus on Olivia's and Ivy's mothers, on the housekeeper, on both of

William's girlfriends, and on his former secretary's son, whose name they'd learned from Sally's obituary, was Kevin Fanwell.

Is he my half brother? Amanda wondered. It was so strange to think that she might have another sibling, a brother. An uncle for Tommy. She would have to deal with those thoughts later.

*And then the thought would have to go right out of her head. In Ethan Black's world, someone related to her—or potentially related to her—had tried to suffocate her with her own pillow.*

Ethan also wanted Amanda to call Paul Swinwood and arrange a visit at the brownstone so they could gauge his expressions and reactions—especially to Ethan himself. Ethan thought that if Paul was their culprit, he wouldn't take very kindly to Ethan's presence, that he'd feel threatened. But Amanda had held him off on Paul for the time being; they had enough people on the list to last them too long as it was, and with Paul came a certain set of emotional baggage that she just wasn't ready to deal with.

She'd waited for Ethan to ask her if she was still in love with Paul, but he hadn't. He'd simply said okay to her request, asked her if she needed anything before he turned in, and then disappeared into the white room without turning back.

Maybe she *had* fantasized the entire afternoon in his hotel room.

By the next morning, a sunny and surprisingly warm day, there was no maybe about it. Ethan again acted as if nothing out of the ordinary had happened between them. He came downstairs with his laptop and ubiquitous notebook, made a pot of coffee, and began doing some research online.

Amanda was busy enough with Tommy's breakfast and helping him build a tower out of blocks. She tried to ignore Ethan's presence, but it was impossible; the man filled every room he was in.

At eight A.M. sharp, the doorbell rang.

"Expecting someone?" Ethan asked.

Amanda shrugged. "No." Ah. Yes she was. "It's Clara," she whispered. "She comes to clean every Wednesday and Saturday."

"Good," he said. "Our suspect comes to us. Very convenient."

"She may be surprised to see you here again," Amanda pointed out. "It's awfully early for a business call."

"Making her wonder about our relationship isn't a bad thing," he said. "It might throw her off guard. If she's our culprit and thinks you seduced me, she may get nervous that you'll have a strong ally to protect you, someone paid to figure out who tried to hurt you. She may try to ally herself with me to turn me against you."

"I didn't seduce you," she snapped and immediately turned red.

He paused for just a moment. "The point is that Clara will probably think you did."

Amanda headed for the front door. She opened it to find Clara standing there in her prim gray coat. "Good morning, Clara. Beautiful day."

The woman nodded and came inside. She hung her coat on the coat rack.

"I appreciate your ringing the doorbell instead of just using your key now that I'm living here," Amanda said.

Ethan strode into the foyer, folding a newspaper

and eating half an English muffin. "Want the other half, Mandy?" he asked. He turned to Clara. "Oh, Ms. Mott. I didn't hear the bell. Nice to see you again."

Clara's face cracked. Just slightly, but Amanda saw it: *surprise.*

Clara nodded at Ethan. "Well, I'd better get straight to work." She headed for the stairs.

The doorbell rang again. Before Amanda could even turn around, Clara had turned around and was at the front door.

"Clara, what a surprise to see you here," said a familiar woman's voice.

"Clara," said another woman, "you're looking well."

Amanda was stunned. Standing in the foyer were her sisters' mothers. Together. That was odd. Odd too was that they had come at all.

Of course, both women knew Clara from summers of dropping off their daughters at Grand Central Station, where Clara would be waiting to chaperone them on their annual summer vacation. The girls would sit in the same car but never in seats next to each other. Once, Amanda had had to sit uncomfortably next to Clara for the first half, from New York to Boston. There were always seats on the train from Boston to Portland.

"Amanda! How nicely you're settling in!" Olivia's mother gushed.

"You seem very comfortable here," Ivy's mother added. "To the manor born."

Amanda had no idea if that was a compliment or a dig. "Can I get you anything to drink?"

"Tea would be lovely," Olivia's mother said.

"Yes, just lovely," Ivy's mother added.

As the women took seats in the living room, each on one of the antique upholstered chairs facing the leather sofa, Amanda took a moment to study them. The two women could pass for sisters themselves, unless you looked closely. They both had the same body type—the tall, thin, regal look William clearly preferred. Both wore their hair in smooth blunt-cut bobs; Olivia's mother had bangs, though, and was a blonde. Ivy's mother was a highlighted brunette. They both wore expensive pants suits in muted colors, and both wore very expensive-looking gold jewelry.

"What a darling baby," Ivy's mother gushed, barely looking at Tommy, who was crawling around the living room. "Small for his age, no?"

"How old?" Olivia's mother asked, making ridiculous goochy-goo faces at Tommy.

"He'll be a year next month," Amanda responded, scooping him up and giving him a kiss on the head before settling him inside the playpen. "And no, he's actually a bit taller and heavier than average."

"Ah," Candace Hearn said, "What do I know from babies? It's been so long since my gorgeous Olivia was in diapers! One year old. My goodness. And what a wonderful birthday present he'll be getting—an entire brownstone. From what I understand, you used to live in a less-desirable building."

"I'll go start the tea," Amanda said.

Just as Amanda was heading into the kitchen, Ethan came out of the room, holding the same folded up newspaper and still holding half an English muffin. "Are you sure you don't want the other half, Aman—" He paused. "Oh, I didn't know you had guests."

"Candace Hearn, Dana Sedgwick," Amanda introduced, "this is Ethan Black. He was retained by William's estate as a sort of caretaker during my stay."

The women glanced at each other, barely concealing their intense curiosity.

"A caretaker?" Ivy's mother said. "What do you do, exactly?"

"I ensure that William Sedgwick's last wishes with regards to Amanda's inheritance are fulfilled."

Ivy's mother smiled. "Ah. So you're the watchdog. Amanda told Olivia and Ivy all about the rules she had to follow and that someone would be watching to make sure she followed those rules. They were at her apartment when she opened the letter from William. Oh dear—I didn't just get you into trouble, did I?"

"Sorry," Ethan said. "Sharing the contents of the letter isn't against William's rules."

"Oh," Ivy's mother said.

"So Olivia and Ivy told you two all about the letter?" Amanda asked as she returned from the kitchen. She hoped the context was less gossipy than Ivy's mother was intimating.

"Good Lord, I had to pry every word out of Ivy," Mrs. Sedgwick said. "You'd think I was asking for personal secrets the way she carried on. She finally told me just to shut me up. My Ivy has always been a little too obsessed with discretion. That job of hers, I guess."

"When Dana shared the rules with me," Olivia's mother said, "I couldn't believe it. Why should sitting on a sofa or not sleeping in a certain bedroom guarantee you a fortune? That's ridiculous!"

"The two of you knew my father a lot better than I did," Amanda said. "Is something like that typical of him? Arbitrary rules? Is he making me jump through hoops?"

"No one *knew* William Sedgwick," Ivy's mother said. "Trust me, I was married to the man for an entire year."

"I think I knew him quite well," Olivia's mother said, smoothing her hair.

"You dated him for three months!" Ivy's mother snapped.

"Perhaps our relationship was more intense than yours?" she suggested.

"May I ask why you've come?" Amanda interrupted. She'd had enough of their squabbling.

"To see how you're doing, of course," Olivia's mother said as though their concern was nothing new.

"I'm a little surprised," Amanda responded. "I've never received a visit from either of you before."

Ivy's mother looked down her nose at Amanda. "My dear, you certainly are direct. I didn't know you well as you were growing up, but I remember you were a bit shy. You've certainly blossomed."

"Thank you," Amanda answered without missing a beat.

Olivia's mother sipped her tea. "To answer your question, Amanda, our daughters have the same father. Dana and I have known each other for years."

So they were friends? Amanda had gotten the

sense they were bitter enemies. What was going on here?

"So, the two of you seem quite cozy," Ivy's mother said, indicating Ethan. "Does William's attorney know that you've become friendly?"

"Meaning?" Amanda asked.

"Meaning that William's last wishes might be compromised," Olivia's mother said. "If you're sleeping with your watchdog, why wouldn't he look the other way when you broke the rules?"

"That's quite an assumption," Ethan said.

"I call it as I see it," Ivy's mother said.

"It's time for Tommy's nap," Amanda lied. "Thank you so much for stopping by."

"You do understand that we'll need to address our concerns to William's lawyer," Ivy's mother said. "For the sake of protecting our daughters' interests."

"Of course," Amanda said. "Whatever you like."

Both women sent Amanda withering glances. And then as suddenly as they'd arrived, they were gone.

"Charming women," Ethan commented when Amanda returned to the living room. "Like mothers like daughters?"

Amanda shook her head. "Not in the least. Olivia and Ivy are both kind. I don't know them well, granted, but they're *not vicious.*"

He nodded and grabbed his notebook. "I'd like to visit William's weekend lady friend later this morning, and then—"

Everything in her life was an *and then.* Before she could stop herself, Amanda burst into tears. It was all just too much. She stood there, in the middle of the living room, tears streaming down her face, grateful that Tommy was engaged by his touch-and-feel book, and completely uncaring that Ethan was staring at her.

He walked over to her, slowly, and held out his arms, and before her brain could tell her to turn around and run, she sank against him and let him hold her. Forcing his hand at showing a spark of emotion seemed more punishment than letting him off the hook of comforting her.

"My life is just getting a little overwhelming," she said, wiping her eyes. "Sorry for turning into a basket case all of a sudden."

"You're hardly a basket case, Amanda. In fact, you're one of the strongest women I've ever met."

"I thought there were no people in your life," she said before she could stop herself. She mentally kicked herself. Why had she said that? What had possessed her to follow up a compliment with a barb? "I'm sorry, Ethan."

He lifted her chin with one finger. "Nothing to be sorry about. You were right to say it. And you *are* one of the strongest women I've ever met. What you're going through right now must be harrowing."

"Well, at least I was taken away from it for a little while the other afternoon," she said.

He looked into her eyes and then looked away. "Amanda, I'm sorry that I've been acting like it never happened. I know that's how it must seem."

She nodded. "That's exactly how it seems."

"I just can't—"

"Can't what, Ethan? Talk to me, please."

"You're going through enough as it is, Amanda. I don't want you to get hurt even more."

She felt her heart constrict in her chest. "What makes you so damned sure you're going to hurt me?"

"I know I will," he said. "It's what I do."

"Cryptic statements like that don't help, Ethan."

"All I've ever done to anyone I've cared about is hurt them. So now I don't get personally involved."

She looked at him. "I'd say we're personally involved."

He stepped back and shoved his hands in his pockets. "We had sex, Amanda."

She felt as though she'd been slapped. "You're so cold."

"At ten-thirty, you'll need to do your hour on the sofa," he said. "After that—"

At the sound of someone clearing her throat, Ethan froze and Amanda whirled around. Clara Mott stood at the top of steps leading downstairs, a Swiffer dust mop in her hand. "I'm suddenly not feeling well. Would you mind if I let things go until next time? I'm feeling a bit faint."

Amanda could barely find her voice. How the hell had both of them forgotten Clara was in the house? Olivia's and Ivy's mothers had thrown them for such a loop, as had Amanda's sudden tears and the awful conversation that followed that they'd completely forgotten about Clara.

Ethan recovered more quickly than Amanda. "Of course that's fine."

The woman glanced at Amanda.

"It's absolutely fine, Clara," Amanda seconded. "I'm sorry you're not feeling well. Please let us know if you need anything."

Clara nodded, retrieved her coat from the hall closet, and left.

"Does it matter that she heard all of that?" Amanda asked him. "If she's the one who attacked me, did we give her anything?"

He shook his head. "I'm sure Clara is used to overhearing very private conversations. And anyway, she probably suspects we're lovers so nothing we said will make a difference. We'll just have to see what happens as far as she's concerned."

"Wait to see what happens? Meaning?" She held up a hand. "Forget it. I know. We'll just have to wait and see if she tries to poison me with Drano or something, right?"

"Amanda, nothing will happen to you while I'm here," he said. "I promise you that I will not take my eyes—any of my senses—off you for a second."

But he already had. She closed her eyes and turned away from him, then picked up Tommy and headed upstairs where some time with her precious son would fill her heart again and remind her that she was whole before Ethan Black and that she would be whole after.

Hurt, but whole.

# CHAPTER 18

At noon, Tommy all bundled up and sleeping in his stroller, Amanda and Ethan set out for their meeting with Lara O'Hara. Lara hadn't wanted to meet at her apartment, so they settled on a nearby Starbucks. Amanda only hoped that at least one of her father's girlfriends had truly cared about him—Lara's initial response to her had been very similar to Mimi Farthwell's.

"Amanda!"

Amanda whirled around at the familiar voice. Paul Swinwood was hurrying up the block toward her. She glanced at Ethan, who seemed suddenly very much on guard.

"Hello Paul," she said.

"Amanda, I'm so glad I ran into you again. I was hoping you'd call, and when I didn't hear from you—" He hesitated, then glanced at Ethan. "Paul Swinwood. I'm Tommy's father."

"Ethan Black."

There were no extended hands.

Paul kneeled down beside Tommy's stroller and caressed his sleeping son's cheek. "Hey there big boy," he whispered. "I have something for you the next time I see you. A really cool talking monkey."

Amanda smiled. "I'm sure he'll love that."

Paul glanced from Ethan to Amanda. "Well, I guess you're on your way somewhere."

She felt a slight nudge at her back and realized Ethan was trying to tell her something. He wanted her to invite Paul over later, she knew. He wanted to observe, investigate.

*How dare you?* she almost screamed at him. *This is my life! This is my son's father!* Tommy deserved to know his dad without Ethan thinking his father was trying to kill Amanda so he could—could what? What could Paul possibly gain by killing her? He wouldn't get custody of Tommy—or would he? Amanda realized she had no idea how that worked. She did have a will that named Jenny as guardian in the event of her death, but that was before Paul had suddenly reappeared in her life. Perhaps if the father of the child wanted custody, he would win hands down. And gain control of whatever assets the mother left behind.

Oh God. Oh God. Oh God.

"Paul, if you're free for dinner tonight, please consider yourself invited to join me and Ethan and Tommy at my place." At the mention of Ethan, Paul frowned, then recovered quickly. "My father passed away recently, and he left me his apartment in his will, and Ethan was retained by the estate to ensure that everything connected to the will goes smoothly."

"I see," Paul said, glancing at Ethan. He turned to Amanda. "I'm so sorry about your father. I didn't know. What time should I come over?"

"How about seven?" Amanda suggested. "Tommy's bedtime is seven-thirty, so that'll give you a good half hour with him before we sit down to dinner."

"Sounds good," Paul said. "Thanks for the invitation, Amanda. I really appreciate it. I'll see you at seven. Nice to meet you, Ethan," he added with a nod before turning around and heading back down the block.

"Interesting that he didn't ask for the address, don't you think?" Ethan whispered.

Amanda's stomach sank. It was, after all, the second time she had just "run into him" on the street. "Paul," Amanda called after him, "I forgot to give you the address!"

He turned around. "I've got it. I saw you come down the steps of the second brownstone," he said, pointing at the house he was practically in front of now. "This one, right? I just assumed."

"Yes, that's the one," Amanda called, brushing aside her concerns. "See you at seven."

He smiled and then disappeared around the corner.

"He saw us leaving," Amanda said as she and Ethan resumed walking. "That's why he didn't need to ask for my address."

"Or he's smart and covered his ass," Ethan said.

Amanda took a deep breath.

Lara O'Hara was yet another tall, thin regal-looking woman. She was also married.

"Don't look so shocked," Lara said, as she handed a wallet-sized wedding photo, perhaps taken ten years ago, to Ethan and Amanda. "Affairs are the spice of a comfortable marriage."

Ethan kept his mouth shut. He glanced at the photo of a younger-looking Lara in her wedding dress, stuffing a piece of cake into the mouth of her groom, a large man around her age.

"I can't get over how cute your son is," Lara commented as she poured two packets of sugar into her tea. "He looks just like you," she added to Ethan. "Despite his blond hair. It's the eyes and the expression. And around the mouth. Yes, he definitely has your chin."

Ethan almost spat out his coffee. "I'm not his father."

Lara's cheeks pinkened. "Oh! Well, he still looks like you."

"Lara," Amanda said, her expression tight, "I hope you don't mind my asking personal questions about my father, but we weren't very close and I'm trying to understand him a bit better now that he's gone. Does that make sense?"

"Oh absolutely," she said. "Your father wanted to do that too."

"Do what?" Amanda asked.

"Get to know you better. You and your sisters," she added. "William—your father—he talked about you girls all the time."

Amanda glanced at Ethan, her face softer now. "He did? Really? What kinds of things he did say?"

"Well, mostly that he regretted not being there for you all," Lara said. "He used to shake his head and say he was a selfish person and even worse than selfish because he didn't want to change, didn't want to deal with all the stuff involved in being a parent. I used to tell him the rewards and the highs were so worth the lows—the chicken pox, the back-talk, the sleep deprivation, the disappointments, the whatever—but he said he'd rather just enjoy himself, devote his life to his corporation, enjoy a nice meal, his friends, girlfriends."

Amanda seemed deflated. "That does sound selfish. He did father children, for God's sake!"

Ethan gently touched Amanda's hand, and she glanced up at him. She was hurting, and right then he was so compelled to comfort her, to take her into his arms and tell her he knew it stunk, but that she had other love in her life. She had good friends, clearly, and a baby who adored her.

A man in her life who made love to her and then slammed a door in her face.

Selfish . . .

Ethan sipped his coffee and forced his attention back to Lara. The woman was as gentle and as sweet-natured as they came. He highly doubted there was evil lurking inside her. She might be cheating on her husband, but it didn't seem to have anything to do with William's money. They'd met at some kind of benefit, hit it off, and began a weekend affair since her husband was so often away on business.

"Lara, if you don't mind my asking," Amanda said, "Did my father leave you anything in his will?"

"Not a thing. When he told me he was drafting a new one, I told him not to include me," she added. "First of all, I'm rich in my own right. Second of all, all I wanted was his company. A memento or a wad of cash can't replace what I lost. I truly adored your father."

Amanda seemed to let that all sink in. "May I ask why? I don't mean that in any sarcastic way. I really want to know. What made you love him?"

Lara sipped her tea and then broke off a piece of her scone and nibbled it. "His honesty. That's it. My husband's a liar. Lies right to my face so effortlessly I'm not even sure he knows he's lying. But William never lied. He told it to you straight. If he said he couldn't make our date because he had to be out of town on business, I knew it was the truth."

"How?" Amanda asked. "How did you know?"

"Because he told me things I didn't want to hear. Early on he said he couldn't make our date because he'd met another woman and wanted to take her out that night. Another time he said I annoyed him the last time and so he wanted to take a little break."

Ethan raised an eyebrow. "That doesn't sound very loveable, Lara."

"But it's honest. William was also brilliant, funny, a terrific listener, and could fix anything around the house, unlike my husband, who couldn't change a lightbulb."

*Fix anything around the house* . . . Nick Marrow's face popped into Ethan's mind. He wondered how the boy was doing, if his dad had come around about the toaster.

Tommy began fussing in his stroller, and even a bite of Amanda's corn muffin didn't interest him. He wanted to leave, Ethan thought. And from Amanda's expression, so did his mom.

"Lara, thanks so much for meeting with us. We'd better get going."

Amanda clearly had been lost in thought. She

started and turned to Lara. "Yes, thank you, Lara. I do feel like I've learned a lot, even if it wasn't quite what I wanted to hear."

A few minutes later, Lara was gone, and Ethan and Amanda stood outside of Starbucks in order to regroup.

Ethan downed the rest of his coffee, which he had taken with him. "Well, at least we can cross her off our list."

Amanda twirled her hair in her fingers. "It's so odd—I keep expecting someone to tell me that my father was this wonderful person and I get so disappointed when I keep hearing negatives. But I already know he wasn't a wonderful person. He fathered three children and then pretended we didn't exist."

"Amanda, your ambivalence makes perfect sense. Your father is supposed to be your hero. You're preprogrammed to love him. And it's supposed to be your birthright that he loves you. Family can be very complicated sometimes."

She glanced up him, and he could tell he'd said the right thing—for once.

# CHAPTER 19

After they left Starbucks, Amanda said she wanted to stop at the supermarket to pick up a few things for tonight's dinner.

With Paul Swinwood, the father of her child.

And though the supermarket was the last place on earth he felt like being, Ethan wasn't about to let her go alone. Not while they still were no closer to figuring out who'd attacked her than they were when it happened. He would have preferred they'd use the time some other way but Amanda swore it would only take a half hour.

A half hour! In the supermarket. The most Ethan had ever spent in a grocery store was ten minutes, and that was to load up his cart for a blizzard warning up in Maine.

Anyway, he was very aware that she needed a break, needed something relatively mindless to do, and so five minutes later they were in the Food Emporium. And of course she asked him to push the stroller while she pushed the cart, and as much as he hadn't wanted to, he did. Pushing the stroller wasn't so bad; the baby faced away from him, after all. He didn't have to look at Tommy's face, hear his coos, his try at words.

And he wouldn't have to wonder if his own baby would have laughed that way or been such a banana addict.

*Ethan Black, Jr., if it's a boy,* Katherine had said. *And Alissa Black if it's a girl, after your mother.*

He was so overwhelmed by sadness, by a bottomless pit of loss, that he was honestly afraid he might break down, right there in the produce aisle. This was how he'd felt on a daily basis in the months after Katherine was killed. Every minute of every day, pitch-black emptiness, quicksand-like, pulling him down further and further into despair. Guilt. Anger. Sadness. Pain like he'd never known. If he thought he'd ever been hurt before, they were mere scrapes.

Woman after woman pushing a cart or carrying a basket smiled at the baby and then up at him. He hadn't been smiled at so much in his entire life as he had been in the few minutes he'd been in the grocery store. So far.

*This is what it would have been like,* he thought. This is what it felt like to have a family, a normal every day family, shopping for groceries like everyone else.

But he wouldn't have been like everyone else, and he knew it. He wouldn't have been in the supermarket for five seconds. He wouldn't be pushing a stroller down the street, in the park, or wherever it was babies went. He would have been at the office or his study, as usual.

"All done!" Amanda said brightly. "See—only twenty minutes. That gives me ten minutes to stop at the bakery on Columbus Avenue for a pie. I definitely won't have time to bake."

Ethan could only nod.

A half-hour ago, Amanda had been covered in gook and gunk and little bits and pieces of what she was making for dinner, which smelled delicious. Ethan had no idea what she was cooking, but his nose had told him it was chicken-related and elaborate. He'd poked his head inside the kitchen and found her hovering over a mixing bowl, blowing a strand of hair from eyes as she read a recipe and stirred something that was apparently requiring muscles.

She was certainly going to a lot of trouble for dinner with the man who'd abandoned her and her child.

He'd watched her for a moment, then left when a funny sensation hit him, almost overwhelming him. He liked seeing Amanda in the kitchen, her attention on cooking. Ethan was no chauvinist; but he liked seeing her engaged by something that she clearly enjoyed, something that didn't involve figuring out who'd tried to stop her from breathing on a permanent basis.

Actually, that wasn't completely true. Yes, he'd liked seeing her in the kitchen. But the overwhelming part, the funny, yet strange part, was that he liked the domesticity of it. That was new. Brand new. Katherine had actually graduated from a culinary institute and had whipped up the most amazing meals in their kitchen, which was beyond state-of-the-art. But something about Amanda, wearing her food-stained apron, her hair half up held in by a pencil, deep in concentration, moved him.

*Shit,* he'd thought, heading upstairs to take a fast shower. He had to stop being moved by her, had to stop letting her affect him. He had to stop looking at her, obviously.

And then he'd come downstairs, and she'd just been dashing up the stairs to shower herself, and when he saw her again, she was standing at the top of the stairs, Tommy on her hip, at seven o'clock.

He stared, frozen for a moment. She was stunning.

So much for not looking at her.

She wore a dress. It was a casual dress, nothing glamorous, but she literally took his breath away. It was a wrap dress, a pale gray, and the thin wool material outlined her figure in a way that had every sense in his body alert. He couldn't take his eyes off her breasts, those amazing large creamy breasts that he'd explored every inch of. And the way the material clung to her hips and legs . . .

She also wore a little make-up, he realized. Not much, but he noticed her eyes were more luminous and her lips a bit redder and glossier, her cheeks more flushed . . .

She looked as she had while he was making love to her.

When she came down the stairs he noticed she'd put on perfume, a light, clean, musky scent.

The dinner, the make-up, the dress, the perfume. For Paul Swinwood.

Was she still in love with the guy? he wondered.

Paul was good-looking, anyone could objectively see that. Tall and muscular. Nicely dressed. And he was Tommy's father. With all that was going on with Amanda and her feelings about her own father, Ethan could understand how important it was to her for Tommy to have his own father in his life.

The doorbell rang, and they glanced at each other.

"I would appreciate it if you didn't treat him like a suspect," Amanda said, smoothing her hair.

"Did I treat anyone else like a suspect?" he countered.

She ignored that and went to the door.

"Amanda, I'm speechless," Ethan heard Paul say. "You look amazing. Just gorgeous."

"I thought you were speechless," Ethan muttered under his breath.

"Wow," Paul said, coming into the foyer. He held a bouquet of flowers. "This is some house."

"I can hardly believe I live here," Amanda said, taking his coat. "I'm still getting used to it."

Ethan watched Paul glance around, taking in the expensive art on the walls, the rugs on the floor, the sculptures. And then the man's gaze landed on Ethan and his entire face changed—hardened was the word for it.

"I'm sorry, I forgot your name," Paul said to Ethan.

Ethan stepped into the living room. "It's Ethan Black."

"I think I might have already told you this, but Ethan was retained by my father's estate as caretaker of this property and my father's will as it relates to me," Amanda said.

"So you come with the brownstone?" Paul asked lightly and smiled.

Ethan searched for tightness or worry in the man's expression but found none. "I guess you can say that."

"Well I guess the romantic evening for two I had in mind is shot," Paul said, winking at Amanda. "Three is sort of a crowd," he added to Ethan.

"You mean four," Ethan corrected.

"Pardon?" Paul asked.

"You forgot Tommy," Ethan explained.

Paul looked momentarily horrified, then regained his composure. "And where is my big boy? Ah, there you are!" he said, reaching for Tommy, who sat with his touch-and-feel book in the playpen. "May I?" he asked Amanda.

Amanda nodded, and Paul picked up Tommy and held him close. "How ya doing, big guy? Yeah, I know. Things are great because you have such a great Mom. That's right. Your mommy and I go way back."

Less than two years was hardly going way back, Ethan thought.

"Who'd like a drink?" Amanda asked.

"I'd love a scotch on the rocks," Paul said.

"Ethan?" Amanda asked.

"No thanks," Ethan said.

"One drink won't hurt you," Paul said.

Ethan ignored him. "Well, I'll let you two enjoy your reunion."

"There's plenty of food," Amanda said, "if you'd like to join us."

"Thanks, but I've got a ton of work of do," he said, and with that he turned and headed upstairs.

Ethan paused at the top of the stairs before opening the door to his bedroom, where he planned to watch the evening's events on his wristwatch screen. He settled in for what he was sure would be a very uncomfortable couple of hours.

"Night, night, little guy," Paul whispered into Tommy's crib as he laid the sleepy baby down.

Tommy looked right at Paul and then closed his eyes, pressed his little fist against his temple and flopped over onto his stomach, his tiny butt raised in the air.

"He's not going to fuss?" Paul asked, looking at Amanda in wonder. "I thought babies were supposed to scream their heads off when you put them to bed."

"Tommy does that too," Amanda said, smiling. "But sometimes he's just good and tired and ready. And you put him in just right, too."

Paul smiled, that genuine I-am-so-happy smile that used to melt Amanda's heart. "Thanks for letting me share in this, Amanda. It means a lot to me." He reached into Tommy's crib and gently caressed his cheek. "I missed so much," he said in a very low voice. He shook his head and stared down at the floor. "What a jerk I've been."

"Hey," Amanda said, touching his arm. "Let's just stick to the present, okay? It's all about baby steps."

Paul smiled and glanced around the room. "I'm surprised there isn't an extra bedroom for a nursery in a place this size."

"There is," Amanda said. "Right down the hall. But I like having Tommy with me."

As they were leaving the room, she wondered if she should mention the break-in earlier this week, to gauge his facial reaction as Ethan would do. To watch for signs of nervousness or guilt or whatever else you were supposed to look for. But what really could Paul's motive be for trying to kill her? It made no sense.

*To get his hands on the money he thinks your father left you. To get his hands on the brownstone he assumes Tommy will inherit in the event of your death. If you die, Tommy gets what's yours. And you have a multi-million-dollar brownstone . . .*

Great. Now she was hearing Ethan's voice in her head as clearly as if he were whispering in her ear.

She was beginning to understand how he thought, what made him tick. Ha. That last bit was a joke. She knew nothing about what made Ethan Black tick.

"Amanda?"

She started and realized that Paul had been asking her a question. "I'm sorry, what did you say?"

Paul smiled. "I was offering a penny for your thoughts. You looked like you were a million miles away just then."

*Actually, just a few feet away . . .*

"I was just thinking that we'd better get downstairs to dinner before it burns," she said.

"I wouldn't mind staying here for just a minute more," he said softly, reaching out his hand to caress her face and run his thumb over her lips.

Just like old times, his touch, voice, and manner aroused her. When they were a couple, he could just look at her a certain way and, as if under a spell, she'd remove her clothes, slowly, the way he liked. He would sit in a chair and she would stand before him and undo the buttons of her shirt, very slowly, and then even more slowly pull apart the sides to reveal her bra. He liked lace and frill, the sexy-looking cheap kind, which was all she could afford. As she'd pull open her shirt he'd stare, his mouth parting slightly, his tongue running over his lips at the sudden dryness as he waited to find out what bra covered her breasts. His favorite, a gift from him, was a see-through fuchsia bit of lace with tiny sequins barely covering the cup center. The moment his eyes feasted on the bra she knew what was coming next, an act that had embaressed her the first time. He would unzip his pants and his hand would disappear inside as he watched and waited. She'd slowly remove her skirt, always a skirt for their dates, to reveal matching see-through thong panties. He'd stare for a few seconds, his hand working before he shoved down his pants. He'd grab her to him, pushing aside with his finger the scrap of lace between her legs and then thrust inside her. He'd move her up and down, back and forth on top of him until she couldn't see straight and would climax.

"You're thinking what I'm thinking, aren't you?" he whispered, a finger lifting her chin. "I can see it in your eyes, Mandy." He ran his gaze over breasts and down her body, then slowly back up. And when he reached a hand to caress one heavy breast, his eyes never leaving hers, she allowed it for one second before stepping back and shaking her head.

"No, Paul," she whispered. "I can't. I don't know that that's what I want."

"I understand," he said. "It's very difficult to keep my hands off you. But I won't take another liberty, I promise you. I'll let you make the next move, if you want to. And if you don't want to, I'll respect that."

She took a deep breath and nodded. "We'd better get downstairs before my chicken cacciatore turns to rubber." She took a final glance at her sleeping son, and then Paul followed her out of the room.

A few minutes later, they were seated across from each other at the dining room table.

"Wow, everything looks delicious," Paul said. "I remember what an amazing cook you are. I've missed your home cooking."

Amanda smiled. "Now if only I can get Tommy to eat anything other than scrambled eggs, cheerios, and bananas."

He laughed. "You know what this table is missing?" He reached into his pocket and withdrew a book of matches, then lit the two candles in the center of the table. "There. Now it couldn't be more perfect."

It was a little too romantic for Amanda's comfort level, but she reminded herself that they were just candles. *They are what you attach to them,* she told herself.

Paul heaped some salad onto his plate. "Amanda, I'm curious. That little joke I made about this Ethan guy coming with the brownstone—he doesn't actually live here, does he?"

"No," Amanda said. "But until certain elements of the will are finalized, he is staying here."

"Ah. That's why he's here now," Paul said. "I

have to say, when I came in and saw him, I was thrown for a major loop. I didn't know if he was your boyfriend or what. I'm very, very relieved to know that he's just an 'or what.' "

An *or what.* It actually fit.

"So he's staying upstairs?" Paul asked. "Right near your bedroom?" He put down his fork and shook his head. "Forget I even said that, okay? I have no right to be proprietary about you or jealous. I apologize, okay?"

She smiled. "Okay."

*He's not the person who attacked me. He can't be.*

*No one is ruled out,* she could hear Ethan saying in her ear.

As Paul began talking about Tommy and how much it meant to him to be able to put him to sleep, Amanda forced herself to put Ethan Black out of her mind. And by the time they finished eating and Paul cleared the table and loaded the dishwasher—he insisted—she realized she hadn't thought of Ethan once in at least a half-hour.

Well, it was a start.

After dessert, they moved into the living room for coffee. Amanda set down a tray with two cups and a sugar bowl and some milk, then sat down on the sofa, and Paul sat next to her, not too close, but close enough for her to be very aware of him.

"Amanda, I can't tell you what this evening has meant to me," he said, sipping his coffee. "I never thought I could be a father because I was such a disappointment to my own father. I didn't think I would know what to *do.* And tonight really helped me see you really don't need to know what to do—you just need to feel."

Amanda picked up her coffee cup and took a sip, even though she really wasn't in the mood for coffee. She needed a buffer between them, even it was just a small china cup.

She offered a smile, mostly because she didn't know what to say. Yes, you needed to feel, but you also needed to be a responsible adult. You needed to be a parent. This didn't seem the time or place for that kind of discussion, though, and perhaps she should just let Paul proceed as he needed to. Baby steps, as she'd said. It wasn't as though she even wanted him to jump right in and actually be Tommy's father in practice.

Arg, she didn't even know what she wanted!

She glanced at her watch. "Wow, it's getting so late. Tommy is such an early bird that I need to get to sleep by ten or I'm a zombie the next day."

He smiled. "Enough said." He stood up and so did she. "Thank you so much for the delicious dinner, Amanda, and this chance to be with you and Tommy again. I—" He paused and tears pooled in his eyes. He blinked them away, wiping at his eyes fast. "I felt like we were family tonight. I didn't think I'd ever really know what that would feel like. And it felt so good."

She reached for his hand and squeezed it. "I'm glad, Paul."

He looked into her eyes. "Can I see you both again soon?"

She nodded. "I'll call you, okay? I just need a little time to process all of this."

"I understand," he said, heading toward the door. He took his coat from the rack, wrapped his scarf around his neck and pulled open the door.

Then he paused and leaned forward. "A kiss good night?" he asked.

She leaned forward, but awkwardly, and the kiss he meant to give her on her cheek landed on her lips. He pulled back a bit, looked into her eyes, and kissed her again. She didn't open her mouth or kiss him back, but she let herself be kissed, let him pull her against him, her breasts crushing against his heavy wool coat. She could feel his erection hard against her thigh and he shifted so that it was directly between her legs.

Her breath catching, she stepped back.

"I'd better go," he said, his brown eyes smoldering with desire for her. "God, Amanda, what you do to me." And with that he turned into the night and was gone.

# CHAPTER 20

Ethan had to force himself not to race down the stairs and pummel Paul Swinwood to a lifeless pulp. He'd watched their entire evening on his wrist-watch screen; the camera pointing at the sofa also covered the dining room and foyer, and as he watched Paul kiss Amanda, pull her against him, he clenched his teeth.

When the two of them had gone upstairs to put Tommy to bed, he'd come really close to going after Paul.

He rewound the tape on his wristwatch and forced himself to watch Paul kiss Amanda again. But he had no idea if he needed to see it because he couldn't believe he was so damned jealous or because he wanted to remind himself that he couldn't let himself care about her, that he had to keep his distance and make sure that what happened between them the other night never happened again.

If he wasn't a cold-blooded killer in sheep's clothing, then maybe they deserved a second chance. The kid would get his mother and father back together. Amanda would get back the man she clearly once loved.

But until Ethan knew for sure that Paul Swinwood wasn't the one who tried to kill Amanda, he'd watch the guy very closely. And he'd make sure Paul kept his hands to himself.

Once he was sure Amanda was in bed for the night, he left his room and did a final check of the doors and windows. And then he headed back upstairs, stopping in front of Amanda's room and wondering whom was she dreaming of.

"Whore."

Amanda felt the whispered breath in her ear a split second before the pillow came down hard on her face.

*Nooo!* she'd screamed against the pressure. But there was no sound. And once again she was no match for whoever stood over her. She couldn't see, couldn't hear, couldn't breathe.

Couldn't call for help.

*Tommy!* she shouted in her mind as tears and adrenaline fought for control of her.

*Ethan! Help me, please!*

She struggled against the taut arms on either side of her, and then with her last thought, she managed to release one arm and waved it beside the bed with force.

Something landed with a thud on the floor. Yes. Yes. She'd knocked over the alarm clock.

*Please, Ethan. Please have heard that and come. Please.*

"Amanda?" he called. "You okay?"

*Come. Please come!*

The arms let go and Amanda bolted upright, her hands flying to her sore neck. She gasped for breath. As Ethan raced into the room, the figure pushed him against the wall and ran out the door and down the stairs.

Ethan ran out in pursuit, and Amanda jumped out of bed and rushed to the crib. Once again, Tommy lay safe, his chest rising and falling steadily.

As Amanda gasped for breath, she realized how easy it would have been for whoever had attacked her to have taken Tommy and gone, just like that.

How the hell was the person getting in? How?

With her key? Amanda wondered, Clara Mott's disapproving face popping into her mind.

*Whore . . .*

Oh God. Whoever it was had called her a whore. Why?

Ethan came running back into the room. "Are you all right?"

She dropped to her knees on the floor in front of Tommy's crib. "I'm so scared, Ethan. Once, okay maybe it was a random break-in. But this was the same M.O. Someone wants me dead."

He kneeled down in front of her and reached out his hand. She took it and let him pull her up into his arms. He carried her to the bed and gently laid her down.

"Tommy and I can't stay in this room," she said.

"I'll camp out on the floor," he offered. "We'll lock the door and barricade it with the desk chair."

She closed her eyes. "Okay."

Ethan locked the door and set a chair under the doorknob, then sat down on the edge of Amanda's bed. "Tell me everything you can remember. Everything. Every smell, every breath. Height, weight. Anything you can remember."

Amanda sat up against the headboard and burst into tears, unable to stop. "Who is trying to kill me? Who hates me that much?" Tears streamed down her cheeks.

"Amanda," Ethan said gently, "this will sound weird, but it may have nothing to do with hate and nothing to do with you at all and everything to do with unadulterated greed."

"Let's call the police," Amanda said. "I want police protection."

Ethan nodded and picked up the telephone and handed it to her.

She dialed 911. "Someone just tried to suffocate me with a pillow," she told the operator. "This is the second time someone broke into my house and tried to kill me." She was assured that the officers were on their way.

As they waited, Ethan asked her again what she remembered. "Whoever it was whispered 'whore' into my ear. Right before I realized that I couldn't breathe, I heard the whisper in my ear."

"Whore," he repeated. "Was it a male voice? Female?"

"I don't know!" she cried. "It was a whisper."

"Was there any trace of accent? Was it said with anger or just stated?"

She shook her head. "I don't know. I'd been sleeping and—I do know the person was tall—not as tall as you, though."

"Yes, I'd say that too. I couldn't get a handle on weight, though. I couldn't judge if it was a man or a woman."

Amanda leaned her head back and stared at the ceiling. "How are they getting in? Is it Clara with her key? If someone had broken in, wouldn't we have heard glass shattering or something?"

"Amanda, let's just wait for the police. They'll determine that. In the meantime, just try to breathe, try to relax."

"Who do you think it is, Ethan?" she asked, searching his eyes.

"I don't know," he told her. "But I do know that from now on, I'm sleeping on this floor. Anyone who wants to hurt you is going to have to kill me first. And trust me, they won't get the chance."

"I just want this to be over," she said. "I want this to be over so I can just leave this house and figure out what to do with my life."

The doorbell rang and they headed downstairs to let in the police. Again they investigated and dusted. "Someone picked the lock or used a key," one of the cops told Amanda.

"You'll call if you find anything?" Ethan asked the police.

They assured them both they would and then left. Then Ethan brewed a fresh pot of coffee. "Paul was on this block earlier today," he reminded her. "He told you he saw us coming out. Perhaps when we parted, he ran around back and got to work on the lock."

"It could have been several other people," Amanda said.

"With that kind of access to the brownstone?"

"Clara had access."

"Clara has a key," Amanda pointed out.

"She's also smart enough to realize she would have to make it look like she broke in," Ethan said. "As far as we know, she's the only one with a key."

"So Paul and Clara," Amanda said, wrapping her trembling hands around her coffee mug. "That's who we're focusing on."

"And your sisters' mothers," Ethan added. "They're a little too invested."

"Well there's still my father's former secretary's son," Amanda said. "And don't forget all the other heirs you claim there could be. It could be anyone."

"You don't want it to be Paul pretty bad," he said.

"Right. I want the father of my child to be the one who keeps trying to kill me."

"I would also add because you're still in love with him," Ethan said.

She whirled to face him. "You have no idea how I feel."

"I saw enough to have a pretty good idea," he snapped. "Including that good-bye kiss at the door."

Her cheeks burned. "Too bad you weren't looking before dinner," she retorted. "When he put his hands on my breasts. You would have gotten an eyeful then."

He glared at her. "Did you sleep with him?"

"I think you would have overheard that, Ethan."

"You're not that loud, Amanda," he said.

She slapped him across the face and then gasped, shocked that she'd done it. "I'm going back upstairs," she said, scooping up sleeping Tommy. "You can lie across my closed and locked door if you want, but I don't want you anywhere near me."

"Fine with me," he snapped.

Furious, tears stinging the backs of her eyes, she cradled her son against her chest and rushed upstairs, closing the door to her room behind her. Once she settled Tommy in his crib, she slid down to the floor and cried.

Since there had been two attempts on her life, Amanda was relieved that the police on "her beat" were going to keep a closer eye on her residence. And Ethan was going to have the locks re-keyed as a precaution. What she wanted most was a burglar alarm system and was baffled as to why the brownstone didn't have one. But until the place was hers, she wasn't allowed to make any changes, even for hers and Tommy's protection. As angry as she was with Ethan, at least he was there and determined to safeguard them. If she didn't drive him away.

# CHAPTER 21

If Ethan had slept outside her bedroom door, Amanda wouldn't have known it. When she emerged in the morning, at six-thirty, he was already downstairs, drinking coffee. She ignored him completely and set Tommy down in the living room where he practiced pulling up to standing, then she headed into the kitchen for a bracing cup of coffee herself.

They didn't say a word to each other for the next two-and-a-half hours. Didn't even look at each other. Ethan was doing some kind of research online, and Amanda busied herself by playing with Tommy and making his breakfast.

The phone rang at nine A.M. sharp. Amanda lunged for it, hoping it was the police with news. But it was George Harris, her father's attorney.

"Ms. Sedgwick," he said, "is Ethan Black there now?"

"Yes, he's right here. Just a moment, please." She covered the phone with her hand. "It's Harris."

He raised an eyebrow, hit the speakerphone button, and replaced the receiver. "Ethan Black here."

"Ethan, it's George Harris. I came in this morning to find my answering machine full of angry calls from the mothers of Olivia and Ivy Sedgwick. They're worried that the terms of the will may be compromised by your personal relationship with Ms. Sedgwick. Is that the case?"

Amanda glared at the phone. How dare they!

"Absolutely not," Ethan bit out.

"Do I have your word?" the lawyer asked.

"How much is my word worth to you?" Ethan asked.

"It's all I need," the man said. "William left explicit instructions that you were to be trusted without question regarding Amanda Sedgwick. If you say the terms haven't been compromised, that you are ensuring she is following the instructions per William's last will and testament, then that's all I need to know."

Amanda glanced at Ethan. Why had her father trusted Ethan? What he could possibly have found in him to trust after meeting him only once? And briefly!

"You have my word that the terms of the will have not been compromised."

"Fine," the lawyer said. "Thank you."

"Listen, while I have you," Ethan continued, "someone has broken into the brownstone twice and attempted to hurt Amanda. The police are working on it, but have nothing so far, and I need to know if you have any reason to suspect anyone."

"Is Ms. Sedgwick all right?" he asked.

"She's fine, but scared out of her mind. Staying

at the brownstone under these conditions is becoming unbearable for her."

*Unbearable* was a good choice of words, Amanda thought.

"Perhaps that's the intruder's intent," the lawyer said. "To scare her away?"

"We don't know," Ethan said, "but it seems more serious than that."

"I wish I could help," Harris said.

Ethan scowled. "Can you at least tell me if anyone has called and asked if William left them anything? Can I get a list of those people?"

"I'm sorry, I'm really not at liberty to discuss that."

"If the police asked for a list, would you supply them with one?" Ethan asked.

"Yes," the lawyer said. "I must go now . . . please give Ms. Sedgwick my best."

When Ethan pressed the speakerphone button again, disengaging the call, Amanda shook her head. "Maybe he'll give you the list once I'm dead."

"I'm sure the police will demand a list," Ethan said. "I'll call the detective on the case and ask him to look into it. At least it will make our own list more complete. Amanda, if you're up to it, I'd like to visit Sally Fanwell's son today. I've been looking for information on him, but so far, nothing."

"I'm up to it," Amanda told him. "I want to get this over with. I want to find this psycho and get on with my sentence here so I can decide what I want to do without it being decided for me."

"I can definitely understand that."

She glanced at him, taking in the shadows under his eyes and his rumpled clothes and disheveled hair. He was exhausted, she knew. And she had no doubt that he had slept on the floor outside her room.

"Maybe Nora at Sedgwick Enterprises has Kevin Fanwell's address," Amanda suggested.

"If Sally listed him as an emergency contact, maybe," Ethan said. He glanced at her. "You're sure you're up for this? I know you want to catch this person, but if you need to rest and just take a day for yourself, I understand. We can lie low for a day."

Amanda shook her head. Then she picked up the phone and dialed Nora's number. The woman, as usual, was full of good cheer and said she'd look in her rolodex, which was Sally's old rolodex.

"Sorry, but there's no number for Kevin. There's a number for a Lorna Fanwell, though. You could try her and ask for Kevin's number. She's probably a relative of Sally's."

"Lorna Fanwell," Amanda repeated, writing down the number. "Thanks so much, Nora."

Before Amanda even hung up, Ethan had looked up Lorna Fanwell online—she lived on the East Side, just across town.

"Let's go nose around the building after you do your time on the sofa," Ethan said. "Get some info from the doorman or neighbors coming and going. Find out if they know anything about Kevin, and how he's related to Lorna. If he's our guy, I don't want to give him a head's up that we're coming. Now that we're sure the first break-in was no random burglary attempt, our psycho is probably pissed as hell that you're still breathing."

"Great," Amanda said.

He put a bracing hand on her arm. "I'm sorry, okay? I didn't mean to put it like that. I'm just beat to hell."

"I know. Me too."

And then they went back to silence. Slightly more companionable, but tense all the same.

At ten-thirty, Amanda took a cup of tea into the living room and settled onto the sofa, grateful for the opportunity to escape Ethan. She hated this mandatory restriction each day. All she could do was stare around the room, a room she was sick of looking at in detail, as beautiful as it was. Out of sheer boredom she chose to look at the portrait above the fireplace. She usually avoided it.

She studied her father, tall and imposing and unknowable. He was twelve years younger in the portrait and looked at least twenty years younger than the last time she saw him a couple of years ago by sheer chance on the street. He hadn't seen her; he'd been walking with what looked like a group of business associates, and she'd been across the street. She watched him smiling and laughing with the group before they disappeared into a restaurant.

She'd never seen him smiling or laughing before, at least not that way, that effortlessly.

She studied Olivia next, the beautiful cool blonde. Olivia also looked unknowable, unapproachable, but she was really quite warm. Amanda wondered if the same were true of her father. Perhaps he was kind . . .

What she was doing? Why did she keep looking

for goodness in a man who his own girlfriends said was selfish?

*Because your father is your father,* a little voice inside her said. And like Ethan said, he was supposed to love her.

Amanda glanced at Tommy, now safely playing in his playpen. *Your father wants to love you,* she said silently to him. *And I need to let him.* She couldn't stand in the way of that, no matter how confused she was about how she felt about him. And no matter how jealous Ethan was.

Was he jealous? Or was he right to suspect Paul? Amanda just didn't know. She definitely was not ready for Paul's sexual advances, though. It would take a long time for those feelings to come back, if they ever did.

She felt like she didn't know anything anymore.

She turned her attention to Ivy, pretty, natural Ivy with the sparkling green eyes. *I do hope your Declan is a good guy,* Amanda said silently to the painted Ivy. There had to be at least one person in this family who got it right.

"Let's walk to the East Side through Central Park," Amanda said as they left the brownstone. Tommy was napping on cue in his stroller. "It's such a beautiful day and I could use some open space and trees right now."

"I'd rather not," Ethan said, zipping up his black leather jacket.

She glanced at him. "Why not?"

"I just would rather not," he said again. "Does

every answer require an explanation? Can't you just accept something?"

She recoiled almost as if he'd slapped her. "Is that what I should do? I should just accept things? I should accept that someone is trying to kill me? I should accept that my father was a selfish prick who then turned around and left me a multi-million-dollar brownstone as long as I didn't open a certain window or cross my legs in a certain room? I should accept that Paul walked out on me without a backward glance when I told him I was pregnant and now wants to be one big happy family? I should accept that we made love but that you want to pretend we didn't? I should accept that people can just use me to suit their purposes?"

He stared at her for a moment. "Okay, let me start with this one: in what way did your father use you?"

"He's atoning for his sins as a parent," Amanda said. "That's why he left me the brownstone. It's guilt. It's not love."

"And how am I using you to suit my purpose?"

"Do I really need to explain that one?" Amanda threw back.

"Yes, you do," Ethan said.

"You wanted to have sex with me in your hotel room. You did. You then didn't want to deal with what that meant. So you didn't. End of story."

Ethan let out a harsh breath. "I didn't mean to hurt you, Amanda. I really didn't."

"But you did."

He recoiled within himself as he was hit with a sense of déjà vu. Of a conversation with his wife, his late wife. *I didn't mean to hurt you, Katherine.*

And her reply: *But you did.*

Ethan closed his eyes for a second, letting the oddly warm December air rush around him.

He glanced up the street, where he could see the tall bare trees in Central Park. He wasn't going anywhere near it ever again.

"Let's just get in a cab or take a bus," Ethan said.

She shook her head. "I'm walking through the park."

"No, you're not," Ethan said.

"You can't tell me what to do, Ethan."

"We have no idea who tried to kill you, Amanda. And whoever it was could be watching and waiting right now."

She glared at him. "Well you know what, I'm not going to live my life in fear of maybes anymore." She began wheeling the stroller up the street. "I'm not going to stand here and argue."

"I'm not walking through the park," he said, his stomach tightening. He suddenly felt sick, felt beads of perspiration form on his neck.

"No one invited you," she tossed back. "Tommy and I will walk through ourselves."

He raced up to her and took her arm. "You're not walking through the park."

"Let go of me! How dare you tell me what I can and can't do!" She pulled away and began angrily heading east.

*Stop,* he wanted to scream at the top of his lungs. *Please stop.*

"My wife was killed in Central Park three years ago," he called, closing his eyes against the tears that stung and burned.

She whirled around, the blood drained from her face.

"She was pregnant with our child," he added, his voice barely a whisper. He dropped down on the bottom step of the stoop and put his face in his hands.

"Ethan, I—"

"Just don't say anything, okay?" he asked. "Not a word."

She reached out her hand and after a moment, he took it. "Let's just go back home."

He nodded, got up, and followed her.

Once inside, Amanda motioned upstairs and carried sleeping Tommy up to his crib, then she came back down and sat beside Ethan on the couch.

"Please tell me," she said gently. "I won't say a word. I just want to listen."

He leaned his head back against the sofa and stared up at the ceiling. "Ever since I was a kid I thought I had to be the best at everything. Best at school and sports. Captain of the football team. I wanted every girl to fall in love with me. I wanted every kid to want to be my friend. And that's the way it was. Through high school, through college, and when I entered the working world. I had to be the best. The top dog."

He glanced over at Amanda. She was staring at him intently. He wanted to get up and leave, get his car out of the parking garage, and drive straight home to Maine without looking back. He didn't want to tell this story, think about this story, live it, breathe it. And that's what would happen if he told Amanda. He'd remember everything and then he'd be in the center of it again and sink down.

If she said a word, if she so much as moved a muscle, he'd just get up and go. Just get the hell out of there.

She didn't so much as flinch.

He glanced up at the portrait of William Sedgwick surrounded by his daughters, the children he didn't want, didn't care about. "If my father ever came back, I wanted him to know what he lost out on. That he could have had this superstar kid, but that it was too late for him, he missed out, too bad, I hate your fucking guts. And by the time I graduated with an MBA from Wharton, the thing I was absolutely best at was being a bastard. I was ruthless with everything and everyone, but I'd gotten so good at convincing people that I was superior that they believed it, I believed it, and so I always had an entourage. I worked my way up to the top in business pretty fast on that. I was the king of hostile takeovers. My company was called Black, just Black, and it was known in the industry as Black and Blue because of the bruises I inflicted. Corporate raiders have to be ruthless, but I was soulless."

He stood up and closed his eyes. *Say something so I can walk out the door and never come back*, he willed Amanda. But she said nothing. He turned around and looked at her. "Soulless. Do you know what that means?"

"Yes, but it's hard to think of you as soulless when all you've done since I've met you is take care of me and Tommy."

"Take care of you?" he threw back. "How is screwing you in my hotel room and then acting like it didn't happen 'taking care of you?'"

"Ethan, I'm not an idiot," she said. "Slamming that door has nothing to do with how you feel about me. It has everything to do with how you feel about yourself."

"You sound a lot like the shrink I went to when Katherine died. I listened to him for about two minutes before I walked out and never went back."

"And three years later you're doing great, Ethan."

He glared at her and she glared back.

"If you don't care about me, why have you not let me out of your sight since the first time I was attacked?" she asked. "If I'm dead, you don't have to watchdog me, do you?"

"I owe your father," he said flatly.

"Why?" she asked. "Tell me why."

Again he glanced up at the painting of William Sedgwick. He dropped down on the sofa next to Amanda. "I was doing business with the . . . let's just say I had a deal going with some dangerous people. I tried to pull my usual fast one on them, which always covered my ass legally and allowed me to walk away much richer, owning another company, and leaving the opponent without a leg to stand on. But these people didn't get out their aggression by suing me the way everyone else did. They hired a sniper to shoot my pregnant wife in Central Park, where she was knitting baby socks on a bench, killing her instantly the police said."

Amanda gasped and her hand flew to her mouth. He saw the color drain from her face and he turned away.

"I thought I was invincible," he said. "I found out I wasn't."

"Oh, Ethan," she said. "I am so, so sorry about your wife, about the baby."

"I didn't even really know that I loved her until she was dead," he said in such a low voice he wasn't sure he even said it aloud. "But I did," he said as tears stung the backs of his eyes. He took a deep breath and the tears fell down his cheeks. "When she told me she was pregnant I wasn't even happy. I thought it would get in my way, distract me. And I found out I felt otherwise once she was dead."

The image sobered him. The police had trouble locating him so, by the time he arrived, she was almost heading for the morgue.

He knew right away that his associates were responsible, but the police couldn't link them beyond circumstantial evidence, and no charges were ever filed. He'd reversed the takeover and then some so that those responsible wouldn't retaliate further; he'd been worried about Katherine's parents' safety and their extended family. And when the paperwork was signed, he'd gotten a call. "It was a pleasure doing business with you," the kingpin had said into the phone.

He'd instructed his lawyers to give six-month severance packages to all Black employees, and then to sell off all his assets. He had so much money that even after the majority was given away, he still had several million sitting in a personal account.

"A few days after Katherine was killed," Ethan said, "I walked down to the East River promenade, which was one of her favorite places. She used to like to run along there, stop at the dog runs and watch the big dogs catching Frisbees, watch the sunbathers on the patches of grass, and look at Roosevelt Island across the water, where she'd lived before we met. And I looked up at the sky, at the moon, which she loved to go out and see every night, and I said, 'I'm sorry, Katherine. I'm sorry. I loved you and I loved our baby, and I'm sorry I failed you,' and then I put one leg over the railing and was about to do the same with the other when your father grabbed my arm."

Amanda gasped again. "My father. My father saved your life?"

Ethan nodded. "He grabbed my arm, and he said, 'Good God, it is you. You're Ethan Black.' "

"And I turned to look at him, and I realized it was the venerable William Sedgwick, also considered one of the most ambitious businessmen in America. I didn't know him personally; we'd never crossed paths before, but we knew of each other. He told me he'd seen the news reports about the murder, and he asked me if I was about to jump because I blamed myself. I said yes, and he asked me if I'd be willing to take a final walk with him first. So I did. And after, instead of jumping, I went home and I packed. And the next day I drove to Maine, and I built a house."

Amanda was staring at him, her mouth hanging open. "What did my father say to you?"

"He told me that if I killed myself, all I'd be doing was dishonoring Katherine. He told me that suicide would be the easy way out, and that he had no doubt I'd never done anything easy before and that now wasn't the time to start. He said I owed it to her to live every day without her, to remember who I'd been and what I'd done. That *that* was the rightful punishment."

"My God," Amanda said. "He stopped you from killing yourself by making you feel even more guilty?"

Ethan shook his head. "I deserved to feel guilty. He was telling me to own up to my responsibility. To feel the consequences, instead of escaping them. He said that one of the best ways to feel was to go into seclusion, to go to a place where there was nothing but earth and sky and build a cabin on the water and live there until it was time."

"Time to what? For what?"

Ethan shrugged. "I don't know. I just know I didn't go beyond a ten-mile radius of the cabin for three years. Until the letter came. Until you."

"Why Maine?" she asked.

"He suggested it. He said it would give me everything I needed. And it has, I guess. Where I live in Maine is just earth and sky and forest and water. The houses are few and far between. My nearest neighbor is one and a half miles away."

"It's hard to imagine my father talking about feeling and responsibility and honoring people," Amanda said.

Ethan glanced up at his portrait. "Those words and sentiments came from inside him, though. You know, in a twisted way, perhaps one of the reasons he kept staying away from you and your sisters was because he didn't feel he deserved you. That was something I spent a lot of time thinking about. The way I worked so hard all my life to spite my father, so that if he ever came back I could rub my greatness in his face and then tell him to fuck off.

That's sick, Amanda. And it comes from bitterness and sadness and a lot of other emotions that get all twisted up."

"I think I understand what you mean."

He glanced at her and reached up to tuck a strand of her silky hair behind her ear. And then he caressed her cheek with the back of his finger. "You are so beautiful. And so soft. Not just your skin. Inside too. You don't have a drop of bitterness inside you, Amanda."

"I'm just trying to do the best I can," she said.

He nodded. "I'd say you're doing pretty damned good."

She leaned forward and cupped his cheek with her hand, and the softness on his hard cheek undid a knot in his chest. He pulled her closer by her hand until she inches from his face and then he kissed her, unable to resist her.

If she hadn't let out a breathy little moan he might have been able to get up and walk away, go upstairs, go downstairs, go wherever. But then she kissed him back, and he felt her breasts against his chest, and there was no way he was walking away.

He slipped both hands under her sweater and then pulled it off. He made quick work of removing her bra and buried his face between her large breasts, teasing the nipples with his fingers before running his tongue along the hardened peaks. She arched against him, and he undid her pants, sliding them down her soft thighs. He ran his hand down her stomach and along her hips, and then he slipped a hand between her legs, and caressed her thighs, and then back up her hips and stomach and breasts.

She moaned and arched her back, and at the sight of her lacy white panties, he groaned and pulled off his shirt, then ripped off his belt and undid his jeans.

A moment later, they were both completely naked, skin to skin. He lay on top of her, kissing her, his hands caressing her breasts, kneading, stroking, probing.

"I want to feel you inside me," she whispered.

He fumbled for his wallet with one hand and, this time prepared, quickly put on a condom, and a moment later he was inside her. She stroked his back and his hair and ground against him, and then she moaned deep in her throat and closed her eyes, her whole body shuddering and convulsing as she came to orgasm. With both hands on her breasts and his mouth hard over hers, he thrust deeply inside her over and over and over until he exploded and then collapsed against her, breathing hard.

"I can't resist you," he whispered in her ear, and she smiled and closed her eyes.

He closed his eyes too and just lay there beside her, aware that for the first time in a long, long time, he wasn't thinking. He was only feeling. And Amanda felt good. Very good.

"Ethan, I just want you to know how much it means to me that you told me about your past," Amanda said, caressing his shoulders. "I know it must have been very difficult to talk about."

He nodded. "So can we go back to not talking and just lie here?"

She smiled. "You are such a guy, Ethan Black."

He smiled too and closed his eyes again.

The doorbell rang and he bolted up. “Who the hell is that?”

She pulled on her bra and sweater and slipped on her pants. “I’m not expecting anyone.”

He dressed quickly, disposed of the condom in his handkerchief, and ran a hand through his hair. “We should see who it is.”

He changed his mind when Amanda opened the door. Paul stood there, holding a bouquet of red tulips. “I had to stop by and see you,” Paul said. “And give you these.”

“Thank you so much, Paul. They’re beautiful,” Amanda said. She didn’t step aside for him to enter, Ethan noticed.

And so, apparently did Paul. “I was hoping I could stay for a few minutes and see Tommy.”

“He’s fast asleep,” Amanda said. “He’ll probably sleep for another hour. Another time?”

Paul craned his neck and his eyes met Ethan’s. And then Ethan noticed him staring at the sofa.

Amanda’s white cotton panties were wedged against the back cushion. And given Amanda’s flushed cheeks, her tousled hair, and the scent of sex in the room, it wouldn’t take much for Paul to make the leap.

Paul stared from the underwear to Ethan and then looked at Amanda. “Look, I need to know right now so that I know where I stand, what I’m up against. Are the two of you involved?”

Amanda’s cheeks turned pink. “Paul, I’d prefer that we didn’t have this conversation right now.”

“Are you sleeping with him?” Paul asked.

“I won’t answer that,” Amanda said. “Paul, you just came back into my life a week ago.”

"Can I talk to you privately?" Paul asked.

Amanda hesitated, then nodded. "Let me grab my coat and we'll talk outside." She put on her wool coat. "Ethan, you'll listen for Tommy?"

Ethan nodded. "Stay close by, though," he said in a warning tone.

*Don't you dare go farther than the bottom step of the stoop until we rule Paul out,* he said to her silently, with his eyes.

"We'll be right outside," Amanda said.

The door closed behind her and Ethan felt sick to his stomach. Ethan had no idea if his problem with Paul was because the guy threatened him, or because he truly was a reasonable suspect.

*Nothing for a year-and-a-half and then he turns up when Amanda inherits a multi-million-dollar home?*

Ethan let out a deep breath. Who the hell knew?

*If she was in love with Paul she wouldn't have just made love to you,* he thought, eyeing her underwear on the couch. *A woman in love with another man doesn't have sex with someone else.*

Unless she didn't know how she felt. Ethan hadn't known that he was in love with Katherine, and he'd come close to cheating on her many times. He'd never had sex with another woman while he was married, but he had flirted.

He peered out the window. They were standing in front of the brownstone next door. Ethan couldn't hear them, and if he cracked the window, they'd hear him. Damn.

Paul looked like he was about to cry. He looked down at the ground a lot, then at Amanda with sad, puppy dog eyes. Was she telling him there was no chance for them? That she loved Ethan?

Where the hell had that come from? Ethan didn't even know how he felt about Amanda!

*What's going on, jerko, is that you're threatened by Paul. He's the father of Amanda's child. And Amanda wants Tommy to have his father. Very rightfully so.*

The sick feeling returned, and Ethan closed his eyes against it, then quickly opened them, afraid to let Amanda out of his sight for even a moment.

Finally, the door opened and Amanda came back in. Her cheeks were no longer flushed and her hair was only tousled by the light wind. She no longer looked like a woman who'd just been thoroughly made love to.

She looked sad. Confused.

Tommy began to cry and she walked past Ethan toward the stairs. "I'd better go see if I can calm him down. It's not quite time for him to wake up yet."

"Amanda, are you all right?" Ethan asked.

She nodded. Then shook her head. "Yes . . . No . . . I don't know."

"Do you want to tell me what you two talked about?"

She looked at him. "No. I mean, I do, but I—I'm pretty confused about Paul. Anyway, his timing couldn't have been worse."

"In general or just now?"

"Both. In general because his reappearance makes him a suspect, which eats my heart out. And also now because we just shared something incredible . . . *you* just shared something incredible with me, and we got interrupted when we could have used some time alone."

"We've got all day," he said gently.

Relief lit her beautiful face. She nodded and headed up to Tommy.

# CHAPTER 22

Ethan was as good as his word. For the rest of the afternoon, there was no notebook, no investigating, no talking about who wanted her dead, no talking. She did her time on the sofa, and Ethan sat across from her, his laptop on the coffee table in front of him, but they barely spoke. This time, though, their silence was very companionable. Comfortable. After the hour was up, she'd hopped up and collected laundry, Ethan's too, and did a few loads, glad for the mindless work.

She needed room to think, room to breathe. The problem was that Amanda couldn't think. She had no idea how she felt about anything because there was just too much going on. Paul. Ethan. The brownstone. The investigation. Her father. Her sisters. . . .

The telephone rang, interrupting her thought. She set her clean pile of clothes on her bed and answered. It was Olivia calling from Paris!

"Amanda, I am so sorry about my mom," Olivia said. "She just called me ranting and raving about how the lawyer is refusing to do anything about your alleged love affair with your watchdog."

Amanda's cheeks burned. She wanted to deny there was a love affair, but she didn't want to lie to her sister. "Olivia, I can assure you that in terms of the will, there is absolutely no conflict of interest. I have followed the rules to a T. And Ethan is making sure that I do."

"In terms of the will?" Olivia asked in a teasing tone. "So does this mean my mother was actually right? Are you and Ethan involved? Forget I asked," Olivia added with a laugh. "That's none of my business. Look, if you two are involved, I hope you're having a great time. According to my mother, he's very good-looking."

Amanda laughed. "How's Paris?"

"Beautiful," Olivia said, but I'm too busy with work to really enjoy it. We just got back from an industry dinner and I'm going to crash. Again, I'm really sorry about my mother. She means well—sometimes. She's just very nosy and very protective of me."

Amanda smiled. "No problem. Have a good time and a safe flight home."

They said their good-byes and Amanda hung up. She realized she was still smiling. Her sister had actually called her. They had a conversation. Chit-chatted. Just like normal sisters did.

She had to remember that no matter what happened, she'd been given a new chance to have her sisters in her life.

No matter what happened. . . . What was going

to happen? Amanda had no idea. She was falling in love with Ethan, and yet she was drawn to Paul in a different way.

She dropped down on her bed, amazed at how clearly the thoughts had come to her. For so long now she'd been torn up, unable to process her feelings. And now, there it was. She loved Ethan Black. And her love for Paul, a love that had once been so strong, so magnetic, had turned into something else. She wasn't sure how to classify it.

Yes, she did, she realized, glancing out the window at a gray day. She was drawn to Paul because he was the father of her baby. Because it meant so much to her for Tommy to have his father in his life. In an every-day way. But she wasn't in love with Paul anymore. She was in love with Ethan. Very much so.

And where was that going to get her? she asked herself. She made such a mistake with Paul, and now she was making a mistake with Ethan. He was so closed up. And though it was heartening that he'd opened up about his past, he did so to avoid going into the park—not because he wanted to talk with Amanda about his life. And he'd made love to her downstairs because he was sexually attracted to her and because she was very willing—not because he was in love with her.

He would do his time, fulfill his obligation to her father, and then move on.

She'd noticed that he didn't refer to what her father had done for him as saving his life. He called it a favor. Her father had told him to honor his late wife's life and memory by living with her loss every day, by feeling her absence, by knowing every single minute what he'd had yet hadn't appreciated. Ethan didn't see, didn't understand that her father had saved his life. Because he wasn't ready to see that. He wasn't ready to live as the new man he'd become. A caring man. A loving man.

She could see love in him. She could feel it when he made love to her, when he looked at her sometimes. And she could feel it in the way that he cared about her, despite what he said.

Amanda took a deep breath and glanced down at Tommy, sleeping so peacefully in his crib.

"I love you so much, Tom," she whispered, caressing his soft cheek. "I want to do what's right for you, what's good for you. Your daddy wants to try again. He just told me. He wants a second chance for us to be the family we should have been all along. That's what he said outside. I owe you that, Tommy. I owe you what I didn't have—what I wanted so much for myself, but my own father wasn't offering. Yours is. And I have no right to take that from you."

*I have no right just because I'm not in love with him anymore. Just because I'm in love with someone else.*

Someone who'll be leaving as soon as his job is finished. Going hundreds of miles away and never looking back.

It was too late to check out the Fanwell's building and Ethan could not keep his mind on the investigation anyway.

It was crazy. If Amanda chose Paul, he got to go home. Back to the air and trees and water and earth and nothing else. If she chose him, he'd be unable to offer her what she wanted, what she needed.

How could Ethan be Tommy's stepfather? Ethan couldn't even look at the baby without his stomach twisting, without remembering, without knowing what he'd lost, what he'd given up, by being such a selfish prick.

*I can't give you anything,* Ethan thought, feeling completely numb. *But Paul can. He can love you. And Tommy gets to have his father. And you get to be a family.*

The smell of onions frying made Ethan realize how hungry he was. Amanda was in the kitchen cooking dinner, and Tommy was in his playpen, playing with a shape-sorter. Ethan sat at the dining room table, his laptop in front of him. He was searching online for information on William Sedgwick, specifically for anything to do with possible other children or paternity claims made by women, but the problem was that typing William Sedgwick into a search engine brought thousands of links.

Suddenly there was the sound of breaking glass coming from downstairs and then a click. Ethan bolted out of his chair and grabbed the baseball bat he kept handy and rushed to the landing of the stairs leading to the lower level. Amanda had come out of the kitchen, a spatula in her hand. She looked terrified. He gestured at Tommy and mouthed, "Get Tommy and go out the front door!" Her expression stricken, she dropped the spatula and did as he asked, careful to close the door very gently behind her.

He stood at the top of the stairs flattened against the wall and waited. *Come on, you son of a bitch. I'm going to break your head open this time.*

As the intruder arrived on the landing, tiptoeing, Ethan grabbed him around the neck and pinned him. The person went completely still, as if out of fear, and then fought wildly, kicking, clawing. But Ethan was stronger and had the intruder pinned.

He pulled off the ski mask and looked into the beligerant face of a teenager.

The kid couldn't have been more than sixteen. He looked no older than Nick Marrow and he was just as tall and scrawny. He was pale with a smattering of freckles across his nose.

"Who the hell are you?" Ethan gritted out.

"I should ask you the same question!" the kid yelled. "Let me go!" He struggled, trying to kick, but Ethan restrained him easily.

"I'm not the one who just broke in," Ethan pointed out.

"You can't break into your own house!" the teenager shouted.

He glanced out the living room window and saw Amanda practically pressed up against the glass, Tommy hoisted in one arm.

"Look kid, I know for a fact that you don't live here."

"But I should! This should be my house!" the boy yelled.

Ethan patted the kid down, making sure he had no weapons. He found nothing. Nothing in his back pockets, nothing in his socks. This was just a scrawny teenager, mad as hell about something. He waved Amanda back in, making sure the boy couldn't possibly escape his hold.

She hurried in, her expression full of surprise.

"You!" he said, staring at her. "I saw you in the paper! You're the one who has the house I should have gotten!"

Amanda looked at the teenager, then at Ethan. She settled Tommy in his playpen, then came closer. "Why?" she asked. "Why should this be your house. Who are you?"

"William Sedgwick is my father," he said. "And this place shoulda gone to me!" He burst into tears then, tears streaming down his face, over his freckles. Sobs wracked his body and he crumpled to a heap on the floor as if overcome by grief.

Amanda and Ethan looked at each other, then back at the boy.

"What's your name?" Amanda asked gently.

"Kevin," he choked out between sobs.

Kevin Fanwell, Ethan realized. This was Sally's son!

"Kevin, as far as I know, William Sedgwick only has three children, three daughters."

"That he *acknowledged*," Kevin spat out. "My mom died last year, and I kept waiting for William Sedgwick to come get me and admit he was my dad but he never did." He broke down in tears again. "And then I overheard that he died."

Ethan and Amanda just stared at each other for a moment. Amanda seemed as unsure of what to say as Ethan was. He hoped he was reading the kid right. Apparently Amanda was reading him the same way because she kneeled down next to him.

"Kevin," she said. "Come sit in the kitchen. Let me get you something to drink. How about some chocolate milk? And then we'll talk."

Sobbing, he let her lead him into the kitchen. He sat down at the table and slumped over, his face buried in his hands.

"Kevin, why do you think William Sedgwick is

your father?" Amanda asked, stirring chocolate syrup into a glass of milk.

"I don't *think* so, I know so," Kevin snapped.

"Why are you so sure?" Ethan asked.

"Because my fake father sucks!" Kevin said. "That's why. There's no way that jerkoff is my real dad. My mother was having a secret affair with her boss and she couldn't tell anyone, so she couldn't admit that her boss was my real father."

"Kevin, who's your 'fake father?'" Ethan asked.

"A total jerk named Scott Cutter," the boy said. "My mom wasn't married to him. He comes to visit me like once a year if he's 'on the coast.' What an asshole! He lives in California with a wife and her kids and doesn't care if I'm dead or alive."

"Who do you live with?" Amanda asked gently.

"My aunt. My mom's sister."

"Is she nice?" Amanda asked.

He nodded, and tears filled his eyes. "She's really nice to me, but I keep telling her that I'm not my dad's son—I'm William Sedgwick's son. My aunt keeps telling me I'm not. But I know I am. I once came here to tell him that I'm his kid, but he said I wasn't."

"Honey, maybe everyone's telling you the truth," Amanda said, her voice soft. "I know that when you don't like the situation you have, you sometimes want something else to be true. But it sounds like William Sedgwick isn't your dad."

"He is! I know it! And he was rich and important and he would have taken me all sorts of places, and we would have had box seats at the Yankees games."

Amanda sat down next to Kevin. "Kevin, you

know what? William Sedgwick might have been rich and important, but he wasn't a very good dad. He wasn't interested in being a father to me or my sisters at all. Being rich doesn't make you a good person."

The boy stared at Amanda. "You're just saying that because you don't want to have to share him or this house. I'm hiring a lawyer. I found one in the Yellow Pages, and I'm calling him today. This place will be mine too."

Amanda touched his arm. "Kevin. I'm not just saying that. My dad never wanted anything to do with me. Or my sisters. I only saw him once a year for a two-week vacation at his summer house. And he wasn't even there much."

Ethan could see that the teenager had moved her. Before Amanda got too weepy over him, he had to make sure of one thing.

"Kevin, have you broken in here before?" Ethan asked.

"Yeah, but the lock was changed so I had to break open the window."

"Wait a minute—you had a key?" Amanda asked.

Kevin nodded. "My mom had it. I stole it and made a copy."

*Whoever had broken in the first time hadn't used a key*, though, Ethan thought. "How many other times have you broken in?"

"Just once, right after I heard my aunt telling someone on the phone that William Sedgwick died."

"What did you do?" Ethan asked.

"Slept upstairs. That's about it. The place was

empty. Except then this old lady was here in the morning, cleaning, so I left when I saw her."

"Did you try to break in again?" Ethan asked.

"I didn't break in," Kevin snapped. "I have a key. *Had* a key until someone changed the lock."

"Kevin, did you ever try to hurt Amanda?"

"Who's Amanda?" he asked.

"I'm Amanda," she said.

Kevin glanced at her. "Oh. No, I've never seen you before. Just your picture."

"Where were you last night?" Ethan asked.

"My aunt made me sleep over at my grandmother's house. She's like a hundred years old. She lives in Connecticut."

Ethan knew he'd have to have a talk with Kevin's aunt. But first, he wanted to get the broken window fixed. As Amanda made Kevin something to eat, Ethan grabbed the phone book, then called someone to come replace the broken glass. Luckily, they were open till seven.

As Amanda put Tommy to bed, Kevin gobbled his grilled cheese sandwich and then his eyes began drooping. Amanda led him to the couch, where he fell asleep, then picked up the phone, and called his aunt. The woman was relieved to hear from her; Kevin had been gone all day without a word, and he'd been very upset lately. She was coming to pick him up right away.

As they waited, Ethan realized that everyone in the brownstone at the moment had been dealt a crappy hand when it came to fathers. Ethan's own had never wanted to know him. Amanda's barely acknowledged she'd been born. Kevin's had another life across the country.

Only Tommy's wanted to make good on being a father. Either that, or he wanted Amanda, and Amanda came with their baby.

*You can't have her,* he thought angrily. *You don't deserve her.*

But he couldn't have her either. And it had nothing to do with Paul Swinwood getting in his way.

It had everything to do with Ethan getting in his own way.

But some people deserved second chances. Whether or not Paul did, Ethan would have to reserve judgment. But Ethan Black didn't deserve a second chance with a wonderful woman and an innocent child.

# CHAPTER 23

An hour and a half later, Kevin had left with his aunt, who seemed like a kind, warm person. They talked openly about Kevin's feelings, and the discussion seemed to have a very good effect on Kevin. He'd said that it had been the first time he felt really listened to. That before today, no one really took what he was saying seriously. And for once, a bunch of grown-ups were sitting in a room talking about nothing else but him and the fact that he believed William Sedgwick was his father.

"Amanda said William Sedgwick was a lousy dad anyway," the boy had said to his aunt during the conversation. "I don't want him to be my dad if he wasn't a good father."

"Sometimes you just have to accept what you've got and work hard to make sure it doesn't get you down," Ethan had said. "I never even knew my dad, and I let it make me really bitter. It completely controlled me. And I lost out on a lot. Instead of focusing on what a great mom I had, I focused on what a bad father I had."

"My mother was great too," Kevin had said, his expression softening. "She was the best mom in the world."

"So honor her by focusing on that instead of focusing on your dad," Ethan said, surprising himself. He felt Amanda's eyes on him, and he met her gaze. "Honor her memory, what a great mom she was. She shouldn't get left out of the picture just because she was good. People tend to do that, right? They focus on what's bad."

"Yeah," the boy said, understanding lighting his face.

"And from everything you've said about your aunt—and from meeting her here now," Ethan said, "it looks to me like she loves you very much and is very happy you're living with her."

The boy looked at his aunt, who had tears in her eyes. "I didn't mean to act like I wasn't glad I'm living with you. I'm sorry. You've always been so nice to me."

"I love you, Kevin," his aunt said, wiping tears from her eyes. She held out her arms.

The boy slumped into his aunt's arms, still hiccoughing a little as he tried to stop crying.

"Why don't we head home, Kev," his aunt said, her eyes glistening. "I'll make your favorite dessert."

"Chocolate chip muffins?"

There were nods and then good-byes and then silence as the door shut behind them.

Ethan sat down on the sofa and shook his head. "I feel like that's one kid saved. If his aunt was a different type of person, who knows where Kevin's anger and frustration would have led him."

Amanda nodded. "You were so good with him. I was so impressed by how easily you were able to speak to him, how you made everything you were trying to say relevant to him so that he'd understand and relate."

"I've had a lot of practice lately," Ethan said, Nicky's freckled face coming to mind. He told Amanda about the boy and his father. "I've donated a lot of money to charities and organizations involving kids and teenagers. Sometimes I think about going back to school for a degree in social work or psychology so that I can become a counselor for teens. I'd offer my services for free so that anyone who needed them could benefit. Ah, but school would take years. I'm just talking off the top of my head."

Amanda smiled. "The years are going to pass whether you go back to school to pursue this new dream or not. So you might as well go back to school, don't you think?"

Ethan turned to face her. "New dream. Huh. I hadn't really thought of it that way. It was always just something in the back of my head."

"You can make it a reality, Ethan."

"I hardly think my background qualifies me to do anything now," Ethan said, the familiar emptiness taking over where moments before he'd felt filled up. "I don't get emotionally involved, I walk away. That doesn't sound like a good counselor to me."

"Actually, Ethan, it does. Counselors need to keep themselves from getting too emotionally involved or they'd never be able to keep going. And if they didn't walk away, they'd never be able to come back to work every day. That separation seems vital to me. Anyway, you just proved by how you handled Kevin that you've got what it takes."

"I don't know," Ethan said. "I'm just talking."

Amanda smiled. "Talking is a start."

Tommy began crying, and Amanda headed upstairs to check on him, leaving Ethan alone with his thought. He was grateful when the glass company arrived to fix the broken window. The last thing he wanted was to be alone with his own thoughts. What he needed were some blinders.

"Ethan! Ethan come quick!" Amanda called.

Ethan bolted up and raced up the stairs to Amanda's bedroom. She had Tommy in her arms, and a thermometer in one hand.

"He's burning with fever and is so listless! I have to get him to the emergency room right now!" Amanda said, her voice frantic. "He's been so well, so healthy since we've been here."

In moments they were out the door, in a taxi, and on the way to the nearest hospital, which Amanda had researched before moving into the brownstone. She knew exactly where to tell the driver to go.

Ethan glanced at Tommy. His face was pale, and he eyes were droopy. He was completely lethargic. "This has happened before?"

"He gets terrible ear infections and he's prone to the flu and bronchitis," Amanda said. "Twice Tommy has been hospitalized for dehydration."

Ethan was out of his element. He had no idea

what to do, what to say, how to make Amanda feel better—how to make Tommy feel better, for that matter.

The taxi came to a stop at the entrance to the emergency room. They raced inside, and Ethan was shocked to learn they'd have to wait before Tommy could be seen. Amanda had to fill out papers, show her insurance card, which she told him was still good through the end of the month.

"Oh God, he's so hot and still!" Amanda cried, touching her hand to Tommy's forehead. "Help us, please," she beseeched the admitting clerk.

Tommy was rushed inside, and Amanda followed. Ethan waited, pacing up and down until someone asked him to stop. A TV was blaring from its perch up in a high corner and he wanted to shoot the damn thing. He couldn't hear himself think.

*Please let Tommy be all right,* he prayed.

Ethan's stomach twisted and sweat broke out on his forehead. For a moment, he felt dizzy, and dropped down on the hard gray chair. *A healthy, vital, pregnant woman isn't supposed to die.*

*Please let Tommy be okay. . . .*

He closed his eyes, burying his face in his hands. He hated being so powerless. But there wasn't a damned thing he could do. The nurse wouldn't let him inside to see how Tommy was doing or to offer Amanda any comfort. The nurse had told him it was going to be a while. That he might as well sit down instead of pacing.

He needed air. He needed to pace in the air.

He stepped outside and gulped in the cold damp December air. He stared up at the sky, feeling the city closing in on him.

*This is all your fault. Katherine's dead, our grandchild is dead, because of you, you selfish, greedy bastard. . . .*

The last time Ethan had been in a hospital, Katherine's father had screamed those words, then told him to leave, that he wasn't wanted there. And so he'd gone, letting the people who'd loved Katherine, who'd been so excited for their first grandchild, to say their final good-byes.

But he'd known in that hospital that he'd loved her too, that he desperately wanted their baby too.

Too late.

# CHAPTER 24

"He's going to be fine," the doctor told Amanda. "We don't know why babies spike with fever sometimes, but it's coming down now."

"He's had that so many times," Amanda said, shaking her head. "It's so hard on his little body."

The doctor advised her about over-the-counter medication, dehydration, a humidifier, and breathing treatments. Then Amanda was assured she could take Tommy home to care for him. She headed into the waiting room, longing to see Ethan's face. Just the sight of him could make her feel better, could build up her reserves, could give her strength.

But he wasn't there.

Had he left? Had he really left her there alone?

She sat down for a moment on the hard chair, Tommy like a rag doll in her arms. She settled Tommy in his stroller, dropping down the backrest so he could try to sleep, and then she grabbed her cell phone and punched in Paul's cell phone number. He lived just blocks away from the hospital. Hopefully he was home or somewhere nearby.

"I'll be there right away!" he said.

Relief flooded her body. For the first time, someone would be there. Tommy's father would be there.

Ethan took another deep breath of the cool air and was about to head inside when he heard his name being called.

He glanced up, and there was Paul Swinwood, heading toward him. "Thank God Tommy's going to be all right."

Ethan hadn't even known that. "Amanda called you?"

Paul nodded. "She said Tommy's been released and she's free to take him home."

Relief flooded Ethan's entire body. "I'll make sure they get home safely."

"She called me," Paul said. "Look man, I know you've got a job to do, but this is my son, okay? I want to be there for him now. I have to show Amanda that when she needs me I'm there. I've changed. Can you just give us some privacy? Please?"

Ethan looked at the guy. Paul seemed so earnest, so sincere, and his expression was so worried that for a moment Ethan wished he could just walk away and give him time with his family.

*His family. . . .*

Ethan's stomach twisted. "I'll follow separately. And I'll make myself scarce at the brownstone.

You'll tell her that I agreed to give you time to yourselves?"

Paul nodded. "And thanks. I appreciate that." He extended his hand, and after a second's hesitation, Ethan shook it. Paul then rushed inside, and Ethan headed up to the window on the other side of the entrance and glanced inside. Amanda and Paul were embracing, and Ethan could see how comforted Amanda was. He watched Paul help Amanda with her coat and tuck a strand of hair behind her ear. And then Paul wiped away tears from under Amanda's eyes and they embraced again.

Paul took control of the stroller, and Amanda wrapped her hand around his arm and they came out. Ethan stepped aside so Amanda couldn't see him. He watched Paul hail the cab and help Amanda and Tommy in, and then get in himself.

Ethan felt a hollow sense of loss when the taxi left the curb. He quickly hailed another and told the driver to follow the taxi just ahead and that there was an extra tip in it for him if he didn't lose the trail. He was relieved to see that the cab pulled up in front of the brownstone. Paul helped Amanda out, retrieved the stroller from the trunk, and then led her inside.

Ethan entered through the door on the lower level. On his wristwatch screen, he saw Amanda heading up the stairs to her room, Tommy in her arms. He could just make out Paul standing in the kitchen, making a pot of coffee.

Amanda came down in a few minutes and sat down at the table. Paul handed her a cup of coffee. Amanda seemed to be crying; Ethan wasn't sure. Then Paul took the coffee from her hand

and held her, then led her into the living room where they sat, on the sofa. Now Ethan was able to see them clearly on the tiny screen.

But there was no talking. Amanda simply sat there and cried, her head resting on Paul's chest, his arms tight around her.

Ethan wanted to scream, wanted to rip Paul away from her.

Wanted Amanda to be happy. And right then, she seemed to have exactly what she needed.

"I'm so, so tired, Paul," he could hear Amanda say. "I just want to go upstairs and be near Tommy and try to rest."

"Okay, sweetheart," Paul said. "Do you want me to come with you? I'll sleep on the floor. I just want to be here for you."

"That means so much to me, Paul," she answered. "But I just need to be alone with Tommy right now, okay. I just need to clear my head. I'll call you tomorrow, all right?"

He kissed the top of her head. "Promise?"

"Promise," she said.

"Okay," he said, standing. "If you need anything, anything at all, you call me. Okay? Promise me that, too."

"I will," she said. "I promise." She walked him to the door, where they were now to the very edge of the camera's range. "Thank you so much for coming to the hospital, Paul, and for seeing me home. I don't know what I would have done without you."

"Don't thank me," he said. "You just get a good night's rest." He kissed her on the cheek and then left, closing the door behind him. Ethan watched Amanda lock the door, then turn away and head upstairs. She burst into tears at the landing, covering her face with her hands.

He wanted to go to her so badly, but everything inside him told him to let her be alone, not to crowd her, not to be a selfish bastard for once and try to be the white knight when her white knight had already come and gone.

Ethan moved swiftly to the front of the house and peered out the window facing the street. He could just make out Paul getting into a cab. Once the car was gone, Ethan checked the doors and windows and then headed upstairs. He paused in front of Amanda's bedroom, dying to knock, to comfort her, but he forced himself into the white bedroom and gently closed the door.

When Amanda came downstairs the next morning, Ethan was awake as usual and online. She said nothing to him.

"How's Tommy?" he asked.

"Do you care?" she tossed back.

"Of course I care!" he said.

"People who care don't just leave emergency room waiting areas while other people are inside, scared out of their minds," she snapped. "When I came back into the waiting room and you were gone, I never felt so—"

*Abandoned,* she finished silently. *And given that my own father abandoned me, and the father of my child abandoned me when I told him I was pregnant, last night hurt worse than anything.*

*It hurt so much because I'm in love with you.*

"Amanda, I stepped outside to get some air,"

Ethan said. "I ran into Paul outside and he asked me to give the three of you a little time alone. I thought that's what you wanted, so I did. I told him to tell you I'd follow you home in a separate cab."

"I thought you didn't trust him," Amanda said. "I thought he was a suspect. I'm surprised you didn't squeeze into the cab with us. And I don't think you and your whereabouts were first and foremost on Paul's mind when he came into the waiting room. Clearly his son was."

"Amanda, I really don't want to fight with you, okay?" Ethan said. "I know you're upset and worried about—"

"You don't know anything about how I feel," Amanda snapped. "And by the way, if Paul wanted to smother me with a pillow, he had ample opportunity last night. I think we can cross him off our list. The way he acted last night was amazing."

"He's still a suspect. Like everyone else on our list, Amanda. But I'm glad your family is back together. I know how happy that must make you."

*I love you, you jerk!* she wanted to scream.

"Jenny's coming over today to help me out with Tommy," Amanda said. "I'd appreciate it if you'd let us have some privacy."

"No problem," he said.

"Yeah, I didn't expect it would be. You like making yourself scarce."

"Amanda, I thought I was giving you breathing room last night. I never intended to just disappear."

"Well, you did," she said and realized she was about to cry. *I will not stand here and cry in front of him, she thought. I'm worried about my son, I'm emo-*

*tionally exhausted, and I just need a good long morning with my best friend. I'll be fine.*

She blinked back any threat of tears, squared her shoulders, and headed back upstairs.

"Oh my God, Amanda!" Jenny whispered. "Why didn't you tell me? I can't believe you've been going through this alone!"

Amanda put her finger to her lips. The last thing she wanted was for Ethan to hear any of this. She and Jenny were sitting in the living room, Amanda on the sofa for her mandated hour, and Jenny on the chair opposite it.

"Do you have any idea who's trying to—God, Amanda, I can't even say it!"

Amanda shook her head. "Ethan has a list of possible suspects, but it could be any of them."

"You must be so scared," Jenny said.

"It has been scary, but Ethan's been there the entire time, well except for last night, and—"

"Amanda," Jenny whispered. "How well do you really know Ethan? I mean, are you absolutely sure you can trust him? What if Ethan's the one who's been trying to hurt you?"

Amanda's stomach clenched. "But what's his motive? He has no motive."

"Maybe he's up to something," Jenny said. "I don't know. Maybe he's romancing you to get his hands on your money. Or maybe he's just putting you through hell, and then at the last second on the last day of your month here, he'll turn around and tell the lawyer that you didn't follow all the rules."

Amanda shook her head. "No, he has no reason to do anything like that."

"Oh really? You said he owed your father a favor. Maybe he thinks he's doing your father a favor by making sure you don't get the brownstone. Maybe he's pissed off that you and your dad were estranged. Maybe he thinks you shouldn't get anything. Who knows? I'm just asking if you're absolutely sure you can trust him."

Amanda took a deep breath. "I'm absolutely sure that I can trust Ethan in that regard. I know I don't have the best record when it comes to men, Jenny, but I've gotten to know Ethan. I've seen inside him, even if he thinks he's impenetrable. And he's totally honest—as good as good gets."

Jenny squeezed her hand. "All right. That's what I wanted to hear. Because that means maybe he's good enough for you."

Amanda sighed. "What I want doesn't matter, Jen. The minute the thirty days are up, Ethan's going to be hundreds of miles away, in some remote cabin. It's Paul I belong with, Jenny. Paul is Tommy's father. Paul was there last night, when I needed someone most."

"But do you love Paul?" Jenny asked.

Amanda shrugged. "He's Tommy's father."

"I know that. But do you love him?"

Amanda glanced up at the painting of the Sedgwicks. What she'd dreamed of her entire life was there in that portrait. A family. Together. But she knew the image in the portrait was false.

"Maybe I just don't know what love is anymore," Amanda said. "After everything I've been through, maybe how I really feel and what's good for me are all mixed up. Maybe I can't even tell the difference."

"Amanda, I've known you for a long time. I've been with you through thick and thin. If you can't trust yourself right now, then trust me and trust this: You *do* know how you feel. And how you feel is valid."

Tommy began crying. Jenny flew upstairs, and Amanda could hear her friend comforting Tommy and offering him a sippy cup.

Ethan could never do that, Amanda thought sadly. He could hardly bear to look at Tommy. It just hurt him too much, reminded him too much of what he lost.

And Tommy deserved more than that.

Though he could have listened to the entire exchange by eavesdropping, Ethan wouldn't invade her privacy and simply watched to make sure that no one was creeping in a window or up the stairs. He would take nothing for granted.

He wondered what Amanda said to Jenny. That she was in love with Paul, after all? That after last night, she knew without a doubt which man was the man for her?

He had to let her go. It wasn't fair to her to try and hold on while he was here but planning to leave anyway.

*Let her go.*

Just as Jenny was leaving, Paul arrived bearing flowers and a huge stuffed dinosaur for Tommy.

The dinosaur barely fit through the door. Amanda and Jenny laughed as Paul tried to squeeze it through.

"Oh, Paul, Tommy is going to love this!" Amanda said. "Paul, you remember Jenny, right?"

"Of course," Paul said, extending a hand, which Jenny shook. "It's nice to see you again."

"You too," Jenny said, a bit coolly.

"Thanks for coming over to cheer up my girl," Paul said, leaning in to kiss Amanda's cheek. "She's been through quite an ordeal."

Jenny eyed Amanda with a smile at the *'my girl.'* "Well, sweetie, I'd better get going. I have to be at work in twenty minutes." She grabbed her coat and hugged Amanda. "You take care of that precious boy." She turned to Paul. "And you make sure she doesn't exhaust herself, okay?"

Paul smiled. "You got it." He closed the door behind Jenny and came inside. "Can I see Tommy? Is he sleeping? How's he feeling? Does he need anything? I can run to CVS or the supermarket—"

Amanda laughed and put a hand on his arm. "He's fine right now. And yes, he's sleeping. He wakes up every hour or so because he's so congested, but he goes back to sleep pretty easily. The humidifier and Robitussin are helping."

"You'll give him this?" Paul asked, pointing at the dinosaur. "You'll tell him it's from Daddy?"

Amanda smiled. "I absolutely will." Truth be told, she couldn't wait. This was the first time Paul had brought something for Tommy, and it couldn't be more appropriate.

Paul caressed Amanda's cheek with the back of his hand. "You're sure you're okay? I can head in late to work. I can take the entire day if you need me. You just say the word."

"I'll be okay," she said, pulling open the door. "Scat. Off to work with you. Oh, and Paul . . . I can't thank you enough for last night. You were really there for me when I was scared to death. And I really appreciate you stopping by this morning. Tommy's going to love his dinosaur."

He gave her a one-armed hug and kissed her gently on the nose. "My pleasure. I'll call later."

As she watched him head toward Columbus, she realized she felt good inside. Not confused. Not tormented. She was not in love with Paul, but she had been once, and perhaps she could get that loving feeling again. For Tommy's sake. Paul was certainly making it easy enough on her.

Amanda was folding laundry when the phone rang. She grabbed the extension on the hall table in the lower level. It was George Harris, her father's attorney.

"Amanda, I'm so glad I caught you in," he said. "Look, there have been a number of developments that I thought I should alert you to. I've tried your sisters, but according to their places of employment, both are out of the country."

"That's right," Amanda said. "Olivia's at a shoot in Paris until next week, and Ivy's in Ireland with her fiancé."

"I apologize for having to heap this on your shoulders then," the lawyer said. "But a woman has come forward insisting that William Sedgwick fathered her child and she's demanding money from the estate or she'll go public."

"Public?" Amanda repeated. "As in the tabloids?"

"And reputable newspapers," the lawyer said. "I told the woman I would arrange a paternity test but she said she wanted fifty thousand dollars or she would tell the world about her affair with William and offer pictures of their 'love child' to prove it."

"Will she talk to me, do you think?" Amanda asked. She wasn't particularly concerned about the field day the tabloids would have with the rumors, but she did want to talk to the woman herself and try to see what truth there might be to her situation and what her relationship had been to William Sedgwick.

It was crazy, but every possible new suspect took the heat off Paul, which she desperately wanted.

"Her name is Tara Birch. I have a telephone number where she can be reached," the lawyer said.

Amanda jotted it down. "Thank you so much, Mr. Harris."

"Before you go, Amanda, there's one more thing. Clara Mott, your housekeeper, tried to commit suicide last night. Her sister found her and got her to the hospital in the nick of time apparently."

Amanda gasped. "That's awful! Which hospital?" Amanda wrote down the information, then said her good-byes and replaced the cordless in its dock. She sat there for a moment, unable to register the terrible news.

Poor Clara. Why had she tried to kill herself?

Amanda raced upstairs to find Ethan. She filled him in, and he was as stunned as she was.

"I'll call Lettie. Maybe she can come stay with Tommy while we go see Clara. Maybe if there's time we can even see Tara Birch." Amanda said. "Lettie has taken care of Tommy before when he's been ill. She's so good with him. I can ask her to come after I'm finished sitting on the sofa."

Ethan agreed and Lettie was more than happy to come over. After she arrived, Amanda instructed her not to let in a single soul, no one, under any circumstances, and then she and Ethan left for the hospital.

# CHAPTER 25

Clara was in room 722. Amanda poked her head inside and saw a woman in her sixties sitting beside Clara's bed, holding her hand. Amanda knocked gently, and the woman glanced up and then came over to the door.

"My name is Amanda Sedgwick," Amanda whispered. "Clara was my father's housekeeper for many years, and now she's been—"

The woman nodded. "Ah, yes. You're now living in the West Side brownstone."

"May I talk to Clara?" Amanda asked. "I honestly don't know what to say, but I just want her to know that I care."

The woman glanced at her sister. "I really don't think that would make Clara feel better." She gestured for Amanda to step back into the hallway and then stepped out of the room, too, closing the door behind her. She glanced at Ethan, who was standing just outside the door. "She told me about the two of you. Talking, plotting, planning, practically having sexual relations while she was there cleaning."

Amanda's cheeks burned. "How dare you—"

"Did you know that Clara was deeply in love with William?" the woman asked Amanda. "I'm sure you didn't. I know my sister wasn't one to wear her heart on her sleeve. She stayed with him for more than twenty years, to his death, cleaning his house through hundreds of his love affairs. Do you know how many women she found sleeping in his bed when she'd go to clean in the mornings? He broke her heart constantly, but she couldn't bear to be away from him and so she stayed."

"My God," Amanda said. "She devoted her life to him."

The woman nodded, her expression grim. "Nothing I ever said got through to her."

"Were they ever involved?" Amanda asked.

"Some years ago, he did make a pass at her," the woman said. "But he was drunk and he called her by another woman's name, his girl of the week, and she got out of there quickly before she let herself be compromised that way. She probably wanted to be intimate with William more than anything, but she wouldn't give up her dignity. Not completely anyway."

Amanda shook her head. "Why she did try to kill herself?" she asked gently.

"I asked her, and I think I understood what she was trying to tell me. She was under sedation and really emotional when she told me, but I think she was saying that she'd always felt like William was hers when she was in that brownstone. She would go in with her key and take care of his house, almost feeling like his wife, and when he died, as devastated as she was, she was still able to access the house, to feel his presence. She'd look at his portrait and he'd fill the room, fill her heart, and it sustained her since his death."

"And then I moved in," Amanda said softly.

The woman nodded. "And suddenly William's presence was gone. He was gone."

"But I'm William's daughter," Amanda said. "Couldn't she find William in me? Why didn't she try to get to know me? I did try to befriend her, but she wouldn't speak to me beyond saying yes or no."

"I think she felt that since you and your sisters were estranged from William there was no connection between you and him for her."

"I know how she feels," Amanda said sadly. "We could have talked about that, if only she'd let me in."

"Well it doesn't matter now," the woman said. "She won't be coming back, by the way. You'll need to find a new housekeeper. I already informed Mr. Harris, your father's attorney."

"Will you tell her that if she ever does want to talk, if she ever needs anything, if she wants anything that belonged to my father, something that meant something to her, all she needs to do is ask."

The woman nodded. "I'll tell her."

As Amanda and Ethan were about to turn away, the door to Clara's room opened, and she stood there, pale and devastated, barely able to hang onto her IV pole. Amanda instinctively grabbed Ethan's hand for support, and he held on tightly.

"Clara! You shouldn't be up," her sister admonished gently.

"I do want something," Clara said. "Something I've looked at repeatedly for twenty-two years."

"Name it," Amanda said.

"I want the portrait," Clara said. "The one that hangs in the living room. I want that portrait."

Amanda stared at her. "Even though my sisters and I are in it as well?"

"He loved you girls," Clara said. "He was incapable of showing love, incapable of understanding how it applied to him, but he loved you. I know it. I always knew it. What I didn't know was that you loved him."

But that didn't make sense. Clara's sister had said she couldn't feel any connection between Amanda and her father. That emptiness she'd felt in the brownstone had led to the despair that led to her suicide attempt.

Clara eyed her and offered the explanation that Amanda had silently asked for. "You wouldn't be here if you didn't love him."

"Wow," Amanda said as she and Ethan left the hospital. "That was intense."

Ethan nodded and zipped up his leather jacket against the chilly wind. "I wanted to ask her if she happened to have tried to kill you a couple of times, but it didn't seem particularly appropriate."

"I really don't know what to make of her," Amanda said. "She seemed to be trying to make some sort of amends with me. But there is such a coldness to her. Do you think she was the one?"

Ethan shrugged. "She certainly seems desperate enough. But I don't know. All I do know is that her story is very sad."

"I can't understand it," Amanda said, drawing her scarf more tightly around her neck. "She's the second woman who loved him despite his inability to love back."

"Sometimes I think that for some people, the love they choose is more about them than about the person they supposedly love," Ethan said. "Was that English?" he asked, smiling. "I mean, perhaps we shouldn't feel so bad for the Claras of the world who choose to love unattainable people. Perhaps that's why they choose them . . . So that they never have to risk themselves, not really. You can't get hurt if the person you're in love with doesn't even see you. You're really just living in your own fantasy world. Does that make any sense?"

She nodded. "I think I understand what you mean. You can't get hurt if you're not really involved with the person you're in love with. You can suffer from unrequited love, but it's different."

"And it's complicated. I think something in all this would explain your father and his relationships—or lack thereof—with his own children. If he refused to be a father, he couldn't get hurt by one of you. He couldn't get disappointed. He couldn't be ignored. He couldn't be shunned. He couldn't be used."

"But what makes someone like that?" she asked. "Why would anyone choose to live like—" She stopped and stared at him.

"Remind you of someone else you know?" he asked grimly.

"You're not like my father, Ethan. You're here. You've been here. You've put your neck on the line for me."

*But there's a difference between my neck and my heart. . . .*

"I think we should call Tara Birch and see if she's available," he asked, changing the subject quite effectively.

"I guess we're done with this conversation," she said.

"That's right," he answered, wondering how she managed to bring every conversation back to him, back to them. She brought him in circles when all he wanted was to continue in a straight line.

"Ethan!" Amanda said suddenly, staring into the restaurant window adjacent to where they were standing. She pushed him gently to the left, then craned her neck to peer into the restaurant again. "I'm 99-percent sure that Olivia's and Ivy's mothers are sitting at a table right by the window!"

Ethan reached into his inside coat pocket for his mini binoculars. He put them to his eyes. "That's them, all right. Thick as thieves."

"Suddenly they're best friends?" Amanda said. "Maybe their little showdown at the reading of the will was all an act, to make me think they hated each other when they're really working together to get me out of the way. Maybe they want more of the pie to go to their daughters."

"Now you're thinking like I do," Ethan said, winking at her.

"Great, you've turned me into a cynic."

He shook his head. "Just a realist, given the situation. Remember, Amanda, all I've been saying is that anything is possible. And when it's life or death, take nothing for granted."

She nodded. "It's also possible they really do fight like cats and dogs but found some common ground after the reading of the will. If my mother were still alive, maybe they would have invited her into the mix. Who knows?"

"It's entirely possible that they decided to join forces to make sure their daughters' interests are protected. They probably see you as a big threat, the one who gets to go first, the one without a big, bad mother to bark and protect." Amanda let out a breath. "Let's get out of here. My head is spinning and I still need to call Tara Birch to see if she's home and will see us.

As luck would have it, Tara was home, and after Amanda had spoken to her Ethan raised his hand to hail a cab. "Just know that you're doing great, Amanda. I know this can't be easy."

A taxi pulled up, and in moments they were headed downtown to the Gramercy Park neighborbood in which Tara Birch lived. The woman had been surprised to hear from Amanda; she'd expected to hear from her only through the lawyer. But she'd agreed to let Amanda and Ethan come over for a chat.

The child in question was three years old.

"So this child would be Tommy's aunt. He'd have a three-year old aunt," Amanda said, shaking her head. The taxi pulled to a stop in front of a tall brick building. Amanda glanced up at it, her expression a combination of nerves and anger.

"Stranger things have happened," Ethan said,

paying the driver. "But Tara Birch could very well be full of crap."

They exited the cab and headed inside the building, which was somewhat shabby. Inside the vestibule, Ethan pressed the button marked *2A—Birch,* and the door buzzed. He pulled it open, and they decided to take the stairs. The smell of food cooking—onions, chicken, and steak—filled the stairwell. At the door to 2A, Amanda knocked.

The door was opened by an adorable little girl. "I'm Lucy," she said.

Amanda kneeled down and smiled. "Hi, Lucy. I'm Amanda and this is Ethan. We're here to talk to your mother."

A woman pulled open the door wider. "Lucy, why don't you go play in your room while Mommy chats with these nice people."

Ethan took a good long look at Lucy. Her hair was black. Jet black. And her skin olive. Her eyes were also black, huge, dark and round. Tara Birch, on the other hand, was one of the fairest women Ethan had ever seen. She had whitish-blond hair, which was so light that you could see her pink scalp. Her eyelashes were so fair that mascara probably didn't even take. And her eyes were a pale blue.

Now, Ethan wasn't a rocket scientist, granted, but did this woman really think that even a total idiot wouldn't know there was no way that she and William Sedgwick's genes, in any combination, produced this child?

"Tara, I'm Amanda Sedgwick. This is Ethan Black. He's been retained by my father's estate as a sort of executor."

"Look, I'm really sorry that things have to be this way," Tara said. "But when the lawyer told me that William didn't leave anything in his will for Lucy's care, I got angry. She's his child," she whispered. "And if he didn't want to acknowledge her, fine. But he still owes child support."

"Tara," Amanda said, "Are you 100 percent sure that William Sedgwick is Lucy's father?"

The woman nodded. "I mean, his name isn't on the birth certificate, of course, but I know who I slept with and when."

Ethan had gotten to know Amanda so well that he could tell she was unaffected by that last comment. When he'd first met her, when they'd first started investigating, a statement like that would have undone Amanda. Not anymore. She was either tougher or just used to it. Or a little of both.

"Please forgive me for saying this," Amanda began, "I'm just going by looks here, but given your coloring and my father's and Lucy's, I'm having a hard time believing that William Sedgwick is Lucy's father."

"Are you calling me a liar?" Tara asked, her lips tight.

"No," Amanda responded. "I'm just saying that on a purely physical basis, it seems impossible that you and my father created this child together."

"Are you saying I'm not the mother?" Tara asked, crossing her arms over her chest. "Because I have a birth certificate saying I am. And I can attest to being in labor for over fifteen hours. Just because she takes after her father doesn't mean—oh shit," she said angrily. "Shit!"

"We'll see ourselves out," Ethan said, getting up.

"I can still go to the papers," Tara said, rising. "I can still put the rumor out there and ruin his good name."

Amanda turned to face Tara. "Can I ask you a personal question?"

The woman looked uneasy. "Go ahead. I don't have to answer."

"Did you have a relationship with William Sedgwick?" Amanda asked.

The woman nodded. "I worked for the company that took care of all the plants at Sedgwick Enterprises. I was responsible for his floor. So I was watering the ficus tree in his office and he came up behind me and he asked if I knew who he was, and I said, 'Yeah, you own the whole company.' And he asked if I wanted to sleep with the man who owned the whole company. At first I was taken aback—I mean, he was like thirty years older than I am, but he was a good-looking man and so powerful, and so we did it in his office bedroom."

"His office bedroom?" Amanda asked, raising an eyebrow.

"I guess he worked such late hours that he slept there sometimes. Or maybe he just slept with women there. It was like a converted walk-in closet. But it had a full size bed and a stall shower. Anyway, every two weeks, when I came in to water the plants, I slept with him in the bedroom. And each time he had little gifts for me—expensive gifts. A heavy gold bracelet. Diamond stud earrings. They all turned out to be real."

"So you were angry he didn't leave you money in his will?" Ethan asked.

"I was so surprised," she said. "I thought I was

special. I know, that sounds really stupid and cliché, but he made me feel like I was his special little treat. He was probably sleeping with every female employee in that back bedroom."

"I'm sorry he hurt you," Amanda said. "But even though he didn't leave you anything, you have a healthy child and your youth and your entire life before you. You can do anything. I've learned that's all that really matters."

"That's because your last name is Sedgwick and you can talk when you're rich as hell," Tara said.

Lucy came into the room, holding a doll and a brush. "Mommy, dolly's hair is all knotted. Can you help me?"

"Sure, sugar plum," Tara said. "I thought you were seeing yourselves out," she added to Amanda and Ethan.

Amanda smiled at the little girl and she and Ethan left, running down the stairs and out the door as fast as they could.

"I don't want to meet another person my father knew," Amanda said. "I've had more than enough. I've learned a little too much about my dear old dad."

Ethan slung his arm around Amanda's shoulder. "Let's go home."

She glanced at him and nodded.

# CHAPTER 26

"I'm so glad you're home," Lettie said when Amanda and Ethan came through the door of the brownstone. Tommy was sleeping in the playpen, his breathing just slightly labored, and Lettie looked nervous.

"Lettie, what it is?" Amanda asked, her heart racing. "Is Tommy okay?"

"Tommy's fine. He's got a slight fever, but he drank a little milk and ate some banana."

"Lettie, what happened?" Amanda asked, putting steadying hands on Lettie's shoulders.

"I think someone tried to break in!" Lettie said. "I kept hearing jiggling downstairs. I was afraid to go down there and look, so for a while I stayed upstairs in your room with Tommy with the door locked. I wasn't sure if I was hearing things, or if it was the wind or what, and I didn't want to call you unnecessarily. Maybe it was just the wind that knocked down a branch and it was banging against the window."

"That's probably what it was," Amanda said. "I'm sorry you had such a scare."

"You know unfamiliar houses," Lettie said. "Always making noises. I'm so used to my own apartment. I'm probably just making a big to-do over nothing."

Amanda hugged Lettie. "Why don't I make you a cup of tea?"

Lettie smiled. "No thanks, dear. I'd better get going. I have some shopping to do. My bridge group is meeting tonight."

Ethan took Lettie's coat from the rack and helped her into it. "Come, Lettie. I'll hail you a cab." He persisted, despite Lettie's assurances that she was all right. He gestured for Amanda to lock up behind him. He was gone for just a few minutes, then knocked. "It's me."

Amanda opened the door, and there he was, filling the doorway, her gorgeous Ethan with his dark eyes and beautiful mouth and all she wanted was to collapse in his arms. "It was wrong of me to leave Lettie here alone with Tommy when I knew someone out there is trying to kill me. What if he or she had gotten in? Lettie could have gotten killed. Tommy could have been killed or kidnapped. What the hell was I thinking?"

"I wasn't thinking either," Ethan said. "We got lucky. Very lucky." He threw his notebook against the wall. "Dammit! Who the hell is it?"

Amanda took a deep breath. "Ethan, what if we don't find out before the month is up. Then what?"

He held her gaze. "I would never leave you in jeopardy, Amanda. Never."

"I'm sorry, Ethan," she said. "I know you want to go home. I know being here, in this city, must be so hard for you. I know what you're going through for me."

He turned away for a moment so that she wouldn't see the expression was on his face. Even if he wasn't quite ready to admit how he felt, she would know from his expression that he was in love.

"I don't want Olivia's and Ivy's mothers to be the ones," Amanda said. "I couldn't bear that for my sisters. And I don't want it to be Paul. I couldn't bear that for Tommy. Is it Clara? Is it one of my father's lady friends? Is it someone we haven't even suspected?"

"I wish I knew, Amanda. And not because I want to run away from you. I want to know because I want you safe. I want to go to bed every night knowing you're safe."

*I want to go to bed with you every night.*

"Oh, Ethan," she said, closing the gap between them.

The doorbell rang before she could do whatever she was about to do, which was wrap her arms around him. Paul stood there.

"I tried calling, but no one answered," he said. "I was scared that that meant you'd taken Tommy back to the hospital. Is he okay?"

Amanda nodded. "He's sleeping now, but he seems to be on the mend."

Paul glanced past Amanda, and when his gaze landed on Ethan's, Amanda noticed Paul's entire body stiffen. "He's always here," Paul whispered. "I feel like I'll never get a chance to be alone with you. I want us to get to know each other again. As these new people we've become."

Amanda smiled, her stomach twisting. "I know, Paul. It's just the terms of the will—"

"You don't have to explain," he said. "I'm sorry. I shouldn't be whining about our relationship when our son is so ill. I'm being very selfish." He lowered his voice. "It's just that you're all I can think about, Amanda. You and Tommy and me as a family." She was sure she saw tears glistening in his eyes. He glanced away sharply, and she knew he was embarrassed.

*Oh Paul. Why does this have to be so confusing?*

"How about a quick cup of coffee," she said, touching his arm.

He smiled. "That would be great."

When she turned around, Ethan was gone. She glanced upstairs in time to see the door to the white bedroom closing. Not all the way of course. It was left slightly ajar. Ethan trusted no one.

She felt Paul's hands on her shoulders. He stood behind her and gave her tired muscles a gentle squeeze. "I'll go start the coffee. Why don't you relax in the living room."

Relax. Right.

She dropped down on the antique chair. Now wasn't the time to sit anywhere where he could sit directly next to her. He would start touching her, and she had no idea where it would lead.

In a few minutes he joined her in the living room. "Coffee's brewing. I also brought you some cookies," he said, "just in case you need a sugar boost."

Amanda stared at the bag of Milanos, the very

ones Ethan had set out for her after the first attempt on her life.

"You look tired," Paul said. "I wish I could erase that worried expression in your eyes."

"I'm okay," she said. "But thanks. I really appreciate all you're doing."

"The coffee's probably ready. You sit. Let me get it. One sugar and a little milk, right?"

She smiled and nodded. "Thanks."

He brought the coffee, which they drank in companionable silence. The entire time Paul didn't so much as touch her. He offered her another cup of coffee, and when she said she was too wired, he collected their cups, brought them to the kitchen, washed them, dried them and put them back in the cupboard. "I'll let you get some rest," he said. "Could I stop by tomorrow to see Tommy?"

She smiled. "How about on your lunch hour?" Amanda suggested. "Tommy usually wakes from his morning nap around one o'clock."

"Perfect," Paul said. "It's a date."

*A date.*

She closed the door and glanced up at Ethan's bedroom door, hoping it would swing open and he'd come out so that they could finish their conversation.

But the door closed all the way.

Ethan decided to fill his head with research on William Sedgwick to keep thoughts of Amanda and Paul out. He sat at the desk, his laptop open to a search engine, and he glanced out the window at the early evening sky. Across the street there were Christmas lights in some windows. He could see a tree with a star atop it, in the window of the brownstone diagonally across from them.

He drew the white curtains and forced his attention back to the laptop. He typed in *William Sedgwick and child*, then hit enter.

He scrolled through entries that didn't relate as usual, his eyes looking for anything that might jump out. Nothing he hadn't seen before. He then did the same for search engines of the three major New York City papers. Nothing.

*Damn!* Ethan muttered, slamming the long desk drawer with his booted foot.

The drawer popped open, and Ethan slammed it closed with such force that it popped open again.

There was a piece of paper in it, folded in half. The name *Karen Anderson* was written on it.

Amanda came running up the stairs and knocked. "Ethan? Are you all right? What's all that banging?"

"Hold on a sec," he called, "it was just the desk drawer." He grabbed the paper, an ordinary piece of white unlined bond paper and left the room. Amanda waited outside. "I found this inside the desk drawer." He handed it to Amanda.

She glanced at it. "It's my father's handwriting.

> *'Dear Karen," she read. "Sorry doesn't even begin to cover what I've done. I know I hurt you. I know I should have left you alone. But you're so beautiful and I'm so weak. I know you want to believe that the baby you're carrying is mine. But it's not.*

*I'm very sorry. I know you want some fairy tale ending where I ask you to marry me. But that can't be. I'm not the father of your baby. I can't be. Please forgive me. I know what a delicate flower you are, and I should have left you alone. My best, William."*

"Wait here," Ethan said. "I want to check something." He ran back inside the white room and typed *Karen Anderson and child* into a search engine. It was such a common name that thousands of entries came up. Ethan added the name *Sedgwick* into the mix. One entry came up.

*May 3, 1984 . . . Anderson, Karen, thirty, of Brooklyn, died unexpectedly Thursday night in her home. A household staff member of William Sedgwick, the New York City entrepreneur, Anderson is survived by month-old daughter, Willa. . . .*

The air whoosed out of Ethan's lungs. He grabbed his laptop and rushed out to the landing. "Read this obituary," he told Amanda.

As she did, the blood drained from her face. "It sounds like she commited suicide. Do you think she did it because of the note he left her? Her baby was only a month old. Oh God, Ethan."

He typed Willa Anderson into the online white pages. His stomach rolled. Willa Anderson lived practically around the corner, on Broadway between Seventy-fourth and Seventy-fifth.

"Maybe it's a coincidence," Ethan said. "And maybe she's been waiting her entire life to make her move. Maybe she's heard her entire life that her mother killed herself because her employer, Willa's father, wouldn't marry her, wouldn't acknowledge their baby. Maybe Willa expected to be remembered in the will. Maybe she wants this house just the way Kevin Fanwell did."

"It's such a horrible story," Amanda said. "I hate it! Why did my father have to be so careless with people's lives? How dare he?"

Ethan put his arm around Amanda's shoulder. "I need you to stay strong. We've come this far, okay? We'll go sniff around Willa's building and learn what we can about her when Tommy's well enough to stay at Lettie's or Jenny's for the day."

She took a deep breath and shook her head. "We can't wait, Ethan. Go check her out now, before it gets too dark. I'll be okay here. The windows and doors are all locked. I'll keep my cell phone in my pocket at all times. If I hear a single jiggle, I'll call 911."

"No, I'm not leaving you here alone."

"Go, Ethan. You'll save me by leaving me."

He looked into her eyes. She was serious, adamant. "If something happens to you, Amanda—"

"I've got the phone," she interrupted. "I've got your baseball bat. I've got double locks. No one is getting in here."

"I'll never forgive myself if something happens to you."

"Ethan, she lives around the corner. You'll do some fast talking, get some info, nose around, and you'll be back in, say, no more than an hour."

"Come downstairs with me," he said. "I want to hear you locking the door and the deadbolt when I'm outside."

She touched his arm. "Okay."

At the door, he looked at her, then gently pulled her to him and kissed her. He took one last look and then rushed off into the gathering dark.

It was still oddly warm for December, and Ethan tried to unzip his heavy leather jacket as he hurried up the block. "Zipper's stuck," he muttered, jabbing at the tiny silver tab. He fought with the stupid thing, then began shrugging out of his coat. His thick wool sweater was all he needed.

The moment he went to pull his arms free of his coat, he was jumped. Someone had grabbed him from the side, as though he'd been lurking between the parked cars and waiting for him. He felt something crash against his head, and everything went black for a moment. He saw a flash of white and his legs gave out.

"Take my money," Ethan barely managed to croak out, spitting out blood. "My wallet's full of cash. Just let me get on my way."

"You're not going anywhere, you bastard," said a voice he recognized too well.

Something heavy came down hard again on his head, and his face hit the concrete. Blood dripped over his forehead, down his eyes, down his cheeks and mingled with the blood in his mouth.

He tried to speak, but couldn't. *Get up,* he told himself as the light in his mind started flickering. *Up . . .*

He could barely keep his eyes open. He saw only at street level, only what was directly in front him, which was a pool of his own blood on the gritty sidewalk.

Suddenly he felt himself being pulled along roughly, his feet dragging. And then there was nothing. Just darkness.

# CHAPTER 27

The moment Amanda locked the door and turned back to the foyer, she felt the difference. How strange it was to be in the brownstone without Ethan. Suddenly the house felt too large, too quiet, too unsettling.

She headed into the living room and glanced out the window on the left. All she wanted was for Ethan to come racing back. She looked up at the portrait of her father, her womanizing, using father who she'd wanted to love so badly, and she knew she was going to give Clara the portrait. It didn't belong in Amanda's home. And if Clara still wanted to love a man who'd done nothing but break her heart and everyone else's he came into contact with, so be it. If it would help keep her alive, then maybe it was worth it.

"I wanted to love you," she told her father's image in the painting. "My whole life I wanted to love you, wanted you to love me. And after all this,

I learned that there was nothing I could have possibly done to win your heart. At least I know I did everything I could."

Her stomach in knots, she went into the kitchen to put on a kettle for tea. She set her cell phone on the counter, checked again to make sure it was on and that the battery was fully charged, then filled the kettle, and decided to do some baking so that she wouldn't spend the next hour pacing the stairs. She decided on a cake, yellow with chocolate icing. Tommy could have a tiny piece tomorrow if he was feeling better.

She looked through the cupboard for mix. Ah, there it was. And there was a cranberry scone mix. And a corn muffin mix. If she had the time, she'd make those too. She set the boxes on the counter, all set to whip up some delectable treats when the tea kettle began shrieking. She hurried to turn it off, afraid the sound would travel upstairs and wake Tommy.

She dashed upstairs into her bedroom and peered into the crib.

Tommy wasn't there.

For a second, Amanda wondered if he climbed out, the way she'd heard babies did. But Tommy had never tried to climb out his crib before.

*Oh God. Oh God. Oh God.*

"Tommy!" she screamed. She ran into the hallway, just in case, then to the stairs in case he had managed to get out of his crib and had fallen down the stairs. But the baby was nowhere to be found.

And the house was quiet. Too quiet.

Amanda felt her back pockets for her cell

phone. Damn! she yelled at herself. She'd left it on the kitchen counter. She raced to the phone on her bedside table to call the police. No dial tone.

She rushed downstairs, so fast that she tripped and fell and hit her head against the wall. She got herself up and ran into the kitchen.

Her cell phone was not where she'd left it.

She looked wildly around the kitchen, on the table, on all the counters.

Her heart beating frantically, Amanda raced into the living room. Perhaps she left it on the piano while she'd been looking at the portrait. She twisted the knob on the floor lamp at the entrance to the living room, but the light bulb must have died.

"Looking for this?" asked a familiar voice in the darkness.

Paul?

The lamp by the window turned on. Paul was sitting on the chair next to it, Tommy fast asleep in his arms. On the chair next to him was a glass of something that looked like scotch. And a gun.

"Paul?" she whispered, her legs trembling. "I'm so surprised to see you." *Act calmly,* she told herself. *Act naturally.* "How did you get in?"

"I stole the keys from your purse while I was making coffee after our hospital visit. Didn't you notice the patio door key was gone? Those other times, I'm a contractor, so I know how to get into locked doors and windows."

*No,* she thought, mentally punching herself for the oversight. She never used that door. After all she and Ethan had been through, how the hell could she have been so carelessly stupid?

"Amanda, I really feel bad that you have to die," he said calmly. "You are really too pretty to be dead. But if you're alive, I can't get custody of Tommy."

She gasped and the air whooshed out of her lungs. *He's crazy*, she told herself. *He's sick. Play along. Talk him through this.*

"Paul, you don't need custody of Tommy. We're going to raise him together."

He snorted. "Together? Who? You, me and that asshole Ethan?"

"Ethan?" Amanda repeated. "What does he have to do with anything?"

"You're screwing him," Paul said. "That's what he has to do with anything. I saw that kiss at the front door, you whore."

"Silly!" she said, forcing a smile. "Screwing him is right. As in screwing him over big time. I'm just using him, playing him, so that he tells my father's lawyer that I served my time here, and I can get the brownstone fair and square."

"What do you mean?" Paul asked.

Amanda explained the terms of the will.

"Why didn't you ever tell me this before?" he asked. "All you said was that he was retained by your father's estate to enforce the will."

"That's right," she said. "Paul, he was always around, listening, watching. I had to be careful with what I said."

He regarded her. "I guess so. I didn't realize he was watching to make sure you jumped through hoops like a monkey. That asshole."

Amanda nodded. "Once I get him to say I did everything I'm supposed to do, I never plan to see him again. He makes me sick."

"Me too."

"You thought I liked him?" Amanda asked, laughing. "Jeez, Paul. You think I could go from being madly in love with you to even liking a guy like that?"

"Do you still love me?" Paul asked.

She nodded. "Very much."

"Then strip for me like you used to. Show me how much you love me."

She almost vomited. *Think, Amanda. Think.*

"Paul," she said, feigning shyness. "Not in front of our baby." She giggled. "I'll strip for you in private."

He gnawed his lower lip. "Go put Tommy in his crib. Then come back down. I want you to start stripping on the stairs. First your shirt."

"I know," she whispered. "I remember that's how you like it."

She slowly walked closer to him, her heart racing so fast she was sure he'd hear it. "Okay, Tommy," she whispered to her son. "Mommy's going to take you up to bed so Daddy and I can play."

Paul smiled and leered at her breasts. When she bent to take Tommy, Paul grabbed the collar of her shirt and pulled her to him, kissing her hard on the mouth.

She forced herself to kiss him back, then gently pulled away. "We don't want our baby to wake up," she whispered to Paul. "I want to make sure I can strip for you and then make love to you without interruption."

He smiled again. "Okay, hurry up." But before she could scoop up Tommy, Paul grabbed her collar again and pulled her to him, kissing her harder on the mouth. As she went to step back, he held her by the back of her head and stuck his tongue deep inside her mouth, a hand hard on her breasts. He pulled back and wiped his mouth. "Forget going upstairs. Just put him in the playpen. I want you to strip right here. Now. And then I'm going to fu—"

Amanda touched a finger to his lips. "Tommy's a light sleeper, honey. And because he's so congested, he wakes up very easily. Let me put him in his crib and close the door so he won't wake up. I don't want any distractions while I'm making you happy."

He leered at her breasts. "Okay, hurry up."

She lifted Tommy into her arms, relief flooding her the moment she had her son away from that sick bastard, and then she slowly turned, praying he wouldn't shoot her in the back. She flew up the stairs and into her bedroom, closing the door and locking it behind her

"Mandy, I'm waiting," Paul called, the sound of his voice sickening her.

"Coming, sweetie," she called, her voice breaking. "Just changing Tommy's diaper."

What the hell was she going to do? She could open the windows and scream for help. Could Paul get inside the bedroom before the police arrived? Probably.

She had to think.

She heard footsteps up the stairs.

*No. No. Please no.*

The doorknob turned. "Amanda, the door's locked."

He knocked. Harder.

Tommy started crying. Amanda rushed to the crib and picked him up.

"Amanda, open the door."

"Paul, I'm scared of the gun I saw downstairs. I saw it when I was coming upstairs, and I got scared. Why do you have a gun, sweetie?"

"How else am I supposed to blow your head off?" he asked.

Amanda's legs gave out and she slid down onto her butt. "Why do you want to kill me?"

"So I get custody of the kid," Paul said. "And then I get the brownstone. And then I sell it for millions. I can probably also get another mil by selling Tommy to some rich couple who can't have kids."

Amanda gasped and closed her eyes. Paul banged on the door. "Let me in, Amanda. Or I'll have to break it down. And then I'll be *really* angry."

"Paul, Ethan will be back here any minute," she said. "Let's leave before he comes back. We can go away together. I remember you always wanted to go to Mexico."

He laughed. "Ethan's not coming back. Ever."

Her stomach flipped over. "What do you mean?"

"He'll be in jail. Charged with your murder. So sad, that crazy drifter Ethan Black, who lost one family and is now unhinged, shot and killed the woman he was supposed to protect. His fingerprints are on the gun downstairs. I made sure of that after I beat him to a bloody pulp."

Amanda tried not to scream. "Where is Ethan?"

"I left him barely breathing behind the garbage cans outside the building on the corner," Paul said. "When Ethan wakes up in a few hours, he'll come rushing over, find you dead, call the police, and when the cops come, his prints will be all over the gun. He'll be arrested for your murder. Really, it's almost too brilliant."

Her legs began trembling wildly. She dropped onto her knees, then pulled herself up. "Paul, what if something goes wrong? What if you get arrested instead of Ethan? Then we'll never get to be together. Let's just run away now. You, me, and Tommy. We can head to the airport right now, before Ethan ever gets a chance to call the police."

"Do you think I'm a moron, you whore?" he asked. "You think you can use reverse psychology on me? I don't want you. I've never wanted you. I did at first, I mean. I thought you were hot and I wanted to screw you. But then you got pregnant." He banged on the door. "And then I read about your father dropping dead and how you were inheriting his brownstone. So I ever so accidentally ran into you and you fell for it like the stupid bitch you are. Just like you fell for all my sob stories, about my dad, about work. Do you really think I would work a day's manual labor? Are you kidding me?"

Amanda backed farther and farther into the room, having nowhere to go.

Paul banged harder on the door. "I've worked too hard at gaining your stupid trust to lose everything now." He began kicking the door, and it shook so hard it vibrated. "Let me in, bitch. Or I'll break it down and you'll really be sorry."

Tommy began wailing, and she tried to soothe him, but he was crying harder and harder.

"Shut that kid up!" Paul screamed. "I can't stand the sound!"

*If he's planning to sell Tommy, he won't hurt him,*

Amanda tried to assure herself. *So just put Tommy's safety out of your head for a moment and think. Think, think, think.*

"I'm going to huff and puff and blow the door down," Paul sing-songed. "And this time I won't smother you in your sleep with a pillow, sweetie. I'll just shoot you in the head. And this time, your boyfriend won't be able to save you."

Her heart racing, Amanda put Tommy in his crib. He stood up, holding onto the rails, crying, and reaching out for her. "I'm sorry, sweetie," Amanda whispered to him. "Mommy just has to make sure everything's okay." She glanced wildly around the room, praying for something, anything to use as a weapon against Paul.

Her eyes landed on the desk chair. It was a plain wood chair, with a cushion on it. She untied the cushion and grabbed the chair and positioned herself in front of Tommy's crib, holding the chair legs out.

Thank goodness for the solid wood doors in the old brownstone, but if Paul managed to get in, and Amanda had no doubt he eventually would, at least she'd have something to fight him with. She'd try to bash him in the head with the legs. The chair was too big for her to manage well, but it was all she had.

She heard him blowing, then laughing. "I'm huffing and puffing, darling. And here I come."

# CHAPTER 28

Ethan's head was pounding, and the rushing in his ears was making him dizzier than he already was. *Where the hell am I?* he wondered, and then he tried to bolt upright, but the pain in his ribs, and the sudden sharp pain on his head kept him down.

No, something else was keeping him down. Something pressing against him. Ethan tried to open his eyes, but one was caked shut. He peered with the other. A huge silver can was lying on its side against him. A garbage can. He tried to shove it, but it was full and heavy. He braced himself, then pushed with all his might, and it clunked heavily to the ground beside his stomach.

He tried to sit up again, but he could barely move. *Get up, man. You have to get up. Get up!* Wincing in pain, he forced himself to sit up and reached for his cell phone. Gone.

Amanda!

Ethan tried again to pry open his eye, and he

realized it was caked shut with his own blood, which was all over his hands. His jacket was also probably covered, but it was too dark to see. Ethan suddenly remembered the brick against his head and almost fell back down to a prone position, but he grabbed a garbage can, and this time was grateful that it was full to support his weight.

*I'm up. Okay. Take a breath and grab onto the rails lining the garbage and move.* He winced with every movement of his ribs. Where was he? he wondered again, looking around for a landmark. He realized he was right on Amanda's block, at the building next door, in their garbage section. He just had to go a few yards down Seventy-fourth Street. *Go. Go. Go,* he told himself. *Fight through the pain.*

Who the hell had hit him? When he first came to he had no idea. Then he remembered the voice of his attacker: Paul Swinwood.

Adrenaline burst through him and he staggered to the brownstone as quickly as he could. No one was on the street. At the stoop to the brownstone, he heard banging. Like someone kicking in a door.

Amanda!

He knew she'd used the safety latch at the front door, so there was no way he'd get in. He went around to the back and used his key and slipped in as quietly as he could. He could hear Tommy screaming. Amanda yelling, "Stop. Please!" And Paul laughing and kicking. "I'd say one more good kick and this door is going down, baby," Paul said. There was murder in his voice. Ethan recognized the tone from his own recent brush with death.

He raced up the stairs as fast as he could, grabbing his bat from under the couch on the way. It would serve him better than a knife. *Okay, Black, here's the plan. Distract him. Let him come after you. You'll provide the cover for Amanda to escape with Tommy. And then it all comes down to what weapon he has. If he has a knife, you have a chance. If he has a gun, you're dead.*

The door to the bedroom flew open and Amanda screamed at the top of her lungs. She came rushing at Paul with the chair and bashed him right in the face with one of the legs. He screamed and went flying backward.

Ethan came running into the room with the bat raised. "Ethan!" she screamed.

Paul was on the floor, his hand to his eye. Blood dripped down his face. He looked up at Ethan, his expression dazed but murderous.

"Get Tommy and run!" Ethan shouted. "Now!" He stood a foot from Paul, the bat at the ready.

Amanda grabbed Tommy and ran, but Paul grabbed her leg. She clutched Tommy tightly against her chest and screamed, praying she wouldn't fall, praying if she did that she could protect Tommy's head.

Ethan wacked Paul with the bat. "Let her go, you son of a bitch!"

Paul screamed and cursed, his hand going slack long enough for Amanda to rush away. She flew down the stairs and fumbled with the chain latch on the front door. Finally she was out and gasping for breath, then ran next door and banged on door, screaming for her neighbors to call the police. No one was home.

She could see a few figures dimly in surrounding windows. "Help!" she screamed. She dropped to her knees, clutching Tommy tightly against her. The cool air seemed to actually calm Tommy down, and he stopped crying.

Finally, a woman came around the corner and headed up the block toward her. She was talking on a cell phone. Amanda bolted to her feet and rushed toward her. "Please call the police! Tell them there's an intruder with a gun at West Seventy-fourth and Central Park. The intruder is the blonde man. Hurry, please!"

The woman looked scared out of her mind. She hung up on whoever she was talking to and punched in 911 and said what Amanda told her to.

Sagging with relief, Amanda raced back to the brownstone and crouched beside a parked car. A crowd of people had formed and a young man asked if she was all right and if the police had been called. She nodded, and he handed her his wool coat. Another woman took off her coat, removed her cardigan sweater, and handed the sweater to Amanda. "Put this on the baby," the woman said. "Those fleece booties might not be warm enough." Amanda mouthed a thank you and wrapped Tommy in the sweater.

She strained to hear anything coming from inside the brownstone. There were sounds of breaking glass. Thuds. Yelling.

And then the sirens obliterated all other noise.

*Please let Ethan be all right,* she prayed. *Please.*

Two police cars pulled up, and as the cops were racing up the stairs, a gunshot was fired. Then another. The cops raced in, their guns drawn.

Amanda stood motionless on the street, a crowd of people around her.

An ambulance pulled up and EMS workers carried a stretcher inside. A moment later, a body was removed from the brownstone, covered with a sheet.

*Who, who, who, who?* Amanda thought wildly. *Who is it?*

She couldn't take it. Her legs gave out. She dropped to her knees, careful to keep Tommy safe.

"Amanda."

She jumped up at the sound of his voice. Ethan stood at the top of the stoop, battered and bruised, but very much alive.

After three hours in the police station, Amanda and Ethan were free to leave. They were told not to go back to the brownstone for at least a week, since it was a crime scene.

"I never plan to step foot in that place again," Amanda said.

Ethan nodded. "I don't blame you."

George Harris, who'd been called in to verify who Ethan was, and the details of the will that solidified Paul's motive, since he was no longer able to speak for himself, held up a hand. "This is quite a conundrum. Nothing in the terms of the will set forth by William covers police-mandated abandonment of the premises."

"Couldn't she do the rest of the thirty days after the brownstone's no longer a crime scene?" a detective threw out.

"I have no interest in doing the rest of the thirty

days," Amanda said. "I'm never going into that brownstone again."

"But, Amanda," the attorney said. "If we can't agree to something to fulfill the terms of the will, I'm afraid you'd be forfeiting."

"Fine with me," she said.

"Amanda, do you realize what you'd be giving up?" the attorney asked.

She nodded. "Bad memories?"

"I'll give you a few days to reconsider, Amanda," Harris said. "Once the police determine it's no longer a crime scene and you're free to move back in, we'll revisit this discussion." He snapped shut his briefcase. "Again, I'm very sorry for all this tragedy. This could not have been what your father wanted for you."

"No," Amanda said. "I'm sure it wasn't."

*But I think I know what was, she suddenly realized. I think my father wanted Ethan for me.*

She glanced at him. He sat on an uncomfortable chair, wincing in pain. He'd been looked over and declared in good enough shape to give his statement, but he was clearly in a lot of pain. When they were released from the precinct, they'd go to the nearest hospital.

She couldn't think beyond that.

They chose a hotel downtown for what was left of the night, far away from the brownstone, far away from Central Park, far away from the East River promenade where Ethan had met William Sedgwick, and far away from anything the city held in memory for either one of them. Their room was small and cozy, with a king-sized bed with a puffy down comforter and lots of pillows, a crib, and a coffee maker, which Amanda knew she'd make good use of in the morning.

As for right then, they needed to sleep. In each other's arms.

And they did.

# CHAPTER 29

"So does this mean the brownstone goes back to William's estate?" Olivia's mother asked.

"Mom!" Olivia hissed, her cheeks turning pink. "I can't believe you. I cannot believe you."

"Don't talk to your mother that way!" Ivy's mother snapped. "It's a reasonable question."

"Mother!" Ivy said, her own cheeks turning red.

Amanda shook her head and smiled at her sisters and they smiled back. Amanda, along with her sisters and their mothers were gathered again in the same conference room they'd sat in weeks ago, this time for the rereading of the will now that Amanda had officially forfeited rights to the brownstone. A week had passed since that terrible night when Paul had been killed by his own bullet that had richocheted off the dresser and hit him in the heart.

"Amanda," Olivia said. "Are you sure you're even up to this? You've been through so much."

Ivy nodded. "We can put this off for another week or two. There's no reason to do this now. You and that darling little boy of yours deserve a nice warm vacation somewhere."

"Don't be silly," Ivy's mother said. "Of course we should do this now. We need to know what becomes of the brownstone now that Amanda's out of the equation."

"Mom," Ivy said, "please."

"No, it's okay," Amanda said. "I want to do this. I want to get it over with so that I can move on with my life."

George Harris walked into the room. "Good morning, ladies. I'll get right to business." He opened his briefcase and withdrew a sheaf of papers. "This is an amendment to the last will and testament of William Sedgwick, to be put into effect upon the negation of the terms of the will as originally stated."

Dana and Candace leaned forward, waiting. Amanda had never seen them look so excited. Olivia and Ivy, on the other hand, appeared mortified at how their mothers were behaving.

George Harris cleared his throat. "Should Amanda veer from the rules beyond the acceptable number of slip-ups, please refer to the following amendment as pertains to the brownstone. In the event that Amanda does not fulfill my last wishes, the brownstone is to be left entirely to Ethan Black. Should anyone inheriting from this will attempt to contest this amendment, their inheritances shall become null and void."

Dana and Candace were speechless. Too stunned to begin complaining. Olivia and Ivy laughed.

"Well, I'd say Dad handled that quite well," Olivia said, winking at Amanda.

Ivy nodded. "It's almost like he worried that some crazy would come out of the woodwork because of greed. So if Amanda forfeited for whatever reason, but most likely out of fear, the man he handpicked to safeguard her would win the brownstone for her. From what I've heard about Ethan, I have no doubt he'll sign the deed right back to you."

Amanda took a deep breath. She wasn't about to tell her sisters that she didn't want the brownstone and never planned to step foot in it again. Her sisters had their own inheritances coming to them, and there was no reason that her own experience had to mar theirs. No one in their father's life had tried to harm her; someone from her own past had taken that prize.

Anyway, the summer house in Maine was modest, as was the place in New Jersey. Whichever property went to which sister wouldn't bring out any psychos. Neither house was worth all that much. Perhaps their father had something else in store for Olivia and Ivy?

"Well I find this appalling," Olivia's mother said. "Now a multi-million-dollar brownstone goes out of the family to some stranger? George, how do I contest?"

"According to the amendment, if an inheriting party or any member of her family contests, that person's inheritance is null and void."

"That bas—" Ivy's mother barked, then caught herself.

"Good day, Ladies," the attorney said, standing.

"Just tell me one thing, Mr. Harris," Amanda asked. "What was the point of the rules? What difference would it make, for example, if I went in the white bedroom?"

The man shrugged. "I guess we'll never know. There's nothing in the will or your father's papers that explains his choices."

"So they were just completely arbitrary?" she asked. "I just don't get it. Why put Ethan to all that troub—"

Ah. She stopped talking and sat back, understanding dawning. Her father had set her up. And he'd set Ethan up. He'd set them up, literally. For some reason, he wanted them together.

*You chose the right man, Dad. Unfortunately, you're not going to get the result you clearly hoped for, but you did choose well. I fell in love. Madly, deeply, truly in love. How you managed that when you never even knew me is pretty impressive.*

Ethan would be going home today. He'd agreed to stay in the city until after today's meeting. There was no way he could have driven such a long distance in his condition before now anyway. And so in a matter of hours he would getting back in his car and driving hundreds of miles away from her. Away from Tommy. Away from his memories.

The attorney smiled at Amanda. Clearly he too thought her father was trying to matchmake. He nodded his chin at the women in the room, then left.

"So there's nothing we can do," Ivy's mother asked Olivia's mother, her expression resigned.

"Unless you want to deny me what my father may have left me," Ivy said to her mother. "And you don't want to do anything that might cut me out of the will, right?"

"Of course not, baby!" the woman said. "We'll just wait and see what you get on your wedding day, sweetie."

Ivy smiled and sent Amanda a private wink. "I'd better get going. I'm meeting Declan to shop for wedding rings!"

"Have fun," Amanda said, hugging Ivy goodbye.

Olivia also embraced Ivy and then said she needed to head out as well. "I've got a nightmare of a meeting with my publisher and my deputy editor," Olivia said. "Something is brewing at the magazine. I am not looking forward to this afternoon at all."

Olivia's mother mock shivered. "Women's magazines are so cutthroat. I don't know how you manage to deal with all those dragon lady types."

The three sisters laughed.

"What in the world is so funny?" Candace Hearn demanded, her hands on her hips.

Amanda, Olivia, and Ivy looked at each other and laughed again.

"How about a quick cup of coffee at the Starbucks downstairs?" Olivia suggested. "The magazine can wait."

Ivy bit her lip. "One quick cup," she said. "After all I'll have Declan waiting for me for the rest of my life, right?"

"Men do not like to be kept waiting, Ivy Sedgwick!" her mother warned as she freshened her frosty lipstick.

Ivy smiled and the three Sedgwick sisters shook

their heads good-naturedly and put on their coats and gloves. And after Ivy and Olivia bid good-bye to their frowning mothers, depositing a kiss on their respective cheeks, Amanda was never more surprised when her sisters stood on either side of her and then linked an arm through her own.

"Are we ready?" she asked them.

"We're ready," they said in unison.

When Amanda returned to the hotel, Ethan was still sleeping. His ribs were still bandaged and would be for weeks to come. He had stitches in his head. A gash, where the brick had slashed his cheek, was just beginning to heal.

He'd saved her life and her son's life. And no matter what happened, even if he really did just up and leave today, she would always be grateful.

Amanda hoped he'd wake up while she was here. She wanted to tell him about his new inheritance, and then she wanted to arrange to have the portrait of her father delivered to Clara's apartment before she headed to Queens to pick up Tommy from Lettie's. She was excited about seeing her old neighborhood. She wasn't planning on moving back there; she still wasn't entirely sure where she would go, but she knew that she would land on her feet. She would get a new job, even if she had to plaster the city's hotels with her resume. Or maybe she'd apply to nursing school and take out loans and worry about paying them later for the rest of her life.

It turned out that Willa Anderson was in nursing school. Amanda had called her yesterday and introduced herself and asked if they could meet in a Starbucks to talk. Willa had been happy to come. Apparently, her mother had been delusional and claimed affairs with everyone from the president to Brad Pitt. Though no one doubted she had actually slept with William Sedgwick—his reputation as a relentless womanizer left no doubt—he had slept with her mother after his vasectomy, which he had proven with a court-ordered subpoena of his medical records to her aunt and uncle who'd raised her after her mother's death. He'd submitted to a paternity test so there would be no doubt, and he was proven not to be the father of Willa Anderson. Willa had grown up thinking that her mother had been in love when she died, and though it was tragic, that had always given her comfort. Amanda gave her the note William had left in the drawer of the white room, and it brought tears to Willa's eyes. Apparently no one had even believed Karen when she'd said that William had seduced her one day in the white bedroom.

And suddenly Amanda had realized that perhaps her father had felt terribly guilty about Karen's suicide and wanted the next woman who slept there to be honored in marriage, unlike Karen.

Amanda had walked home from her meeting with Willa feeling the weight of the world had been lifted off her heart. She had been dreading visiting Willa, hearing another story of a broken heart and dashed hopes, but instead Willa had seen the positive aspects of her mother's love for William. And in turn, that had allowed Amanda to walk away from this chapter of her life on a good note.

She would never look into her father's life again. She would never wonder why he hadn't loved her. She would accept that he was who he was and that his own limitations had cost him dearly.

She had a son to raise. She knew she would tell Tommy that his father had died when he was less than a year old and that they hadn't married, but that she had loved him very much once.

Ethan stirred and opened his eyes, those beautiful dark eyes. "How was the meeting?"

"In the event that I don't fulfill the terms of the will for whatever reason, guess who the brownstone goes to?"

"Your sisters split it," he said.

She shook her head. "It goes to you."

"What?" he barked. "Me?"

She shrugged. "And this amendment to the will can't be contested or my sisters forfeit their inheritances."

"What the hell am I supposed to do with a brownstone in New York City?" he said. "What was William thinking? I'll just sign it over to you. You can sell it. You'll be set for life."

"I'm already set for life," she told him. "I can always find a job and a place to live. I don't want the brownstone. You know that."

"Well what am I supposed to do with it? I don't mean to sound like a jerk, but I don't need the brownstone or the money. I've got plenty already."

"I know what you could do with it," she said with a smile.

He listened as she spoke, not saying a word until she was done. And then he held out his arms and she went into them gently so she wouldn't hurt his ribs.

Ethan signed the papers at Harris's office, officially donating use of the brownstone to the Children's Center, a beloved organization in New York that offered free counseling to children and teenagers. There was a center downtown, but now there would be one uptown as well.

Ethan stood in the center of the living room of the brownstone, which looked remarkably different without the portrait. Without that huge painting of the patriarch and his children, which now hung in Clara Mott's living room, the brownstone now felt free of a past and ready for a future.

"I know why you brought me here, William," Ethan said to the air in the room. "And it wasn't just about matchmaking or about making me face my past now that I'd had three years to heal. You must have seen something in me and seen something in Amanda and known that we belong together. Despite not knowing your daughter, you knew her very well. I don't know how you managed that, but you did. Because I love her with all my heart. And I love Tommy too. I love him as though he were my own. And if Amanda will have me, I want to take her home to that land of earth and sky and water and forest and make her happy for the rest of her life."

When Ethan turned around to go, Amanda stood there, Tommy in his stroller.

"I'll have you," she said, smiling."I love you too," she said, tears pooling in her eyes.

"Come with me, Amanda. We'll live in the cabin until we build our dream house a little closer to civilization. You have to come, or I can't go."

"I wouldn't mind being away from civilization for a while," Amanda said, smiling. "And I could use a little water and air and forest. Plus, I'm just in the mood for a long, long drive."

He kissed her. "What do you say, Tommy?" he asked, unlatching the harness and lifting the baby out. He held the precious boy against his chest and kissed the top of his head. "I think you'll like Maine," he told Tommy. "I can teach you how to fish."

Amanda smiled. "Let's go before I start bawling.

And as they left the brownstone and walked up Seventy-fourth, Ethan carrying Tommy, Amanda slipped her arm through Ethan's, and the family headed for home.